Oxford Messed Up

a novel

ANDREA KAYNE KAUFMAN

GRANT
PLACE
PRESS

Grant Place Press
500 North Michigan Avenue, Suite 300
Chicago, Illinois 60611
www.GrantPlacePress.com

Library of Congress Control Number: 2011915264

Printed in U.S.A.
ISBN: 978-0-984-67510-4
Design by Ruth Efrati Epstein and Patricia Frey

For (and because of) my extraordinary family:

Jacob, Ariel, and Josh

CONTENTS

PART ONE:
AUGUST
To Pee or Not to Pee

I'm a dweller on the threshold
And I'm waiting at the door.
And I'm standing in the darkness
I don't want to wait no more.

Van Morrison, 1982
From "Dweller on the Threshold"

I saw a man pursuing the horizon;
Round and round they sped.
I was disturbed at this;
I accosted the man.
"It is futile," I said.

Stephen Crane, 1895
From "I saw a man pursuing the horizon"

1.

Gloria watched the swollen white orb of a hot-air balloon rising over Navy Pier and knew she had to break it off with Oliver, for he was the type who would never enjoy hot-air balloons, Van Morrison songs, or mess, whether from orgasm or otherwise. But who was she to be dreaming about mess today?

She had more pressing matters to contemplate, like traveling to Oxford University as a Rhodes Scholar. And she was not going to Oxford for love. All she wanted to do in Oxford was pee. And who else but Oliver could accompany her on such an important journey, across such a difficult threshold?

Poor Oliver! Loyal, reliable, and protective Oliver. He may not have cared about her pleasure, but he was preoccupied with her safety, often calling it his raison d'être. No, today was not the day to say goodbye to him when she was already saying goodbye to so much—including a sweltering August in Chicago and her equally stifling parents. But her parents did try; they meant well enough. And Oliver meant well too.

She had to admit she was grateful for his company as they all drove toward O'Hare Airport. Peeking at him through stray wispy bangs that had somehow broken free from otherwise perfectly brushed and secure hair, Gloria felt indebted to Oliver for sticking by her through so many difficult years and thresholds. She wanted to feel happy to have him. She tried to convince herself she was happy to fly with Oliver today.

After all, with more sophisticated technology and superior air power, airplanes flew farther distances and at greater heights than hot-air balloons. Hot-air balloons were insignificant, aimless carnival attractions, mere sideshows. Airplanes actually took you places. Real places. England. Oxford. But with their compressed air and metallic odors, they were more confining. Even steadfast Oliver would agree that airplanes were more confining.

As Gloria pressed the button to close the tinted window, the hot-air balloon receded from her view, blending into the clouds. Her eyes fell in line with the rhythm of the passing buildings, a braided chain of concrete and sky. Concrete and sky. Concrete and sky. It was then that twenty-two-year-old Gloria Zimmerman knew for certain she would have to contemplate her freedom on another sunny August day. Today, she had responsibilities. Today, she was a superstar.

So she smiled at Oliver awkwardly and nervously, rubbing her hands in the backseat of her father's brand new shiny, black S55 AMG Mercedes, surrounded by travel bags on the seats and floor.

Gloria was pretty, with long, wavy dark brown hair and big blue-gray eyes. Long lashes made her eyes luminescent in a penetrating, soulful way that hid a note of sadness. Today, her eyes were a sad that registered nervous and uptight rather than her usual thoughtful and resigned.

Oliver thought Gloria was pretty, especially when perfectly put together, with everything in its proper place. In contrast, most other people thought Gloria would be even prettier if she were not so put together—if she relaxed a little and let her hair down, literally and figuratively. They thought her look, like her demeanor, was too uptight and just plain tight. Tight jeans. Tight tank under fitted blazer. Hair perfectly coiffed in a tight ponytail at the base of her neck like the choke chain for a dog.

Latent energy palpable, Gloria was wound so tight that at any moment she might explode. And with sad, nervous eyes, she spent most of her time navigating this edge, scared to death that her tight coil of self-composure would come undone. Scared to death of losing control. A dutiful Oliver helped her keep things together, tight and in control. Oliver was always there to help her calm down and maintain control, even if he could be a bit stifling.

But much to Oliver's dismay, Gloria also had other companions who served this purpose. For example, Van Morrison calmed her down. Oliver did not approve of the Belfast Cowboy's music, preferring instead uptight, angry British punk from the 1970s, like the Sex Pistols and the Clash. He listened to the Clash constantly, especially in the weeks leading up to Oxford.

His screeching rendition of "London Calling" induced massive headaches. When it came to the Clash and to so many things, what Oliver thought was clever and witty, Gloria found annoying and clawing. But he did mean well.

In spite of his protestations, Gloria did not think Oliver a faithful Clash fan at all. What would Joe Strummer and Mick Jones think of Oliver applying their iconic political anthem about socioeconomic dislocation and nuclear proliferation to the plight of a Jewish-American girl traveling business class to study at Oxford?

Gloria, on the other hand, respected their music, especially the poignant, poetic lyrics. But she could only listen to pulsating, angry ranting in small doses. It was hard enough dealing with Oliver's pulsating, angry ranting in a steady stream. Gloria considered Van Morrison's music quite the opposite.

Van Morrison's lyrics were poetic genius as well, but his bluesy, soulful, and often improvised melodies not only calmed but inspired. Her favorite description of Morrison's brilliance came from music journalist and cultural critic Greil Marcus, who described Morrison as transporting listeners to a "realm beyond ordinary expression, reaching out as if to close your hand around such a moment to grab for its air, then opening your fist to find a butterfly in it." Gloria liked that metaphor and feared that filling her brain with Van Morrison was the closest she would ever get to unfettered flight.

They never spoke about it, but she sensed Oliver's jealousy. His insecurity only exacerbated his ranting, so she tried not to listen to Van Morrison in front of him. Gloria had a theory that Oliver did not like *happy*—whether happy Van Morrison songs, happy butterflies, or happy girls. Surely, Oliver would not like a happy Gloria. He wasn't mean or sadistic, really. It's just that such a state would undermine his raison d'être. Such a state would undermine Gloria's dependence.

So promoting all things sad and composed, Oliver was quite pleased that the tragic confessional poetry of Sylvia Plath, who had stuck her head in an oven with her children down the hall, also calmed Gloria down. Tragic confessional poetry might actually be called Gloria's raison d'être, as it was to be her area of study at Oxford.

If Van Morrison and hot-air balloons reflected her dreams, Oliver's solicitude and dead women poets were her reality. And hand sanitizer. She couldn't forget the hand sanitizer, which calmed her down more than anyone or anything.

Like Oliver and Sylvia Plath, hand sanitizer was harsh but soothing. But there was a catch. With hand sanitizer, she always needed more. She was never quite able to assuage an endless thirst for Purell. It had to be Purell or another brand with maximum chemicals. The natural lavender-scented hand sanitizer her mother had bought from Whole Foods was unacceptable, even if more gentle on the skin.

For Gloria, it was all about eradicating—actually killing, downright *annihilating*—germs. Evil germs. Germs had been her enemy since adolescence. That's when it all started. The flood. The music. The poetry. Her relationship with Oliver. And her frantic need to stay tight and in control.

Just thinking about grimy airplane germs made her empty the Purell bottle she was clutching with an increased urgency. Four drops on the right hand and two more on the left. Rubbing her palms in a counterclockwise motion, she chanted:

> *I saw a man pursuing the horizon;*
> *Round and round they sped.*

Gloria had no idea whether this Stephen Crane poem was about hope or futility, and she didn't really care. She kept rubbing—

> *I was disturbed at this;*
> *I accosted the man.*
> *"It is futile," I said.*
> *"You can never——"*

"You lie," he cried,
And ran on.

The poem perfectly described Gloria's suffocating lifestyle—the sad plight of a hamster on a spinning wheel, running round and round but never really going anywhere.

But the mantra's real utility was that its length was just right. Not too long but long enough to calm her nerves so she could finally put the beloved and dreaded hand sanitizer away—at least for a little while. At least until the next time she felt out of control and compelled to pursue the elusive, out-of-reach, and utterly cruel horizon.

As the car approached the turnoff for O'Hare Airport, Gloria's hand-rubbing was picking up speed and intensity, well past the time it took to recite Crane's poem. Alone in the back of her father's six-digit-and-then-some car, which he took better care of than his daughter, she noticed that some hand sanitizer had spilled on to the fancy white topstitching of the soft leather seat.

Her father would not be pleased. And this gave her a modicum of secret satisfaction as she rubbed the residue into the pretentious leather with an ugly red hand while sharing a conspiratorial grin with Oliver.

In contrast to the perfectly tight and put-together look of everything else about her, Gloria's hands were a mess. They were red, chapped, and peeling with the sore knuckles of a bare-knuckled boxer. Instead of looking like the hands of a Yale graduate—a nice Jewish girl from the Gold Coast neighborhood in Chicago, whose mother had taken her to a salon on Oak Street three days ago for a deluxe spa manicure with aromatherapy and paraffin wax—her hands looked like those of a rancher, a bricklayer, or someone who had been burned in a fire.

It was only Oliver who loved Gloria and her ugly red hands. Oliver took good care of her, burning hands and all, albeit in his protective, dominating sort of way.

He whispered in her ear so her parents would not hear, "You're not parachuting into Afghanistan. You're just going to England. What's so bloody dangerous about that? You just need to stay in control. Away from germs. *London's calling to the faraway towns.*" He laughed, "Clash not soothing enough? I'll keep singing until you let me take care of you. *I fought the law and the law won.* I just want what's best for you. Always."

Although Oliver tried to lay down the law, he did help her calm down, walking her through the cyclical steps of staying away from germs and in control. And even though Oliver could be harsh, he was also soothing, taking better care of her than almost anyone, especially her parents.

To her parents, Gloria was someone—rather some*thing*—they were alternately proud to own and show off to their dearest friends and rivals at the club or could not wait to be rid of. The shiny new Mercedes or last year's model to be traded in for something sleeker, preferably with normal hands and a more outgoing personality.

Frank and Gladys Zimmerman sat in the spacious front seat of the car with its more intricate topstitching and burled elm dashboard. For Gloria, hunched in the backseat and riveted on Oliver and her hands, the car might as well have had a glass partition. It had been difficult enough dealing with her parents since moving home after graduation, let alone on this arduous day when she was traveling all the way to Oxford.

Her father was yelling through bad reception into his cell phone: "Pay the goddamn margin call. Our business is about risk. How'd I get here? Risk, risk, risk!"

Her mother turned to face her in the backseat. Although her forced smile conveyed good intentions, her voice came through as a reprimand. "Those hands. Jesus, Gloria. Don't skip your medication."

Her mother never made it explicit, but Gloria knew Gladys considered her hands an embarrassment. She felt judged whenever Gladys stared at her ugly red hands. Oliver reminded her that her mother took no responsibility for her hands because Gloria was the sick one. As Oliver often reminded her, her mother thought she was a *sick, wretched, embarrassment. A freak. A leper.*

Gloria was not the only one with an obsessive streak; her mother was obsessed with medicating her. Oliver tried to convince Gloria that the only reason Gladys cared about the stupid pills was so that Gloria would at least appear normal and Gladys would be able to dine with her at the club. Oliver often said that for Gladys, the epitome of life's triumphs was to be able to show off her Yale graduate, Rhodes Scholar, and nice Jewish daughter *who has beautiful fucking hands.*

As they pulled up to the curb outside the terminal, Gladys reached over the seat to hand Gloria a bottle of Klonopin, which delivered immediate relief from her panic attacks. Gloria wondered whether Frank owned stock in Roche, the pharmaceutical company that markets Klonopin. The container was so huge it looked like an oversized baby bottle. Gladys seemed proud of her motherly concern (at least someone was).

Shaking a second pill bottle like a maraca, Gladys announced, "Really, you won't do well without your Luvox pills either, sweetheart. I made sure we're covered through New Year's, Gloria. Two hundred and fifty pills." And for the benefit of airport personnel assisting airplanes taxiing to their gates, Gladys leaned in even further, screaming in Gloria's taut face, "Did you hear me, Gloria? Two hundred and fifty pills!"

Gloria hoped her parents couldn't hear Oliver as he whispered, "Thank you, Gladys. Only the best mothers medicate their children so they can avoid taking responsibility for how miserably they treat them."

Oliver's indictment of her mother was not entirely fair. Gloria was supposed to take the Luvox every day to maintain control, and it was a powerful weapon against germs and other enemies. But even though the pills worked, Gloria did not like taking them unless absolutely necessary. They made her want to break free from Oliver, and he didn't deserve that. He was not the enemy, in spite of what everyone said. In fact, he was the one who cared the most and was always there. She knew this would hurt her parents, but it was true.

But on this difficult day, Oliver's companionship might not be enough. Traveling to Oxford would be overwhelming for both of them. So with ambivalence, Gloria reached for the pills with her ugly red hands.

As always, Frank defended Gloria, highlighting her stellar résumé. "Not do well, Gladys? Yale, Phi Beta Kappa, Rhodes Scholar. Found that missing manuscript. Special doctoral research assistant for that...feminine...feminist poetry...bullshit...whatever. You know what I mean."

Frank smiled at Gloria in the rearview mirror, completely oblivious to the look of terror on his daughter's face.

"But Oxford, damn," he said in awe, mostly to himself.

Unlike Gladys, Frank wasn't embarrassed by Gloria. Quite the opposite, he was proud of her achievements. He loved her achievements. He lived through her achievements. Her academic success meant everything to him. And of course, it was much more important than her mental health and happiness, although he would never admit that to others or even to himself.

Gloria knew she had a high *Blue Book* value. Like the Mercedes, luxury powerboat moored at Belmont Harbor, and 9,000-square-foot penthouse on East Lake Shore Drive, Gloria was a prize that told the world Frank Moshe Zimmerman, originally from Skokie, Illinois, had become somebody to be revered and envied at the Standard Club and even beyond Chicago's Loop.

He was successful in his investment business and powerful in his own provincial circles. Most importantly, he owned great stuff, including a shiny car with enough horsepower to reach sixty miles per hour in less than five seconds and a smart daughter, whose accomplishments were equally impressive if not useless.

Gloria's "minor hand problem" paled next to her major academic accomplishments and high IQ. The calculus that measured her ugly red hands against her prestigious Rhodes Scholarship most assuredly worked in her favor, at least as far as Frank was concerned. Oliver reminded her that for her father, *Blue Book* value—what the members of his club would pay—meant everything.

Frank whistled, turning to smile at Gloria, and said, "My Superstar."

Frank continued whistling as he climbed out of the car. When her father began unloading her bags, Gloria sat frozen in the backseat. Oliver was confusing her, encouraging her to go but holding her back at the same time. Oliver loathed mass transportation but loved Oxford. How would she manage this conundrum? She made a stoic audience to Oliver's sarcastic monologue.

"With your crackerjack education, you can figure it out. You should know airport restrooms are filthy, disgusting, vile, fetid, germ-infested rat holes—unless, of course, you're a conservative senator trying to have clandestine sex. Airport and airplane restrooms must be avoided at all costs. Oxford, however, should not be avoided. It's very prestigious, Superstar. Sir Andrew Lloyd Weber and Frank Moshe Zimmerman would both agree, Superstar. Is it worth the risk? Risk, risk, risk! How do you think we got here? I'll protect you from all risk."

Immobile, Gloria stared at her parents outside the car, pondering these people sending her to the other side of the world yet again. Who were they? The same people who shipped her off to the Big Sur horseback-riding camp 2,000 miles away, where she didn't know a soul and was terrified of what Oliver called, "those dirty, vile, fetid, germ-infested equine"?

The same people who visited her only twice during college, hastily dumping the terrified freshman and dutifully retrieving her four years later at graduation? In fairness, the Zimmermans did travel to New York quite frequently during Gloria's time at Yale. They often encouraged her to endure the germ-infested Metro North train to have dinner with them in the city.

But it went without saying that these invitations would sometimes be revoked if they happened to be dining with anyone who "really mattered" and might have been repulsed by Gloria's ugly hands and peculiar eating habits.

Aside from a few meals alone with Gloria, it was easier for her parents to enjoy their accomplished, if somewhat strange, Yale student from afar. Gloria was always far more appealing as an abstraction rather than as a real person.

So Gloria sat in Frank's museum-piece car while he smiled at her uncomfortably from the curb, impatiently playing with something in his pocket. Keys, perhaps? Gladys adjusted her light sweater, discreetly checking her watch. Gloria wondered what they had lined up for that evening. Dinner at the club? At Hugo's Frog Bar? Or did her mother have to clean out the bottom drawer in their guest room? She knew Oliver was thinking they could not wait to be rid of her. Gloria wasn't sure what to think and did not budge.

Frank and Gladys crouched down to address Gloria through the back window. They looked like gorillas at the Lincoln Park Zoo, hitting the glass to make contact. Or was Gloria the gorilla? She stopped rubbing her hands and put down the window.

Frank spoke gently. "It's time, Superstar."

Gladys tried to be kind through her strained Botox smile. "Sweetheart, you're acting sick again. I want you to be okay. I want you to be well. Please take your Luvox so you can be well, so you can be okay."

With pursed lips, Frank gave Gladys a look. "Enough, Gladys. She's okay. She's fine. She's better than fine. She's the best. She's my Superstar."

Gloria's father offered her his hand. She refused it and pretended not to notice the slight sting of rejection in his eyes. Didn't he know that her ugly red hands were rough and coarse, such a far cry from the soft, buttery leather of his car seat? She felt awkward holding hands with him or anyone. Why couldn't he see that she was not okay?

But she smiled at her oblivious father as she stepped out from his ridiculous car. She still couldn't help but freeze up like a statue as she received a heartfelt squeeze from him and loving air pats from her mother, who puckered her shiny red lips for dramatic effect. Gloria took a deep breath as she watched her parents get back in their prized car and drive away, both sad and relieved to once again be rid of them.

She pivoted to focus on an even bigger menace, the airport terminal. She surveyed the contents of her safety pouch, a black nylon handbag slung over her shoulder—ticket, wallet, passport, iPhone, and hand sanitizer. Plenty of hand sanitizer. She was well armed. In spite of her loathing for all her pills, she thought taking a Klonopin might be necessary for the difficult flying ahead.

Gloria struggled to open the childproof Walgreens bottle with a shaky red hand, but when she finally pried the top loose, the tablets tumbled onto the ground, scattering everywhere. All of her Klonopins were rolling in different directions, as if running for their lives. Running from Oliver. Damn Oliver! It was all his fault.

For several suspended moments Gloria was panicked and paralyzed, having no idea what to do. Finally, with labored breathing, she reached down to pick up the pills, or as many possible, or just a few, or two, or one. But she just couldn't bring herself to touch the germ-infested ground.

Oliver's voice rang in her ears. He was not helping.

She always sells you short, Superstar. The frigid bitch is wrong. You don't need your pills. You're better than that. Think of all the dog feces on the shoes that have touched this hallowed ground. You know all the lovely worms dog feces bring: heartworms, whipworms, hookworms, roundworms, and tapeworms.

Gloria was clutching the empty Klonopin bottle and shaking as she feebly stood up. She needed to calm down without her pills. She needed to calm down without Oliver's ranting.

She was angry with Oliver and wanted to let him go. But she couldn't just yet. He was all she had to make it through. He was all she had to make it to Oxford. Well, at least she could try to shut him out for the moment to punish him.

So ignoring Oliver and listening to Van Morrison, Gloria Zimmerman used her ugly red hands to drag her heavy baggage into the terminal, en route to Oxford University. *I'm a dweller on the threshold and I'm waiting at the door and I'm standing in the darkness. I don't want to wait no more.*

2.

Twenty-five-year-old Henry Young sat on the swing suspended from a large oak tree in the front garden of his family's eighteenth-century Oxfordshire estate playing Van Morrison on his guitar, believing he too was a dweller on the threshold. The Jacobean house, which had been in his late mother's family for over four generations, was called *Equanimity*, probably due to its serene panoramic views of green on all sides, including acres of tranquil gardens with bright variegated flower beds, unspoiled grounds with mature trees, and large areas of open grazing.

Henry thought equanimity, as both house and concept, was a load of shit. Instead of bringing images of mental serenity, the large, cold house conjured quite the opposite for him and his older sister, Claire. *Apprehension. Uneasiness. Fearfulness. Disquiet. Perturbation. Angst. Tension.* Those would have been better names.

Equanimity could be quite useful, however. It was their favorite code for saying *fuck you* to their father. Henry and Claire often played a game of sorts, trying to see who could bring it up at a family meal without its real meaning being detected. Henry usually won those dysfunctional family games. He was merciless in ways his sister was not.

His sister, preferring other sport, had too big a heart to go for the jugular. In contrast, their father was lacking in heart altogether and therefore had no qualms about aiming for the jugular, especially Henry's. From an early age, Henry had learned how to defend himself. Distinguished professor and don Nicholas Young—chair of the Department of Music, Jesus College, Oxford University—was truly Henry and equanimity's greatest opponent.

Nicholas may have been an accomplished and commanding academic, but he was a substandard father. Even righteous Saint Claire would have to admit that. What a pity there was no doctoral requirement for fatherhood. No tenure portfolio to submit. No manuscript for publication consideration. No need to articulate one's theoretical framework and contribution to the field. Indeed, any moron with live sperm and convenient twat could become a father.

Henry felt guilty implying that his beloved mother had been a twat when she had been quite the opposite, and while his father may have been a lot of things, he certainly wasn't a moron. Just an arrogant pompous arse with live sperm. Henry thought that without Claire, Nicholas' deplorable record as a father might be complicated by Henry's own delinquencies and, for lack of a better phrase, *fucked-upness.*

But what about Claire, Henry's nearly perfect older sister who tried so bloody hard to please Nicholas? Top of her class at Jesus College with double first-class honors. Top of her class in her psychology internship at Oxford Radcliffe Infirmary and Hospital. At just thirty years old, patients and fellow doctors sang her praises, already nominating her for several promotions and awards at the very start of her professional life. The chair of her department adored Claire—at times a little too much for Henry's comfort.

And even though she was just five years Henry's senior, she took good care of him as well. She tried to, anyway. He could be an especially difficult patient and unruly younger brother. She became his surrogate mother of sorts when their mother died.

Since that time, she accompanied him to his many appointments and reminded him to do this and that. She relentlessly nagged him about taking better care of himself and staying out of trouble. It could be annoying and invasive as bloody hell, but it came from a place of real concern and love, and Henry knew that. Indeed, he loved and cherished his smothering, annoying, intrusive older sister very much.

Claire also tried to take some responsibility for their lonely father. But like he did with all the equanimity in his life, Nicholas rejected her and pushed her away. It was sad, more like pathetic, for Henry to see his accomplished sister's self-worth be instantly extinguished by one sadistic look or cruel utterance.

Perhaps that's one of the reasons Henry did not even try when it came to Nicholas...or anyone else, for that matter. And he always pretended not to care. The only way to win dysfunctional family games with his father was to pretend not to care and to leave his messed-up version of equanimity as quickly and as far behind as possible.

Henry was not moving far, but he was moving quickly. Today was the day he would move to St. Cross and spend the next several months avoiding his father until his hearing in early December. He was grateful Claire was able to use her connections at university housing to find him a room in the crowded postgraduate college. He desperately needed a change in his Oxford society.

Between his father's looming presence and his own sordid history, Jesus College had become extremely claustrophobic. His father was not at all pleased he was moving to St. Cross. He considered the college "substantially less prestigious than Jesus" and "overrun with foreign students from God knows where."

Henry was pleased St. Cross had such a large international population. The snobby British incestuous groupings had become suffocating. It was bad enough taking classes with those bloody bastards at Jesus. He couldn't bear the thought of living with them any longer. He needed a peaceful, anonymous place to listen to his music and bide his time.

As he waited on the swing, Henry played a red spruce Martin acoustic guitar. He was flanked by five milk crates filled with records that had mostly been his mother's. In a moment, he would pack them in the boot of Claire's car and say goodbye to his cold house and cold father. Aside from his sister, his records were what he loved most in the world, especially his extensive collection of Van Morrison vinyl.

Ironically, Van Morrison's "Precious Time" was released right before their mother died. Henry remembered playing it for her in hospital. Claire thought his memory was faulty, that they never played her music in those final days when she was barely lucid.

Henry did not like arguing with Claire, especially on the topic of their late mother. But Claire could be a bit patronizing as the self-appointed guardian of their childhood memories and losses. Real or imagined, playing "Precious Time" for his mother was a lovely memory that Henry was not willing to part with, whether Claire approved or not.

His father may have been chair of the music department, but his mother was the one who had filled their house with music. In a strange and comforting way, he felt connected to her when listening to her records, as if he were having an out-of-body experience and communicating with her from beyond. He had read that Van Morrison believed in out-of-body experiences, which, of course, led to one of his most important and early albums, *Astral Weeks*.

His mum's *Astral Weeks* was severely scratched, but Henry liked its scratches. They told him which songs she had played over and over again. Even more than photos, the scratches were proof that she was real, or had been real. That, at one time, she had been alive listening to the very same records, the very same music he played over and over again.

In addition to her records and love of music, Henry had also inherited his mother's green eyes, wavy auburn hair, and infectious dimpled smile, which he used to fake his way through many awkward situations and major fuckups. Whether a blessing or curse, his crafty smile worked more often than it should have.

Henry also had some of his father in him. He was tall and lean like Nicholas, with the long and delicate fingers of a musician. Like Nicholas, Henry played guitar, cello, piano, and organ. All in all, Henry was handsome, putting aside his perpetual adolescence and apathy. How long could a twenty-five-year-old get away with wearing vintage concert T-shirts and not brushing, let alone washing, his hair for days on end?

He was a handsome, charming mess with no intention of cleaning up or growing up any time soon. At thirty, he would inherit the estate and other property from his mother's side. Until then, he was in a holding pattern, trying to stay out of his father's way and trying to stay healthy, all things considered.

Claire was also tall and lean, with their mother's red hair and green eyes, but she seemed more put together than Henry on both the outside and inside. It was only when she came back to their family home that she was a wreck. Upon entering *Equanimity*, the accomplished Oxford-educated psychologist became a frightened schoolgirl in desperate need of Daddy's approval and love, which he was unwilling (Henry's theory) or unable (Claire's theory) to give.

As a gifted psychologist, she knew the pattern well. But as a daughter, she couldn't quite turn theory into practice, falling prey again and again to Nicholas' barbs. Sitting on an oak bench adjacent to the tree, Claire smoked a cigarette with nervous, jumpy fingers. She only smoked at *Equanimity*, or so she said. Henry knew she was listening for their father so she could quickly flick the cigarette behind the tree. As always, the thirty-year-old schoolgirl cowered at the prospect of Daddy's wrath.

Nicholas was someone most people feared. Henry tried to remember the last time he saw his father smile at something genuinely happy and good. The sadistic smiles that would flicker on his face when he cut someone down did not count. Those came often. Henry had to go back years for such a recollection of a real smile, even before his mother was diagnosed with breast cancer. It was sad for all of them that such a memory was extinct, but it was mostly sad for Nicholas.

Claire felt bad for Nicholas. She thought that saying a proper goodbye to their father was the least Henry could do to smooth things over a bit and not part on such unpleasant terms. According to Claire, the fact that Henry was no longer living at Jesus College was difficult for Nicholas as a "lifelong Jesus man" who "did worry about Henry's welfare in his own way."

So to please his sister, Henry sat on the swing in the front garden waiting to say goodbye to the xenophobic sperm donor and Jesus College alum he called "Dad."

It seemed like ages, but Henry's illustrious father finally emerged through the front door. Without saying a word, Nicholas marched toward the tree, scowled at his son, and slammed a bottle of pills on the end of the oak bench. The perfect start of another happy day at *Equanimity*.

3.

The business-class security line was more crowded than Gloria thought it would be. Her parents had told her she would sail through, but the line was moving slowly in fits and starts. When Gloria finally reached the TSA officer, she quickly turned off Van Morrison and once again began to panic.

With baggage checked and ticket and passport in hand, Oliver was on high alert, even more so than the Transportation Security Administration, which had announced that the travel safety threat was orange.

Look at all the vile people sneezing germs, coughing germs, and picking germs out of their noses. And those disgusting fat slobs coming out of the airport bathrooms. Vile, fetid, heinous, germ-infested airport and airplane bathrooms. No public bathrooms for you. The next time you pee will be in your own bathroom in Oxford.

She was somewhat relieved when they finally reached the security conveyer belt. Carefully and methodically, Gloria placed carry-ons, laptop, shoes, and jacket in the gray trays, touching them with only her fingertips and, even then, as little as possible.

The prospect of sharing germs with family and friends, let alone strangers in airports, was terrifying.

Sealing herself off from the germ-infested people to the maximum extent possible, Gloria tried not to breathe through her mouth or touch anything extraneous. She hoped to pass through this last part of security quickly and unnoticed. But, of course, she was called over by a TSA officer, a middle-aged man with a no-nonsense demeanor and graying moustache.

With a contrived smile and forced politeness, as if according to regulations and following a script, he asked, "And how are you today, Miss? May I check inside your bag?"

He did not care how she was, and they both knew he was looking in her bag whether she wanted him to or not. The only outstanding questions were whether he would view her as a terrorist or freak and just how much of her germ-killing arsenal he would seize.

She nodded, and the TSA officer opened her stuffed tote, which contained a bevy of cleaning products. He and some fellow travelers gaped at the amount of hand sanitizer—at least thirty bottles. Surprise turned to concern when the TSA officer also found over ten boxes of antibacterial wipes, a stack of white gloves, and five aerosol cans of Lysol disinfectant, extra-strength original scent.

The intense staring and unwanted attention made Gloria even more anxious. Didn't they know how filthy and dangerous germ-infested airports and airplanes were? She hoped Lysol was not regularly used to make bombs; they were all giving her such peculiar looks, like she was dangerous.

Her ugly red hands trembling, she watched nervously as the TSA officer called over a colleague. In addition to hoping they didn't think she was a terrorist, she hoped they would not take her artillery, weapons to help her make it through this torturous travel. She had contaminated her pills. Van Morrison wasn't working. And damn, she already needed to pee, and it would be at least another ten hours until Oxford. And as usual, Oliver's sarcastic muttering was exacerbating more than it was helping.

Why is he worried about you? He's the one who looks like fucking precaptured Saddam Hussein with his oversized curly moustache and sadistic grin. Vile, fetid, germ-infested dictators, terrorists, and Transportation Security Administration officers. It's wrong for them to take your stuff. You have constitutional rights, you know. You're still in the goddamn United States.

She tried to ignore Oliver, making it clear that this wasn't the time or place for his ranting. She was trying to pay attention to the TSA officer; she had to make it through.

As if following the "screening for terrorist while wary of ACLU attorney" line of questioning, the TSA officer probed gently but firmly, "And where are you flying and for what purpose?"

Gloria's posture betrayed her wish to disappear. Her eyes darted from her bag to the TSA officer to Oliver and to the other faces in the security line, which were looking on with more curiosity than consternation now. But she hated this attention. Right now she was the gorilla at the zoo—the psychotic, dangerous gorilla crouching in the corner waiting to be euthanized.

Unable to make eye contact, she mumbled to the TSA officer, who strained to hear her incoherent response as she rubbed her temples with her ugly red hands.

"Oxford. I mean London. Flying to London, driving to Oxford. Well actually, a driver is picking me up in London and taking me to Oxford. The city and university, I mean. Going to study at St. Cross College. Of course, St. Cross is part of Oxford University. I'm a Rhodes Scholar studying feminine—I mean *feminist* poetry."

She did not know whether it was her long-winded response or ugly red hands, but the TSA officer seemed to believe her. He even stifled a smirk handling her Sylvia Plath books while removing contraband cleaning weapons from her bag.

For the briefest moment, Gloria was insulted by his seemingly misogynistic suggestion that a female terrorist would not be reading Sylvia Plath. What else would she be reading? Gloria was certain those female suicide bombers, even the illiterate ones, understood *Ariel* and *The Bell Jar* all too well. Why else would someone opt to die and leave her children by blowing herself up or putting her head in an oven?

The TSA officer cleared his throat before rendering his final verdict: "No Lysol. And only 3.4 ounces of hand sanitizer. I have to take all the rest of these unless you'd like to check them."

Gloria kept rubbing her ugly red hands as she tried to make sense of what to do. She looked back at the long security line; it was so crowded with so many germ-infested people. No way she could start over, but she needed her cleaning weapons, her survival gear. Oliver reminded her that she desperately needed her gear.

What are you doing? Just giving your stuff away. Who cares about the fact that airplanes are not routinely cleaned and sanitized between flights? Who cares about the fact that viruses like influenza can survive for hours on all airplane surfaces? Who cares about communicable diseases, germs, and early death? And don't forget SARS. That's a glorious way to go. SARS for Superstar.

Trapped and resigned, Gloria quietly answered the TSA officer, "You can take them."

As soon as she left security, however, Gloria dashed to the nearest airport kiosk like a woman on a mission. She studied the display of personal products on a wall behind a distracted cashier. Toothpaste. Toothbrushes. Tampons. Tylenol. Tums. And hand sanitizer! She stared at the hand sanitizer with the wide, lustful eyes of a junkie. She needed it. She craved it. As much as she could get to replenish her cache. Practically salivating, Gloria asked the cashier for Purell.

When the cashier placed one bottle on the counter, Gloria added, "All of them, please."

The young cashier either did not hear or chose not to, as she continued reading from a weathered issue of last month's *People*.

Gloria demanded, "All of the bottles of hand sanitizer, please. I'll be late for my flight. I need them now! Please."

The apathetic Latina teenager shrugged as she put all eight bottles on the counter, lining them up in a row. When Gloria asked whether there were more bottles in back, the cashier shook her long black hair and put down her magazine, glaring at Gloria like she was crazy.

And at least at this moment, Gloria was crazy. At Oliver's urging, crazy, crazed Gloria spent the next hour running from airport kiosk to airport kiosk buying as much hand sanitizer as she could to replenish her stock. By the time she boarded her flight an hour later, she had essentially cleaned out all the available hand sanitizer in Terminal C at O'Hare Airport.

4.

Henry continued playing guitar, trying hard to show his scowling father that he did not give a damn.

"You forgot something, Henry. Didn't you?"

Henry continued to play, ignoring his angry father.

"Henry has a lot on his mind, Dad. Moving into St. Cross College today. Preparing for his hearing in a few months," Claire anxiously explained in a futile attempt to smooth things over.

"A mere formality for Henry, given my status as chair. I gave him the research and outline, practically wrote the bloody paper for him. But I can't take his medication for him." Nicholas was looking directly at Henry now. "You need to adjust your priorities, Henry."

Henry continued to play guitar as his father's anger mounted.

"I'm talking with you," Nicholas growled.

Henry quietly said, "*At.*"

"Excuse me, did I miss something?" Nicholas asked, hostility rising.

Henry stopped playing. His father was a daft prick. More like an arrogant prick.

"You are talking *at* me. Not *with* me."

"How terrible of me to question the fact that my son remembers his 500 useless records while leaving behind crucial medication," Nicholas seethed as he kicked one of the record crates for dramatic effect and to infuriate Henry, no doubt.

Trying to contain his own anger, Henry stubbornly moved the crate out of his father's reach and resumed strumming his guitar over his father's shouting.

"Henry, I am talking *to* you. No matter where you live, I am your father!"

Henry stopped playing. He looked at his father with scorn and went for the jugular.

"*About*. You're talking *about* me. In the third person. Like I'm not even here."

The Achilles' heel that belonged to both of them, Nicholas could not respond to this. If they were keeping score, Henry won—but not really. In this particular dysfunctional family game, nobody won. At the end, everyone remained despondent, disillusioned, and utterly resigned. Accordingly, a defeated and noticeably more subdued Nicholas shrugged his shoulders.

"Take your medication. Don't take your medication. It is up to you, Henry. At twenty-five, you need to take responsibility for your own life. For once."

"Why should I when you're so much more capable, Dad?" Henry asked, trying to suppress the acid in his own voice.

Nicholas waved him off, saying, "Goodbye, Claire. Henry."

Claire and Henry watched Nicholas march down the long gravel driveway to his car.

Before getting in, Nicholas turned back to reproach, "And please no cigarette butts by the tree, Claire." Clearing his throat as if cocking a gun to deploy maximum guilt, he added, "Don't you know that was your mother's favorite?"

Lambasting Henry was not enough. He had to berate Claire as well, as if she were desecrating their mother's corpse with bloody cigarette ashes. What a prick. After he drove away, Henry resumed playing his guitar, stealing glances at his nervous older sister. Claire's hands were shaking, making it nearly impossible to light another cigarette.

Although he appeared cool, Henry was shaking on the inside. His father always made him feel that way. But he dared not admit it to Claire. She would use it against him one way or another, trying to force more disastrous family reunions. Silly girl. Didn't she know that not wanting to be together was the only thing upon which both father and son agreed? Take that away, and there truly would be nothing left.

Henry put down his guitar, reached for his sister's trembling hand, and with his classic dimpled sneer said, "God, I love that man."

Indeed, he was very grateful to be moving into St. Cross College. He had to get away from those arrogant pricks at Jesus College. He had to get away from his father, the biggest prick of all. He had to get away from *Equanimity*.

He recalled the solicitor saying that under the terms of his mother's will and arrangements made by his maternal grandfather, the house was technically—legally—his, as sole male heir, his ownership fully vesting when he turned thirty. Henry turned around and looked back at what many would call a beautiful and grand old house.

But if it were up to him, he would torch the place, collect the insurance proceeds, and spend whatever money and time he had left on the planet listening to Van Morrison as far away from *Equanimity* and Oxford as possible.

5.

Boarding was well under way, but Gloria found her business-class aisle seat quickly. Fortunately and unexpectedly, she was the first to arrive in her two-person row. Oliver always sat behind her on airplanes so he could more easily whisper in her ear to calm her down and keep her focused.

At Oliver's urging, Gloria used newly purchased antibacterial wipes to disinfect her seat, armrests, personal video monitor, and tray table. She also wiped the seat, armrests, video monitor, tray table, and window next to her before the seat's occupant, an attractive woman in her late twenties carrying a stack of fashion magazines and a Louis Vuitton Neverfull tote, tapped her on the shoulder.

"Excuse me, I think this is my seat," she said kindly as she examined her boarding pass to double-check.

Embarrassed, Gloria apologized and quickly got out of the way so her rowmate could sit down. The woman introduced herself as Madison and began making conversation with Gloria. While Gloria tried to be polite and keep up with her neighbor's small talk, she felt self-conscious about her presumptuous and utterly fanatical cleaning rituals. Gloria tried to hide behind her worn copy of *The Bell Jar* to avoid any more trivial conversation, but it did not work.

Madison ignored Gloria's pretext and tried to get to know her, to draw her out even. Gloria thought it ironic and slightly irritating that chatty Madison was going out of her way to make Gloria feel comfortable and less embarrassed, when all she was doing was making her feel less comfortable and more embarrassed.

The flight was already going to be hell, and Madison's polite banter and extroverted people skills were not making it any easier. Admittedly, Madison was innocuous enough and meant well. Nice, smart, pretty, successful, outgoing, *blah, blah, blah*—exactly the kind of person of whom Gloria should be jealous. More precisely, she was exactly the kind of person Gladys, her mother, would be proud to take to dinner at the club or in Manhattan with important clients.

Gloria was not jealous of Madison's well-paying advertising position at the London office of *Vogue* magazine. She was not jealous of her "incredibly accomplished" fiancé with an MBA from the University of Chicago and Jewish-sounding last name. She was not jealous of Madison's soft white hands and the gleaming engagement ring that adorned the left hand.

Gloria put very little stock in those Sigma Delta Tau Jewish Barbie Doll fantasies. She had resigned herself long ago to the fact that her own hands, like her life, were far too messed up to be entwined with any true love and accompanying piece of platinum.

At the moment, the only aspect of Madison's life arousing Gloria's jealousy was her Diet Coke. Gloria gazed on as Madison raised the drink to her lips as if in slow motion; the bubbles and splash were intoxicating, like a beer commercial during the Super Bowl.

Throughout the flight, Gloria stared with unabashed lust and envy as her seatmate tossed down Diet Coke after Diet Coke. It was torture, pure hell. And Gloria was jealous. Oliver whispered in her ear, trying to keep her disciplined and focused.

You're stronger than you think, Superstar. Forget the Diet Coke. What if you have to pee on this dirty, fetid, germ-infested airplane, this vile compression chamber with its recycled air and recycled germs? Can't you smell the stench coming from the bathroom? Putrid stench with a little potpourri thrown in to make you think you're getting value in this overpriced business-class torture chamber.

No Diet Coke until Oxford, where you can pee in your germ-free bathroom that you clean with your own hands.

In spite of his intentions, Oliver was not a comfort. Van Morrison's music wasn't working either. She had no pills. And reading Sylvia Plath only made her want to jump out the window. As the premature night set in, she was the only person awake in the dark business-class cabin, sitting in the yellow glow of her lone reading light.

Gloria lathered on hand sanitizer and silently chanted Stephen Crane's mantra. She was going round and round and making no progress whatsoever. She hoped the pilots were making better progress flying to England. In England—at Oxford—she would pee, but she could not think about that now.

She looked over at Madison, who was sound asleep, stretched out in her fully reclined seat wearing the red American Airlines sleep mask with the matching red blanket pulled to her neck. Gloria was appalled and curious at how Madison could put the germ-infested fabric—used for multiple flights and multiple people—on and around her face, so close to her nose and mouth. Staring at Madison with repulsion and envy, Gloria squirmed and wriggled through most of the night, plagued by her bursting bladder and ravenous thirst.

At the moment, she did not feel like Frank Moshe Zimmerman's Superstar. How ironic that he had redeemed 150,000 American AAdvantage miles for Gloria to be stuck in this business-class hell. She might as well have been sitting in a middle seat in economy with two obese sleepers drooling on either side. It made no difference.

Actually, she might have been best off stowed in the belly of the plane, barricaded by the dusty, dirty luggage and the germ-infested caged beasts. At least then she would not have to stare longingly at the illuminated *Vacancy* sign on the bathroom door, whose cruel mission was to taunt and beckon her all through the long, torturous night.

It had not been a torturous night for Madison, who awoke with the sunrise. Refreshed from a full night of sleep, she was eating an omelet and once again being entirely too chatty for Gloria's liking.

"Gloria, do you LashDip?" Madison asked, staring at Gloria's eyes with too much intensity for so early in the morning.

"Lash *what*?" Gloria asked, trying to sound polite in spite of the incomprehensible and seemingly ridiculous question.

Madison responded with a mouth full of food, which only exacerbated the language barrier; Gloria could barely understand what she was saying through her loud swallowing.

"LashDip? Semipermanent mascara? You look so well rested. And I know you didn't sneak off to the bathroom to redo your makeup. You've been parked in your seat the whole trip."

Could Madison be even more of a freak than Gloria? Gloria was anything but well rested, and her bladder was about to explode. Hadn't observant, chatty Madison noticed the squirming? Tired and uncomfortable, Gloria pretended to sip black coffee as she squirmed in her seat some more, listening to Madison drone on. She desperately concealed her need to pee as she politely played her part in the meaningless conversation. Oliver was resting quietly, and Gloria didn't know what to do with herself. In a way, the idiotic banter was a welcome distraction.

"Assistant sales manager at British *Vogue* is a huge stepping stone if I want *Vogue Vogue*."

"*Vogue Vogue*?" Gloria asked, crossing her legs for the umpteenth time.

"Headquarters in New York. My parents want me to stay in Chicago and think it's self-centered transferring to London now and possibly New York in a few years. They just don't understand. If you really want to be someone in journalism, you need to be in New York," Madison explained matter-of-factly as she shoved a large, indelicate bite of germ-infested omelet in her mouth.

Gloria noticed some stray egg on Madison's lip in the shape of Big Ben's clock tower. She thought it might be a Freudian hallucination, manifested by her overwhelming desire to be in England already—to pee in England already.

Obsessed with the stray egg, Gloria answered Madison distractedly, "It sounds like your fiancé understands." Gloria continued speaking while watching Madison level Big Ben with her tongue. "You moving to London for a while?"

"Andrew's absolutely incredible. Totally has faith in us. He'll be in Chicago for the year. I'll be in London. Doesn't matter because we're in love, and that fact alone can see us through...anything. Before saying goodbye, he quoted Shakespeare's famous poem, 'Love is not love....' Damn, how does it go? You must know the one."

Gloria, a Phi Beta Kappa English Language and Literature major at Yale, Rhodes Scholar, and special research assistant to Margo Mitchell, professor of Poetry at Oxford, knew Shakespeare's sonnets well. And Sonnet 116 was one of her favorites. She smiled at Madison as she recited the poem in a strong melodic voice, sounding much more confident than her usual speaking voice, which was quiet and reserved.

> Let me not to the marriage of true minds
> Admit impediments. Love is not love
> Which alters when it alteration finds,
> Or bends with the remover to remove:
> O no! It is an ever-fixed mark
> That looks on tempests and is never shaken;
> It is the star to every wandering bark,
> Whose worth's unknown, although his height be taken.
>
> Love's not Time's fool, though rosy lips and cheeks
> Within his bending sickle's compass come:
> Love alters not with his brief hours and weeks,
> But bears it out even to the edge of doom.
> If this be error and upon me proved,
> I never writ, nor no man ever loved.

"You are good. Real Oxford material," Madison remarked in admiration, wiping her lips with the red germ-infested polyester napkin.

Her smile slowly waned, though, as she turned toward the porthole window, gazing at the orange and pink sunrise peeking through a vast carpet of clouds.

"Going to miss Andrew," she sighed, examining her engagement ring and then kissing it with her germ-infested-omelet-residue-saliva lips.

After admiring her own hands, Madison automatically looked over at Gloria's. Although they had been together for hours, it was the first time she really noticed Gloria's hands.

Madison gasped out loud and said, "Gloria, you're such a pretty girl, but your hands? Were you burned in a fire or something?"

Gloria avoided Madison's horrified gaze as she quietly and timidly muttered, "Something."

"I'm sorry. I hope I didn't overstep..." Madison said with contrition.

Gloria was accustomed to damage control when it came to her shocking hands. Perhaps she should have put on her white gloves, but those attracted attention as well, especially in summer.

She put her unsightly hands in her pockets and reassured, "No. It's fine. Please don't worry, Madison."

At least Madison was kind about Gloria's hands. Unlike Gloria's mother, who had been mortified when the manicurist, holding Gloria's coarse hands, compared them to sandpaper. Her mother's embarrassment only made it worse, made her rub her hands more intensely and with more hand sanitizer, making them redder and rougher. *I saw a man pursuing the horizon. Round and round they sped.*

It was a vicious cycle. *Round and round.* And at the pompous salon on Oak Street, Gloria kept rubbing and rubbing like Lady fucking Macbeth. Her hands were certainly a sorry sight, as Shakespeare would say, but when did mental illness become murder? And who was to blame for Gloria's mental illness?

Perhaps that question did not even matter. It was already too late, and Gloria at twenty-two was irrevocably messed up. As Lady Macbeth put it, "Things without all remedy should be without regard—what's done is done."

Madison flashed another apologetic smile. "I'm also sorry because I have to use the bathroom again before we land. Do you mind holding my tray so I can get out of my seat? You must be sick and tired of me getting up so much to pee. Too much to drink. Next time I'll get an aisle seat, I promise. I'm so sorry, Gloria."

"No problem," Gloria replied, as she forced another reassuring smile and reached for Madison's tray with her ugly red hands.

6.

Reluctantly, Claire left Henry and his crates in the new flat at St. Cross. She lit a nervous cigarette as she rambled toward her office at Radcliffe Infirmary and Hospital not knowing what to do with her unwanted sisterly concern. She had intended to help Henry unpack and organize his belongings, but he had insisted on doing it—or, rather, not doing it—himself.

Henry's new flat, like his life, was chaotic, disorganized, and an utter mess. He had said that while he appreciated Claire's good intentions, he was quite capable of sorting out or living with his own mess, whether at St. Cross, *Equanimity*, or anywhere. As usual, her little brother, who stood much taller, looked down at her with gentle humor in his green eyes, urging her to act as sister rather than mother.

Claire wanted to give Henry his independence, but she had difficulty letting him go. Indeed, his past history and current problems were complicated. As she strode past the mathematics building, Claire thought that all the abacuses in all of Oxford could not possibly keep count of the many times she had almost lost him. Henry had more lives and chances than the craftiest, luckiest cat.

She may have been employed as a psychologist at Radcliffe, but saving Henry was her real job, her most important job. Claire didn't think of herself as martyr or hero; it's just that she was desperate. And Henry was reckless.

Claire knew very well that Henry was more capable than most gave him credit for. Christ, he was more capable than he gave himself credit for. She was the needy one. She needed Henry so she could nag him and care for him and laugh with him and poke fun at their overbearing father with him.

She needed Henry so they could listen to those bloody Van Morrison records and remember Mum. Although lately, she was tiring of Van Morrison, especially the songs Henry played constantly and insisted she have played at his funeral with accompanying lyrics engraved on his headstone. Much to Henry's sadistic delight, she found his macabre requests more disturbing than amusing. And they only fueled her incessant worry.

Claire suddenly stopped in her tracks, worrying about Henry's medication. Did he remember to bring it to St. Cross? Did he leave his medication on the bench in the front garden of *Equanimity*? She meant to ask him about it. She meant to place it in the loo in a conspicuous location where, of course, he would not forget.

Henry was always forgetting important things: His pills. His appointments. To call her back. To call their father. To go to class. To work on his candidacy paper. He could be so lax. It wasn't that he didn't care. If anything, he cared too much, which only caused him to shut down and tune out. And when Claire mentioned this to him, he put his Van Morrison on and tuned her out.

Sitting on a bench in front of Ashmolean Museum, Claire lit another cigarette and thought of the afternoons their mother took them to Ashmolean when they were children. One of the oldest buildings at Oxford, Ashmolean was the world's first university museum, built in the 1600s to display Elias Ashmole's "Cabinet of Curiosities." Claire and Henry treasured the exotic collection of zoological specimens.

Young Henry was obsessed with the Dodo bird, the most infamous part of Ashmole's gift. Ashmole had bequeathed the stuffed body of the last Dodo bird ever seen in Europe. But by 1755 the Dodo bird was so moth-eaten that, except for its head and one claw, it was practically destroyed. Henry always felt sorry for the extinct flightless bird with its strange hooked bill and even stranger name.

He would endlessly dwell on that bloody Dodo and its humiliating decay. Claire felt a pang of guilt recalling her childhood teasing, calling Henry "Dodo Brain" and making him cry. It had been a long time since she'd seen him cry, in spite of all the grown-up tragedies they had endured and all the people and feelings that were now extinct.

Sitting across from Ashmolean's entrance, Claire took out her mobile to ring Henry to remind him of his medication. But she clicked off before he could answer. He would not be pleased she was mothering him again, only thirty minutes after his plea for freedom. Would she ever learn? Sifting through her satchel, she replaced her nagging phone with a hardback ruled journal titled *Wednesday Worry List*.

Wednesday Worry List was devised by her supervising psychologist, Dr. Downing, who had been concerned about Claire's own escalating anxiety, especially since Claire's professional expertise was supposed to be in treating anxiety. Dr. Downing had insisted that Claire write all her worries in a journal and not think about them or do anything to resolve them until the following Wednesday. At first Claire was skeptical, but much to her surprise, she found that Dr. Downing was quite right.

When she examined her journal on each subsequent Wednesday, many of the worries had resolved themselves and could be crossed off. Although Claire had to admit this rarely applied to worries about Henry. Still, she promised Downing she would honor the process even when it came to her reckless brother.

As Claire started writing, the worries about Dodo Brain flowed:

8. *Will Henry find and regularly take his medication?*

9. *Will Henry remember his next medical appointment at Radcliffe with Dr. Witherspoon in a fortnight's time?*

10. *Will Henry write and defend his candidacy paper or defer yet again?*

11. *Will Henry initiate contact with Dad this term without intervention or prompting?*

12. *Will Dad support Henry's—*

Claire's mad scribbling was interrupted by the pulsating ringtone of her mobile. Damn, it was Alfred! Alfred was the last person with whom she wanted to speak.

Sitting amidst the columns of Ashmolean's ancient façade, she decided she much preferred their company to Alfred's. They may have been quiet, but unlike Alfred, they were good listeners. They were sturdy and reliable and would always be there for her. For shelter. For support. A landmark when she was lost. She could not say the same about Alfred. After all, he comprised worries #4, #5, and #6 on her list. And her worries about Alfred kept multiplying, requiring almost as many abacus beads as her worries about Henry.

True, Henry was still the object of more worries than Alfred, but at least her little brother was there for Claire and loved her. She could not say the same about Alfred. No, not at all. Ignoring Alfred's second call, Claire took another long drag of her cigarette, comtemplating how she was the real Dodo Brain in the family.

7.

anding at Heathrow was not enough to resolve Gloria's
discomfort. Bladder bursting, she walked through Heathrow
straight past the many *Toilet* signs in her path. Men, women,
and children came out of the bathrooms with what seemed like
exaggerated expressions of relief and comfort. Oliver was still wary,
reminding her of dangerous airport germs.

*English airport toilets are not cleaner than those in the States,
even if the Brits seem more polite and civilized. You can wait until your
own germ-free bathroom in Oxford. You're almost there, Superstar.
You can pee in Oxford. Keep moving. Luggage, customs, car, toilet.*

Baggage Reclaim at Heathrow was crowded with a throng of
hot, sweaty travelers in desperate need of their luggage, hydration,
and better air-conditioning. Although Gloria was also hot and
dehydrated, she put on her white cotton gloves, a fitted linen blazer,
large sunglasses, and a light-blue Hermes scarf before grabbing a
luggage cart.

Several travelers standing by the luggage carousel stared at
Gloria. She looked like a wannabe 1950s movie star, alluringly

covered up. She self-consciously dodged their eyes, noticing a nearby Muslim family, the only other travelers at the carousel more covered up than she. She inched over to stand nearer to them in a futile attempt to blend in.

A hired driver waited for her outside of passport control and customs. He looked like a formal English gentleman from central casting, immune to the August heat in his dark suit, chauffeur cap, and his own ridiculous white gloves. Gloria refused to shake his hand even through their two layers of impenetrable fabric and offered instead a polite wave.

Seated in the back of the fancy black sedan, she rhythmically crossed and uncrossed her legs to contain her agonizing bladder. She could barely hold on. She was completely unaware of the green and lush English landscape of gentle rolling hills speckled with charming limestone villages outside her window. She rubbed her hands with hand sanitizer as she chanted Stephen Crane incessantly in her mind. *I saw a man pursuing the horizon.*

Sitting in the backseat of a strange car in a strange land with a bursting bladder and bottle of hand sanitizer, Gloria felt scared and alone. The Zimmermans had always said they were forcing Gloria into daunting new places "for her own good." They wanted to provide her with "all the enriching, stimulating, and challenging worldly experiences" their working-class Skokie immigrant parents were unable to provide for them or even contemplate.

They "knew she could do it" and constantly urged her to "struggle through difficult challenges" in order to prove she was "their Superstar." She had to prove her status again and again. Her life had been one long job interview. But as long as she was taking her pills, hiding her hands, and earning As, there did not seem to be any problem from her parents' perspective.

Her earliest memory of this tough-love *Great Santini* parenting strategy was when she was six years old, spending a scorching July 4th weekend at her aunt's Lakeside, Michigan, summerhouse. Ignoring her protests and declarations of dependence, her father decided to throw her into the pool to prove to her and all the older cousins that she too was a "superstar swimmer" who could navigate the deep end "like the big kids."

Gloria vividly remembered making contact with the overly chlorinated water on that revolutionary day and how her fragile six-year-old body landing in the water sounded like a slap in the face. For Gloria, it had been revolutionary in ways her father did not intend and could not even imagine.

She also remembered being equally transformed several years later when she read "The Swimming Lesson" by Mary Oliver. The poet's uncanny accuracy and empathy astounded her. It was as if Mary Oliver had lived inside Gloria's own gut since she hit the water on that fateful July 4th when she was six.

> *Feeling the icy kick, the endless waves*
> *Reaching around my life, I moved my arms*
> *And coughed, and in the end saw land.*
>
> *Somebody, I suppose,*
> *Remembering the medieval maxim,*
> *Had tossed me in,*
> *Had wanted me to learn to swim,*

Gloria recalled the taste of chlorine in the back of her throat when she snorted cold water, immersed in the deep pool. She felt like she was drowning.

> *Not knowing that none of us, who ever came back*
> *From that long lonely fall and frenzied rising,*
> *Ever learned anything at all*
> *About swimming, but only*
> *How to put off, one by one,*
> *Dreams and pity, love and grace—*
> *How to survive in any place.*

Mary Oliver understood. Mary Oliver's poem spoke to, about, and for Gloria, especially when she was first diagnosed with Obsessive-Compulsive Disorder. Mary Oliver uniquely understood the mounting pressure from the outside world and her anxious brain. And so Mary Oliver became her close friend in the seventh grade when the pressure from all fronts had peaked beyond control.

Mary Oliver was the only one she could hold on to when the capricious winds of adolescence blew the real friends away, their cruel epithets lingering in the chilly atmosphere. Oliver's poetry helped Gloria calm down, making sense of the stormy tempests in her head and in her world.

The psychologist who had originally diagnosed the OCD when Gloria was thirteen had encouraged her to externalize her OCD by *naming it*. The first name that came to mind was *Oliver*. The psychologist had wanted Gloria to consider Oliver her adversary. But whenever possible, Gloria threw away the pills, keeping Oliver close as her friend, her only real, reliable, and germ-fighting friend.

Frank had fired that psychologist the moment she challenged him to "face the facts about his sick daughter" and had suggested there was a part of Gloria that "wanted to be sick." Wanted to embarrass her mother at the club. Wanted people to see her ugly red hands. Wanted people to see her. Wanted her parents to see her, *really* see her.

The psychologist, who Frank had cast aside as an "alarmist bitch," had a point: without Oliver—without her OCD—Gloria was afraid she might totally disappear. While Gloria liked that psychologist, she also liked Oliver. She loved Oliver—*most of the time*. At least her father couldn't fire Oliver; he was under her jurisdiction—*most of the time*. And unlike her parents or the psychologist, Oliver had always been there, protecting her. Trying to, anyways.

Her parents were now tossing her into a new deep end: Oxford. She knew from experience that she would survive, but she was not ready to be thrown off the platform just yet. She needed some time to take in the enormity of her fall. And she needed to pee.

Interrupting her frantic meditation, the driver struck up polite conversation. "So, Miss Zimmerman, comfortable travels? First time in Oxford?"

Gloria smiled at him awkwardly, nodding her head. Under the circumstances, it was the best she could do without totally losing control. As they approached Oxford proper, Gloria wanted to be the poetry scholar she purported to be. She wanted to be the poetry scholar working for the professor of Poetry at Oxford.

She wanted to be the poetry scholar who could appreciate those famous words of Matthew Arnold, the first professor of Poetry at Oxford. He had immortalized this ancient city and exalted university, describing it as "that sweet city with her dreaming spires, she need not June for beauty's heightening."

But June was over; it was already late August. And Gloria, tormented by Oliver, her strict OCD, and bursting bladder, stared out the window without seeing the dreaming spires—without seeing a damn thing. It was impossible to contemplate Oxford's beauty and what the university held in store for her when all she could hope for was the germ-free splendor of white porcelain, water, and a flush mechanism.

8.

Margo Mitchell left lunch with Rebecca Greenberg wondering whether it was possible to file for divorce from an editor—a pushy, brilliant, armchair-psychologist New York book editor. True, it had been over twenty years, and they had been through a great deal together.

Their prolific partnership had resulted in over ten books, six reprints, editions translated into more than five languages, over 300 published poems, a MacArthur Genius Grant, and a Pulitzer Prize. Of course, the biggest professional crown was Margo's installation as professor of Poetry at Oxford University and Master of St. Cross College. They also had been through six rounds of chemotherapy, thirty-three days of radiation, six deaths of parents and siblings, and four domestic partners.

Over the years, Becca had become a very close friend. Unlike her decorous British publisher, who was also a good friend, Becca was a tough New Yorker who could be brutally frank and direct with both her admiration and admonition. Margo usually appreciated this refreshing American candor, knowing it came from a place of genuine concern.

In Becca, she had found a kindred intellectual spirit, poetic soul sister, and writing midwife who had stayed with her during some very difficult times in her writing life and in her *life* life. Aside from Margo's partner, Patricia, Becca was the person with whom Margo shared some of her most intimate musings about poetry and everything.

But this time her pushy chum, with her thick New York accent and lack of social filters, had gone too far and said too much. How dare she accuse Margo of—How did she put it?—"encouraging young women to drown in tragedy, suspended in a fallacious web of sadness when you yourself have broken free."

Margo was livid. Rebecca, one of the finest editors in New York, knew better than to insult a Pulitzer Prize–winning poet with a ghastly mixed metaphor. And how dare she accuse Margo of being a fraud and unworthy mentor to her readers, students, and research assistants?

Margo had great affection for her readers, students, and research assistants. Moreover, Margo's students and research assistants adored her and learned a great deal under her tutelage. Some had even become accomplished poets in their own right. Ironically, heavy-handed Rebecca Greenberg had even published some of their poetry, even if composed of morose reflections on "drowning in a web of sadness." Bollocks!

Just because Becca had recently begun a new relationship and course of antidepressants did not mean that Margo was obligated to inform the world of her own happiness. Becca had accused Margo of "cruelty in refusing to share her transformation from confessional poet to transcendental poet. From Anne Sexton's tragedy to Maxine Kumin's hope. From sadness to happiness. From breast cancer to life beyond chemotherapy and radiation." The ghastly clichés were giving Margo indigestion.

Margo thought it must have been about money. Although Rebecca Greenberg led a successful eponymous imprint, the corporate publishing giant that owned her press was experiencing the economic impact of a truncated and changing publishing industry: The proliferation of eBooks. Large bookstore chains closing. Diminishing marketing budgets. The widespread phenomenon of self-publishing and social media.

But wasn't Becca already selling enough books on Margo's behalf? Margo's tragic confessional poetry books provided her publisher decent returns on multiple reprints and editions, eBooks, audiobooks, and translations. Critical praise did enhance sales, especially when compared to other academics. Margo's books were regularly assigned in poetry classes in universities around the world. Why was Becca trying to force her to publish more? Greedy American.

Margo stormed through the gates of St. Cross College huffing and puffing, trying to fill her lungs with more rage, like she was blowing up a balloon. But when she reached the sundial in the center of the quad, she sighed as she collapsed onto the nearest teak bench. She could no longer hold on to the air or anger—the untied balloon whizzed and swirled and shrunk toward its inevitable reunion with the ground.

A calmer Margo stared at the sundial, not knowing what to think. An ancient Egyptian invention, the sundial situated one in time and place. Like Becca, it seemed to be challenging Margo to think about where she was in contrast to where she had been. Perhaps she did have a responsibility to share this journey through her more recent poems?

Bugger! Why did she show them to Becca in the first place? Of course such a lunch would include a loud Jewish woman's "come to Jesus" speech, imploring her to publish a new book of "happy" poetry, whatever that meant.

Margo was no longer angry, but she was not particularly happy at the moment. She was out of sorts. Their argument had sabotaged the day, and she was not feeling ready to receive her new research assistants, who would be arriving to St. Cross shortly. Margo was interested, however, in one new research assistant in particular—Rhodes Scholar Gloria Zimmerman from Chicago. Even without having met her, Margo was indebted to Gloria for miraculously finding the missing Teasdale manuscript at Yale. Margo wondered what Gloria was like.

A colleague in the English department at Yale had described Gloria as "an obsessive and brilliant girl who's tortured—but in a *good* way." What a strange thing to say about a young woman. Was it a compliment? Was there a clinical diagnosis buried in the admiration? Was being tortured a good thing? Did one have to be tortured to understand feminist confessional poetry? Was this a precondition in their field?

Margo was curious and concerned about Gloria's affliction. Would their research together alleviate or exacerbate her suffering? Were Margo and her fellow confessional poets unconsciously encouraging membership for these young women in a sisterhood of sadness? Was her pushy editor and dear friend on to something?

These questions gnawed at her as she took out a copy of Gloria's Rhodes application from a file folder in her handbag. While Gloria's essay may have been a bit stiff and lifeless, her personal poetry was quite vibrant. There was something astir in her poem about Lake Michigan.

> *Looking at the lake*
> *Waves swishing by*
> *Like a point of no return*
> *Swirled into the dust storm of tomorrow*
> *You never know what might happen*
> *Looking around in pure unfamiliarity*
> *It seems so far from home*
> *But it will clear up and the rain is sometimes fun*
> *Just everyday might not be the one*

In her essay, Gloria had described herself as emulating the confessional poets, but Margo Mitchell disagreed. Gloria's lively images (and perhaps a novice mixed metaphor or two) conjured the spark of something. Even the smallest flame can build to fire. For a tortured girl and a formerly tortured Pulitzer Prize-winning poet, *pure unfamiliarity* held promise. It was a place to start.

9.

Students and faculty were milling in and around the main courtyard of St. Cross, but blind to her surroundings, Gloria did not notice. All she wanted to see was her toilet. While she had endured the long trip from Chicago without giving in or peeing in her pants, the prospect now of getting from the front gate of St. Cross into her new room seemed quite impossible.

Probably sensing her bewilderment, the driver helped her drag her many bags through the busy quad and handed her luggage to a waiting porter, who offered to take it to her new accommodations. Keys in hand, she was on the last leg of her journey in search of her toilet.

Frank and Gladys had assured her that they "paid through the nose for the best room in the house," a minisuite with a bedroom, kitchenette, and bathroom. With her security pouch still firmly across her about-to-explode body and clutching her carry-ons filled with emergency short-term cleaning products and other antigerm paraphernalia she was able to assemble at the airport, she scurried through the courtyard in search of relief.

So focused on meeting and cleaning her new toilet, she was completely oblivious to the courtyard's splendor—its summer greenery with splashes of vivid color from blooming rhododendrons and azaleas, the sphere sundial encased by wooden benches, and all the surrounding Gothic-style buildings.

A black German shepherd was enjoying the activity in the courtyard and followed Gloria as she dashed through the crowded quad. Oliver hated dogs even more than people and did not hesitate to remind Gloria.

Heartworms, whipworms, hookworms, roundworms, and tapeworms.

Gloria tried to ignore Oliver as well as the dog, as the promise of near relief was unbearable. She began sprinting toward her new room.

Finally in her new suite, she frenetically grabbed the antibacterial wipes and toilet paper from her bag. She opened the door to the bathroom. But when she came barreling through, all plans were foiled.

Dumbstruck, Gloria rubbed her eyes with ugly red hands, not trusting her sight. A young man with red hair and wearing a vintage Who shirt was sitting on her germ-infested toilet and playing Van Morrison's 1968 love anthem, "Sweet Thing," on a red Martin acoustic guitar.

10.

Claire was embarrassed as she walked back to her office with the other psychologists from her department. The colleagues who were not falsely congratulating her were staring at her with puzzled expressions. Once again, thirty-year-old Dr. Claire Young was winning at leapfrog, landing an undeserved promotion.

Many of the doctors were quite kind about it; only a few looked at her with unabashed envy and scorn. Most were smiling but dumbfounded. Although quite capable and hardworking, Claire did not have the experience or even the expertise for this plum assignment. Her prestigious appointment did not make sense. Department chair Dr. Mars had announced that Claire was to head a high-profile task force on proactive strategies for postgraduate mental health, reporting directly to the vice chancellor.

The vice chancellor and other high-ranking officers at the university were very concerned and feeling a great deal of external pressure in the wake of a doctoral student's recent suicide. The Japanese biophysics student had drowned in her bathtub. The internal university investigation had concluded that the tragic submersion was intentional.

Claire wondered how they knew about the student's intention. It was hard enough figuring out intentions when people were alive. Christ, it was hard enough figuring out one's own intentions. How could they know with any certainty what that student intended or suffered?

The most disturbing part of the investigation was that when fellow students were asked about whether she had ever talked about suicide, depression, stress, or just feeling sad and lonely, no one ever remembered having had a conversation with her unrelated to course content or dissertation research. No small talk about the weather, the latest cinema, a recommended good book. Nobody recalled having lunch, going to a pub, having tea, or visiting her flat. It was as if the poor girl had been invisible, dead before she was dead.

The university knew it had to improve its outreach to postgraduate students, who tended to keep their mental illness and stress hidden away. In addition, many postgraduate students did not have the support system and sense of community enjoyed by younger students. Claire was to lead an esteemed group that would develop such a support network and devise a system to identify those lonely, suffering postgraduates.

Her brother was just such a lonely, suffering postgraduate, so Claire felt ready for her task. She hoped her colleagues at Radcliffe and on the committee would come to think of her as a worthy leader. More than anything, she wanted credibility with them. But it was hard for her even to give credibility to herself. After all, she and that arse Dr. Alfred Mars, chair of her department, had been sleeping together for over three weeks. And her perceptive colleagues were starting to look at her as if they knew.

11.

·

Seeing Gloria, the redhead with the red guitar stopped playing and smiled with a mixture of embarrassment and amusement. But it was mostly amusement Gloria detected in his bright green eyes. She, on the other hand, was a deer in headlights. Motionless. Speechless. Totally and utterly shocked and embarrassed, her face turned as red as her ugly hands and the young man's acoustic guitar.

He apologized with a full smile, revealing deep dimples. "So sorry, didn't lock the loo door. Just finishing now."

He may have gotten his disgusting germs all over her toilet, but he had a warm, handsome smile and good taste in music. Oliver's assessment was not as generous.

Hey, sweet thing, let's look past the Van Morrison and dangerous dimples, shall we? Wake up and smell the feces. He may be handsome if you like overgrown adolescents who haven't shaved, washed their hands, or used toilet paper for the past month.

Gloria averted her eyes. "No, I'm sorry—I thought this was my private bathroom."

He was laughing. "Apparently not. I think we both have bedrooms that connect to this loo. I guess we're loomates." He pointed to Gloria's toilet paper and asked as he cleared his throat, "Do you mind, Loomate?"

Realizing it was time for him to wipe, she threw him the toilet paper and hurried out of the bathroom, mortified. Mortified because he had just flushed and mortified because there was a part of her that had not wanted to leave, that wanted to stay in the bathroom listening to him play Van Morrison on her toilet. *Their* toilet. *Their vile, fetid, germ-infested toilet.*

Confused, ashamed, and still desperate to pee, Gloria danced and squirmed around her new bedroom to distract herself. Although dusty and dirty, she had to admit it was charming with its vintage details, aged wood cabinetry, and expansive view of the St. Cross courtyard, including a handful of Oxford's dreaming spires.

She particularly liked the old fireplace with its statuary marble mantle. Probably white originally, after steadily aging over the years, it was now the lightest shade of yellow, almost like creamy butter.

She recalled seeing a fireplace in the bathroom as well. Oliver hated fireplaces. Being a germophobe, they were too unsanitary and dirty for real use or comfort. But there was a secret part of Gloria that really liked fireplaces, or at least the idea of them. She thought a fireplace was a metaphor for something important, though she just couldn't remember what.

She thought the pee must have been filling her brain as she jumped on the worn oak floorboards, making them squeak like a scared mouse running from a cat. As she continued leaping about, she remembered seeing a traditional claw-foot tub in the bathroom as well.

Even during her brief and shocking encounter with the redhead and his dangerous dimples, she observed that the antique bathtub was filthy but striking set against the vintage black and white octagonal tile on the floor.

Thoughts of the bathtub were interrupted when she perceived someone behind her. She practically peed in her pants when she heard the redhead quietly chuckling. Even more embarrassed than before, she wondered how long he had been watching her hop around the room, probably thinking she was some kind of American idiot.

But when she turned around, she was relieved to find no judgment in his demeanor, just his warm, handsome smile animated with those dangerous dimples.

His Queen's English accent had a slight undercurrent that was throaty and soulful, calling to mind a Van Morrison song or hinting at a grandparent who'd spent some time singing blues in Chicago.

"I am so sorry to startle you again," he said as he reached out his hand to shake hers. With a smile, he added, "By the way, I am Henry Young from Oxfordshire. I am so sorry about my informal and inappropriate welcome."

As much as she wanted to shake his hand, Oliver would positively not allow it.

Oh my God, I cannot believe you're even considering touching his disgusting, vile, fetid, heinous, germ-infested, feces hand. Your charming British friend did not even wash his germ-infested hands. There was no soap in that toxic-waste dump of a bathroom. He probably doesn't even own soap. Keep your hands and your mind clean.

Instead of receiving his hand, Gloria offered him a box of antibacterial wipes with an apologetic half-grin. Henry took the wipes and laughed as he wiped his hands thoroughly in between each of his long fingers. As fascinating as his long, delicate guitar-playing fingers were, her bladder could not wait a moment longer.

Gloria uttered a strained, "Excuse me!" as she blew by Henry and headed into the bathroom with a second box of wipes.

After quickly but meticulously wiping the top and bottom of the toilet seat with several antibacterial wipes, Gloria finally took the orgasmic pee that had been building inside her for the last fifteen hours. It seemed like it had been days, and she let out an audible sigh.

And then once again she heard Henry playing Van Morrison's "Sweet Thing" on his guitar. This time the music was coming from her new bedroom, and she had to smile when she heard him sing along in his gravelly voice. He may not have been the cleanest neighbor, but he was talented and had excellent taste in music.

> *And I will stroll the merry way*
> *And jump the hedges first*
> *And I will drink the clear*
> *Clean water for to quench my thirst*

She listened to him sing with rapt attention, briefly forgetting she was on a strange toilet in a strange land. The music transported her. She was sailing in her white balloon.

> And I shall watch the ferryboats
> And they'll get high
> On a bluer ocean
> Against tomorrow's sky.

Gloria went back into her new bedroom perceptibly more relaxed and comfortable. Henry put down his guitar and handed her the box of wipes with a Cheshire-cat grin, again revealing his dangerous dimples. She wiped her hands and smiled back at him tentatively, sparing him the fact that she already wiped her hands with the second box of antibacterial wipes that she had left in the bathroom.

"You are so prepared. You must think I'm an unrefined oaf in comparison," he said, laughing.

"An unrefined oaf with excellent taste in music," she corrected. "Van Morrison expunges all sins; you are forgiven for not washing your hands, Henry Young, unrefined oaf from Oxfordshire."

"We have more in common than just a toilet, I see."

She started to blush. "Please don't remind me. I'm starting to feel embarrassed again. It had been subsiding listening to your rendition of 'Sweet Thing.'"

"You're embarrassed? I was the one on the bloody toilet, and I still don't know your name or where you're from." He revealed his wide, dimpled smile again.

"Gloria Zimmerman, anal suitemate from Chicago."

"Any relation to Robert Allen?" He raised his eyebrows, as if testing her.

"Zimmerman? Big Bob Dylan fan, but no. And I should ask you, Henry Young, any relation to Neil Percival?" she challenged back, confident she could hold her own when it came to music trivia.

She stifled a laugh that sounded like a cough as she thought she was much more self-assured about music trivia than encountering half-naked men on toilets. He picked up his guitar and started playing a few chords from Neil Young's "After the Gold Rush."

"What a great father Neil Young would be, but no relation," he said as he played.

"Not so sure about that, Henry. Did you read *Shakey* by Jimmy McDonough? Probably not the best father," Gloria said authoritatively and then shrugged her shoulders, trying not to sound too didactic or bookish. She didn't want him to stop playing.

"I did. And *Neil and Me*. And *Neil Young Nation*. I guarantee my father has more issues and no compensating musical genius," Henry declared with the air and authority of a fellow music scholar as he stopped playing and took his guitar in one hand.

Gloria gave him a knowing look as she pulled on her ponytail, pleased that they both had a similar taste in music and also pleased that they both had father issues. A perverse connection, for sure, but not nearly as perverse as sharing a germ-infested toilet.

"I can relate to that," she said as they locked eyes. "And just out of curiosity, do you always play the guitar while you're..."

Henry laughed. "Only when meeting fascinating new Oxford students from Chicago who adore Van Morrison and desperately need to pee. I should let you move in now. Please let me know if you need anything. Anything at all."

He took his red guitar and headed back through the bathroom to his own bedroom, staring at Gloria as he slowly closed the door. After he was gone, she took out her ponytail and loosened her hair, looking at the door to his room for a long moment.

The ubiquitous loneliness that usually enveloped her as a warm and snug blanket felt uncomfortable and a bit stifling as she contemplated Henry Young on the other side of the bathroom door. But like a needy child, loneliness was the security blanket she took everywhere. She wasn't sure she could survive without it, especially if she lost control.

She wondered whether she should say something about sharing the flat to her mother or the head porter. After all, she was supposed to have a private bathroom, and she knew her mother would throw a fit at having paid for the best suite in the college. And, of course, Oliver would throw a fit.

In spite of being an unrefined, germ-infested oaf, Henry Young was intriguing. She wanted to know him better. But she doubted Oliver would let that occur. Her bathroom, like her life, had space for only one toilet and one love.

12.

Henry could listen to Gloria Zimmerman from Chicago scrub the loo floor all night. Like Chicago blues great Muddy Waters, her scrubbing had a stomp and stammer beat as she jived across the floor. He listened to her downstroke rhythms and thought of her on her hands and knees, trying to imagine what she was wearing. Tight tank revealing supple breasts as she scrubbed forward? Tight jeans encasing firm arse as she moved across the floor? Long hair cascading down her back when she stopped to catch her breath every several minutes?

Wanker! What was he thinking? The poor girl's hands were red and sore, and she'd been cleaning the bloody loo for the past three hours. The mysterious scene on the other side of the door was not erotic and sexy; it was more like pathetic and sad. The unfortunate girl obviously had demons and was ill. Perhaps that's why they got on so well. But they also had Van Morrison in common.

Trying to distract himself from listening to Gloria, Henry started unpacking his Van Morrison vinyl. It was the only part of the unpacking process he could focus on and sustain for more than several minutes at a time. Clothes and sheets and books and research and rubbish were strewn all over his untidy room. And he had no idea about the location of his bloody medicine. He regretted not accepting Claire's offer to help him unpack and organize.

Everything would have been tidy by now and he would be peacefully resting, dreaming about his new neighbor and her Chicago blues. If given the opportunity, Claire would have already alphabetized his books, records, rock T-shirts, and medication. Everything in its place, except his deranged mind, and if she could alphabetize that too, she most certainly would.

Henry suspected that Gloria, having sanitized every surface, had already organized her room and belongings with her stacks and stacks of toilet tissue and wipes. He hoped she was paying her damaged hands overtime for all their excruciating work. After a long while, it finally sounded like their workday was over; no more scrubbing blues coming from the loo.

Henry missed the sound of Gloria in the loo, so he decided to put on a record. He played Van Morrison's overlooked masterpiece, *Veedon Fleece*. He didn't want to be rude playing the music too loud, but he wanted Gloria to hear. He wanted to share the poetry with her.

He had researched Gloria through Oxford's secure student website and learned that she was a Rhodes Scholar doctoral candidate for the Oxford professor of Poetry. No wonder she appreciated the Belfast Cowboy. To hell with Margo Mitchell, Van Morrison was the real visionary poet. *Veedon Fleece* was one of Morrison's most lyrical works, with its stream-of-consciousness lyrics and complex musical textures. And Henry knew Gloria would understand and appreciate Morrison's dialogue with and references to fellow poets like Blake, Yeats, and Thoreau.

He wanted to talk with her about Van Morrison's poetry and other poetry. He wanted to talk with her about Van Morrison's music and other music. He wanted to talk and not talk. He wanted to stare at her tight tank top.

With the abandon of a child, Henry sashayed through the loo, practically skating on the slippery floor, to knock on Gloria's bedroom door. But looking back through the loo into his own bedroom at his disorganized belongings strewn everywhere, he hesitated. And then he spotted it.

He finally found his bottle of medication. Just like his father, it taunted him and made him question everything, as it lay arrogantly on top of an old ripped Oxford sweatshirt spread out on the floor. Who did he think he was? What made him think he had the right or expertise to talk with Gloria about poetry? She was an Oxford poetry scholar. He was an Oxford mess.

13.

"And I will stroll the merry way and jump the hedges first, and I will drink the clear clean water for to quench my thirst." Gloria awoke to a reprise of Van Morrison's "Sweet Thing." Unfortunately, the quenching melody was not coming from her handsome neighbor; it was coming from her iPhone, which also told her it was six in the morning. Startled, disoriented, and utterly exhausted, the jet lag had taken its toll.

Oliver had no sympathy for her jet lag or for the fact that she had stayed up late into the evening cleaning and organizing her new bedroom. It was her first full day at Oxford, and Oliver was a drill sergeant, insisting on establishing a precedent for routine and tight control.

Just because you're in England, does not make you the queen or even a lesser Jewish princess. Are you here to sleep or work? Some Rhodes Scholar you are. You need to wake up and get going. Both you and the bathroom are very dirty indeed.

Gloria pleaded, "But I am so, so tired."

In willful defiance, she stayed seated on the edge of her bed flirting with the idea of lying back down, if only for a little while. She was so tired. Perhaps she could hire a cleaning person? Slip the janitor a bonus commission? In addition to her generous bank account and credit cards, Frank had shoved a wad of $100 bills in her safety pouch "just in case." But drill sergeant Oliver would not hear of it.

Do not even think about it. You need to clean with your own hands. As they say over here, your own bloody hands. You need to clean until your hands are bloody. Bloody, bloody hands. Now!

A contrite Gloria obeyed strict Oliver. She entered the bathroom armed with a blue bucket filled with cleaning products and other antigerm weaponry. But once inside, she noticed Henry's bedroom door slightly ajar. In a rare mood to rebel against Oliver, she tapped on his door ever so lightly with two ugly red fingertips.

Peering in his room, she surveyed the piles of records, books, and clothes scattered all over his messy floor. She finally found the biggest mess of all, a sleeping Henry lying on top of a scrunched-up blue duvet. She was slightly revolted but kind of amused when she noticed he was wearing the same long-sleeved Who shirt he had worn the day before.

Oliver did not approve of his dirty shirt. Nor did Oliver approve of Gloria's dangerous diversion.

Who are you? Who, who, who, who? Why don't you just enter his toxic-waste dump of a room? I'm sure he would love to spread the germs and cuddle. Isn't that why you came to Oxford? To cuddle with a filthy overgrown adolescent in his filthy room wearing his filthy shirt on his filthy blanket? Forget the dirty boy and his dirty, feces, germ-infested hands. Focus on this dirty bathroom. Sharing a bathroom is a bad idea.

Gloria stole one last glance of Henry in his dirty long-sleeved T-shirt before quietly closing his bedroom door for good. Once again, it was time to pursue the fucking horizon.

It was time to settle in to begin the arduous and sacred task of cleaning the bathroom. She used a strong disinfectant cleanser on the tub, sink, and floor to eradicate all germs, eviscerate any dirt, and wipe away grimy evidence of soap scum.

But the most important part of her ritual was cleaning the toilet. In order to prevent the spread of bacteria and viruses, it had to be done with absolute thoroughness and precision. Cleaning the toilet was a test of her competence and loyalty to Oliver, her god, and the precept of staying in control.

Gloria began cleaning the toilet by squeezing green liquid cleanser into the bowl, closing the rim, and flushing with the lid down to trap errant spray. While the powerful green solution was soaking into the toilet grime, she wiped the outside of the toilet as if she were painting it, making sure to cover every inch of exposed surface.

She started her technique at the top to prevent dripping onto the clean surfaces. She sprayed the tank, handle, and tank edges with a purple cleanser before carefully wiping them down. She then used the same spray to clean the outside lid and outside bowl from the sides to the bottom edges where the toilet met the floor.

Next was the toilet seat. Truly, it would be sacrilege to neglect the toilet seat, as it was the one part of the toilet that regularly came into direct contact with germ-infested people. Gloria raised the seat and kneeled down as if in prayer. She sprayed the seat, inside lid, and rim with her purple cleanser, hoping a generous five squirts on each would be enough to eradicate vile people germs. She then wiped the lid, seat, and hinges at the back with devotion, knowing that the most important task was yet to come.

Finally, it was time to clean the holiest of holies, the inside of the toilet bowl. Akin to a *bimah* in a synagogue, altar in a church, or the central dome of a mosque, the very inside of the toilet bowl was the site of her most sacred worship. She entered from the top down, thoroughly scrubbing the rim.

Devoutly and carefully, she examined under the rim to eviscerate all germ-infested stains, grime, and other evidence of infidels. Finally, she was ready to worship the hole at the very bottom, a sacred passageway for germs and longing. She bowed her head in reverence, closed the lid, and gave one more flush for good luck and long life.

Gloria purposefully cleaned without gloves, even though the harsh cleaning products and vigorous scrubbing destroyed her already damaged hands. An Opus Dei Jew, she wanted to destroy her hands. To feel the pain. To prove to her god and herself that she was a devout pilgrim and would endure endless hours of self-flagellation to advance sacred beliefs and unyielding truths.

Indeed, she cleaned the tub, sink, floor, and toilet with religious devotion and zealous aggression as if she were attacking a heretic.

She then stripped down and took a bath that was anything but soothing. She washed her hair and body with the same intensity and agitation with which she cleaned the bathroom, as if her body were the enemy.

Finally, she cleaned the bathroom once again—including the tub, sink, toilet, and floor—for the benefit of Henry's use. After all the cleaning, her skin looked withered and worn, and her ugly red hands appeared even more so. This was the painful and cleansing way Oliver forced her to say her prayers every morning.

14.

The St. Cross Refectory was a fairly large cafeteria known for its vast selection of international food because over 60 percent of the students who lived at St. Cross were, like Gloria, from someplace else. She had read somewhere that St. Cross served some of the best sushi in Oxford every Thursday night. Gloria did not eat sushi or much of anything.

Oliver did not permit most food or strangers, especially in combination, and kept Gloria away from social meals whenever possible. She tried to assume that a cafeteria worker was being friendly and not labeling her patently Jewish when she placed a bagel and cream cheese on Gloria's tray without asking. Gloria politely refused the bagel, pushing it back, and then discreetly retrieved a new, clean, and uncontaminated tray.

She avoided the cafeteria worker's gaze as she found herself again in the food line, this time preoccupied with choosing a perfect orange. Gloria was so preoccupied, in fact, that she was holding up the line, oblivious to the curious eyes of various students, faculty, and even the friendly cafeteria worker.

Once again she found herself behind Plexiglas, the gorilla in the zoo, although this zoo was very proper—the students and staff politely trying to hide their quiet chuckling as she slowly, deliberately, and absurdly mulled over which orange to choose from a large wooden bowl.

Oliver had been strict this first full day at Oxford. The orange had to be just right. Perfect.

These are the most pathetic, sorry oranges I've ever seen. Disgusting, vile, fetid, heinous, pathetic oranges. Oxford is supposed to be civilized. How will you survive here with such pathetic, imperfect oranges? Too much green. Too yellow. Too reddish. Too small. Not round. Strange white marks. Black marks. Need the perfect orange. Needs to be perfect. Perfect. Perfect. Perfect. You're perfect, Superstar. You need a Superstar-perfect orange. Everything about you, everything you eat, must be just right, must be perfect. Perfect. Perfect. Perfect.

Gloria finally selected the perfect orange, carefully extracting it from the middle of the bowl with white-gloved hands as if performing gallbladder surgery. She added the perfect orange to her tray, which included a factory-sealed box of Special K breakfast cereal, black coffee, and her own package of antibacterial wipes, which she had brought from her room.

Once she had her food, Gloria was not sure where to sit in the large dining room with its long teak tables and low-hanging wrought-iron chandeliers. Because of the large international population, Gloria heard at least three different languages as she made her way to a seat by herself in the back corner. She felt more comfortable away from the various crowds and clusters that sat together happily chatting and eating while reading newspapers, journals, and text messages. Gloria was slightly envious of the groups of comfortable diners but knew she could not join them. She would never be a comfortable diner.

She fastidiously wiped her seat, table, dishes, and utensils with antibacterial wipes before eating her own austere breakfast alone. But she was not totally alone.

Oliver ranted to fill the silence.

Finally, you found something decent to eat in this vile, fetid, heinous, dirty cafeteria. So uncivilized. Such strange, smelly food.

Such strange, smelly people. Make sure to stack the peels just so. Just right. Perfect.

Gloria wiped her hands with hand sanitizer before peeling her perfect orange, which she ate slowly and carefully after stacking the peels just so.

15.

It was already too late when Henry woke up, completely disoriented and with a massive erection. He started stroking himself, thinking about his new American loomate and how she reminded him of Chicago blues. Little Walter. Muddy Waters. *I just want to make love to you.* Van Morrison talked about how Chicago blues exuded a restlessness and curiosity—moving forward but surviving.

As accomplished as Rhodes Scholar Gloria Zimmerman was, he knew that, like him, she was just a scrappy street fighter, a survivor. Her red hands and endless supply of toilet tissue bore the scars. Fuck. Enough with this pseudointellectual masturbation. He had to get to class. He moved his hand faster and faster, finally finishing himself off, thinking about Gloria's wide blue eyes and luscious breasts. Ejaculations were ejaculations, even for mediocre doctoral students at Oxford.

Of course he could not find any tissue in his room, so he had to wipe himself on his dirty blanket. He laughed at the thought of anal Gloria, who probably had a stack of tissue boxes in her wardrobe for him to nick, which would be entirely justified, as she was the source of his most recent mess.

He checked under his disheveled blanket, side table, and shelf, searching for his watch or mobile, of which he could find neither. He knew he was late for class but did not know how late. He did not even know the bloody time. He reached for the laptop on the floor, whose battery was drained. Plugging his computer in to power it up, he saw that it was already well past ten o'clock.

Henry yelled, "Fuck me!" as he jumped out of bed, grabbed his stained, wrinkled khakis and bottle of pills from the floor, and rushed to the loo. His T-shirt was clean enough to carry him through another day. He had to get to class quickly; Cook was going to kill him.

16.

Professor of music and don John Cook stood at the head of an oval walnut table in a small but distinguished seminar room at Jesus College with a stained-glass crest on the back wall. He was flanked by nine eager doctoral students in stiff high-back chairs who took detailed notes while listening to an obscure recording that sounded like someone breaking glass in a rainforest.

As if leading his congregation in silent prayer, Professor Cook was listening intently with his eyes closed and arms spread. Midsong, Henry tried to sneak in the room unnoticed, strategically avoiding the judgmental gazes of his colleagues around the table.

When the recording ended, Cook, whose eyes remained closed, spoke with the low, intimidating voice of a has-been baritone. "Thank you for coming, Mr. Young."

Professor Cook opened his eyes wide, staring straight at a disheveled, unprepared Henry, who was even more disheveled and unprepared than usual.

"We were hoping you would share with us your studied opinion of Stockhausen's *Aus den Sieben Tagen*."

"I apologize, Professor Cook. I have this problem with my new flatmate, you see. She...she has got this germ issue. And I had to wait an interminable time—over an hour, actually—to use the loo, and..."

Henry felt guilty using Gloria's eccentricity as his excuse. But in a way, it was her fault he was late. He had been quite distracted by her and Chicago blues. Sure Cook was a wanker, but Henry thought he himself was one too, and this morning quite literally. But it was not his fault Gloria had beautiful, kind eyes and what looked like luscious swollen breasts under her white tank top, which was much too tight. *My, my, my, my sweet thing.*

Professor Cook laughed with derision and said, "Have you thought about transferring to the Department of English Language and Literature, Mr. Young? You tell awfully good stories."

Henry returned Professor Cook's sarcastic smile and then hid his embarrassed face behind an unread book. He was a fraud, and they all knew it. Every one of those pricks around the table in that pretentious seminar room in the haughty music program at pompous Jesus College knew it. And he agreed with them. That fact and a shared loathing for his arrogant, intimidating father were the only things they had in common, the only things about which they agreed.

Henry truly thought his pride was inexorable, calling himself a doctoral student at Oxford University. He knew fair well that no matter how charming he could be or how prominent his father, he just did not belong. He did not belong in this seminar room at Jesus College. He did not belong in the St. Cross flat sharing a loo with Gloria. And no matter what the solicitor decreed, he did not belong at *Equanimity.*

Always a dweller on the threshold—messed up, fucked up, fraudulent, and sick—Henry Young just didn't belong.

17.

At Oxford's Bodleian Library, Gloria, wearing her ridiculous white gloves, finally looked normal. She was in the rare-book archive, which was located off the main reading room known as Radder. For the first time since she arrived, Gloria truly felt the import of Oxford's majestic spires. She was really here, sitting among her faculty advisor, Margo Mitchell, Oxford professor of Poetry, and fellow research assistants Elizabeth Seton and Samantha John, all of whom also donned white gloves.

Professor Mitchell seemed pleased, maybe to excess, to have Gloria at Oxford. In addition to singing Gloria's praises to the other research assistants, she looked at Gloria with a penetrating and protective stare as if she knew and would honor Gloria's secrets. The staring made Gloria feel flattered but uncomfortable, even more uncomfortable than usual. Why would this famous poet want to know her? Was Gloria that much of a freak?

Professor Mitchell, Elizabeth, and Samantha seemed visibly impressed as Gloria carefully handled and read from an original Sara Teasdale manuscript that had been missing for over forty years, which she had found the previous spring, misfiled in Yale's rare poetry collection. It had been loaned to Yale from Oxford in 1966 and had been missing until Gloria discovered it misfiled in the wrong room.

Gloria thought about Sara Teasdale's suicide, an overdose of sleeping pills, as she read aloud from the formerly missing manuscript. She was reading Teasdale's most famous poem, "Barter."

> *Life has loveliness to sell,*
> *All beautiful and splendid things,*
> *Blue waves whitened on a cliff,*
> *Soaring fire that sways and sings,*
> *And children's faces looking up*
> *Holding wonder like a cup.*
>
> *Life has loveliness to sell,*
> *Music like a curve of gold,*
> *Scent of pine trees in the rain,*
> *Eyes that love you, arms that hold,*
> *And for your spirit's still delight,*
> *Holy thoughts that star the night.*
>
> *Spend all you have for loveliness,*
> *Buy it and never count the cost;*
> *For one white singing hour of peace*
> *Count many a year of strife well lost,*
> *And for a breath of ecstasy*
> *Give all you have been, or could be.*

When Gloria finished reading, she outlined Sara Teasdale's original signature with a white-gloved index finger, tracing the exaggerated loopy S several times.

Gloria had met Mitchell and her fellow research assistants for lunch before examining the recently discovered Teasdale text. Professor Mitchell talked about how she wanted to be close to her research assistants, how they needed to share their "demons and longings" and why they were moved by poetry.

Mitchell, of course, spoke of her struggles with breast cancer. At Mitchell's urging, tall, thin Elizabeth told them about her eating disorder and its relationship to her still being in the closet with her family. Samantha spoke of dreams she had, trying to save all the suicidal poets she read.

When it came time for Gloria's confession, she didn't know what to say, so she dodged the question with a generic, "I just find Plath's imagery very moving."

How could she share her secret life with Oliver? How could she explain why her hands were so red, and why she didn't have any friends? She wondered whether Professor Mitchell, Elizabeth, and Samantha would still be impressed if they knew Gloria was a fraud. If they knew that the only reason she found the rare and valuable Teasdale manuscript was because she has severe Obsessive-Compulsive Disorder and had spent most Friday and Saturday evenings for the past four years in Beinecke, Yale's rare-book library, dusting and shelving every lifeless, lonely book in its poetry collection many times over.

Beinecke defined her existence at Yale. The Yale University Beinecke Rare Book and Manuscript Library was one of the largest buildings in the world dedicated to rare books and manuscripts, holding over 600,000 volumes, including the *Gutenberg Bible*, the first Western book printed from movable type. Its impressive collection was as prestigious but slightly subordinate to similar collections at Oxford's Bodleian Library, British Museum, and British Library.

Beinecke's stunning and provocative modern building, designed by Chicago architecture firm Skidmore, Owings & Merrill, was built as if "lifting up a treasure box from the Renaissance" according to Yale architecture dean Robert A.M. Stern. Ingeniously, the structure of Beinecke was also its enclosure. The renowned and somewhat controversial building had been cleverly designed so that the treasure chest's white and gray marble panels filtered the light in a way that enabled it to display its rare gems while at the same time protecting them from damage.

Inside Beinecke, a glass tower of valuable books and documents rose through the center of the building like a queen's bejeweled scepter, enabling all who entered to see and admire its valuable collection. But seeing and admiring were decidedly different from using and enjoying. Everything about Beinecke, from its state-of-the-art temperature and humidity controls to its stringent security procedures, was designed to display its treasures but to keep them out of reach, undamaged, and safe.

Gloria had spent most days and evenings and times in between in this beautiful but aloof and entirely hermetically sealed world, where the air was brisk and dry and she was safe. This is where she lived her life, if you can call it that, at Yale. Books were safer than people; books had cleaner germs.

Oliver kept her in this prison, continually thwarting her attempts to make friends and forcing her to say no to most invitations, formal and otherwise. She said no to New Haven's famous pizza and was one of the few Yalies who had no opinion as to whether she preferred Sally's to Pepe's. No to all other dinners. No to movies. No to beers. No to parties. No to everything and everyone. No to boys—no to men. Her only love interests were from Jane Austen fiction, and her closest friends at Yale had been her beloved dead women poets, Van Morrison, and Oliver. They were the exclusive members of her sorority, dining club, and secret society.

She was utterly terrified of living, breathing human beings and the damage they could do to rare books and rare girls. Her thoughts immediately turned to her new suitemate, which is to say flatmate, which is to say loomate, Henry. Unfortunately, he was a living, breathing human being with living, breathing germs. She could not share a meal with him, let alone a toilet. *Impossibly dangerous.* No matter how intriguing or kind or handsome or musical he was, she knew—Oliver knew—he and his germs and his dimples were impossibly dangerous.

She would have to make alternative living arrangements without offending him, and as quickly as possible. She absolutely did not want him kicked out of the flat they shared. She would have to leave and lie about it to her parents. If Gladys knew Henry was her flatmate, she would have him kicked to the curb in a heartbeat. It was the Zimmerman way.

Perhaps Gloria could rent a flat close to campus and come up with some excuse to explain to her parents and to Henry. She recalled reading about a university housing office that helped students find rentals in the area. What would she tell Henry? What would she tell her parents? Was there enough money in her account to do this without them knowing?

Then an enticing (but utterly terrifying) thought crept into her deliberation: could she share the flat with Henry? Technically, it was not really a flat or suite after all; it was just a bathroom. *Just a toilet, for Christ's sake.* What was the big deal? She was an expert at cleaning toilets.

Surely, Oliver could be assuaged. She would clean it every day, three times a day. Thirty times a day. Whatever it took to make everyone happy and comfortable. The three of them could peacefully coexist as long as she got rid of germs. It had worked at Yale, where she had different roommates the three years she lived in Branford College. She knew she could do it here. It would be her responsibility to get rid of germs. Oliver would be satisfied, assuaged, okay as long as she kept the germs to a minimum.

But Gloria's confidence waned as she reexamined Teasdale's naïve presuicidal signature, knowing she was being naïve herself. She would have to pose the ultimate question: *To pee or not to pee in the same toilet as Henry Young?*

But it was a ridiculous and futile question and as cruel as the fucking horizon. And considering Teasdale's demise and Oliver's stranglehold, the answer was obvious. Once again Gloria would have to remain alone in her rare-book library, where the hermetically sealed atmosphere was germ free and she always said no.

PART TWO:
SEPTEMBER
Dead Women Poets

I am not sorry for my soul,
But oh, my body that must go
Back to a little drift of dust
Without the joy it longed to know.

Sara Teasdale, 1915
From "Longing"

But, precious time is slipping away.
You know she's only queen for a day.
It doesn't matter to which god you pray
Precious time is slipping away.

Van Morrison, 1998
From "Precious Time"

1.

Many joys would forever go unsatisfied under the thumb of Oliver's unrelenting discipline. But one of the joys Gloria refused to give up was living in the St. Cross flat she shared with Henry.

The flat was spacious and convenient. It was close to Margo Mitchell's office and residence at the Master's house as well as to Bodleian Library. It was a short distance to all of Gloria's classes as well as to the Rhodes House, where Gloria gathered with the other Rhodes Scholars for various programs and special events.

But if she were being completely honest, the most compelling reason for sharing a flat with Henry was the Van Morrison he played almost every night. And he was not just listening to the Van Morrison canon—*Astral Weeks*, *Moondance*, and *Tupelo Honey*. Henry was a true aficionado, appreciating Van Morrison's full and complete repertoire—*Veedon Fleece*, *Poetic Champions Compose*, *Into the Music*, *A Sense of Wonder*.

Oliver was not enthusiastic about Van Morrison or Henry, especially in combination. Oliver thought sharing an interest in Van

Morrison as well as a toilet with Henry was quite dangerous for everyone involved.

Sure, her new loomate came with as many threats as pleasures. But these were storms Gloria could weather. It's not like they were sharing the rickety basket of a hot-air balloon; it was only a bathroom. Gloria appreciated Oliver's solicitude, but she was becoming increasingly frustrated as he acted more like surly bodyguard or jealous lover than protective parent...or even drill sergeant.

This was especially true when it came to the precious time Gloria spent with Henry. She had to persuade, cajole, and hoodwink Oliver so she could enjoy those precious moments when she and Henry accidentally ran into each other around the university. Gloria adhered to a set of strict "rules" for interacting with Henry that she had hoped would assuage Oliver's concerns but ultimately allow her to spend precious, albeit limited, time with Henry.

First rule: Gloria could never seek out Henry. She was at Oxford as a Rhodes Scholar to study poetry and thus had to focus primarily on her academics. If she happened to bump into him, there was no reason she could not enjoy his company. He was a fellow St. Cross student, and it wasn't stipulated in Oliver's manifesto that she had to be rude. But above all else, she had to be a superstar, rigidly adhering to her unyielding, demanding, and entirely self-imposed academic schedule.

Second rule: Gloria could not accept Henry's ubiquitous invitations to breakfasts, lunches, dinners, teas, coffees, pubs, clubs, concerts, or other germ-infested events, which she would certainly regret no matter how generous or thoughtful the invitation. Public unwrapped food and crowds and their extensive germs would send her over the edge, causing her to lose control. It had happened before and led to disastrous results. No matter how much a part of her wanted to accept Henry's invitations and live in the world, she could not take that risk. Ever. It would be too dangerous for Gloria, Henry, and especially Oliver.

Third rule: As much as Henry wanted to share his impressive record collection and VPI Classic turntable with Gloria, she could not, under any circumstances, enter Henry's messy, dirty, germ-infested room for music or under any other pretext. Entering Henry's room was a dangerous, slippery slope that could only lead to more and more dangerous, germ-infested activity. The mere thought of this made Gloria douse her hands with extra hand sanitizer. *I saw a man pursuing the horizon. Round and round they sped. Round and round.*

Oliver accepted these rules skeptically, viewing them as a Faustian bargain of sorts but knowing that if he pushed too hard, he might push her into making the very risky choices he was trying to prevent. And it was not just Oliver who was wary of Henry and his germ-infested room and the slippery slope they suggested.

Gloria herself knew she had to avoid Henry's room, particularly under the intoxicating influence of Van Morrison vinyl and his dangerous dimples. Henry and his room and Van Morrison were dangerous, especially in combination. It was just too risky.

So although they shared a bathroom with bedrooms in close proximity, Gloria would only interact with Henry in "safe" places—St. Cross refectory, St. Cross quad by the sundial, or outside Bodleian Library near the tables—and only when they happened to run into each other by chance.

Of course, Gloria never ran into Henry *inside* Bodleian Library. Henry had told her he was allergic to books and anything related to academic research. She did not buy into his lazy, apathetic, anti-intellectual façade. It was a cover. Henry was smart but maybe just a little scared.

During her first weeks at Oxford, Gloria found herself counting on these happenstance moments with Henry more and more. And fate seemed to oblige; whenever she turned around, he was there with his bright green eyes and dangerous dimples. They talked about music—always relating to Van Morrison somehow. He knew so much. They talked about their messed-up, dysfunctional families, carefully respecting boundaries, never probing too deep in any one sitting. And they always ended up laughing.

Even when the subject matter was intense or macabre, Henry's sick and twisted and often politically incorrect sense of humor was infectious, much to Oliver's dismay. Gloria laughed more in these first weeks at Oxford than she remembered laughing almost anywhere. While it could sometimes be hard on her bladder, especially late in the afternoon, it felt good to let loose for once.

But as enjoyable as Henry was, Gloria understood and even somewhat agreed with Oliver's caginess. In spite of her rules, spending time with Henry was not only precious but also dangerous as hell. She worried that she enjoyed spending time with him a little too much.

That is precisely why she felt both delight and dread as Henry approached her table at the dining hall on an unusually warm September day with his messy lunch tray and wide dimpled smile. He was dangerous as hell.

2.

Margo Mitchell sat in her plush library at the Master's house, reading from an old box of poems. She had started writing poetry when she was eleven years old, shortly after her mother had been consumed by an advanced breast cancer that spread through her frail body like an indiscriminate forest fire.

The afternoon of her mother's funeral, while her sisters and father received grieving visitors in the living room, Margo locked herself in her small attic bedroom, away from the sympathetic gathering, which she found nauseating, no matter how well intentioned.

She refused to be with anyone except for Molly, a doll that had been her mother's as a girl and had been given to Margo for her eleventh birthday, just a few weeks before her mother had passed.

Margo felt terrible that, unlike her father and sisters, she could not cry and grieve publicly. But alone with Molly in the safety of her hideout, she was able to grieve in her own way. She gripped her pen with one hand and clutched Molly with the other, holding on to both for dear life.

There may not have been tears, but when she started writing about Molly and her mother, the words flowed, soaking and drenching the page of her lined journal.

Decaying hair pulled away
Embarrassed to be slowly melting downward
The confidence on her face worn down
Her plastic gold decorations sparkling against
the silky brown dress
She wants to move and come to life
Be what she used to be
Though she can't
Just many more days of sitting there
Lifeless
Until every speck of her is gone
Somewhere we don't know
In a place far from here
Until then, she waits
On and on and on
She tries to push the tip of her finger to move
It doesn't
She uses all of her little strength but no
It doesn't
Lifeless again
Rejected on the shelf
Waiting

Grown-up Margo went to the bookcase to retrieve her old friend, who stood guard on the very top shelf. The sad, faraway look in the old doll's porcelain face reminded her of someone, but she couldn't quite make the connection. Of whom was she thinking? Her mother as a young girl? A portrait of a young Sara Teasdale? Did beautiful Molly remind her of her own beautiful Patricia?

Running her fingers gently through Molly's silky black hair, it came to her. The fragile doll, with its lifeless look and lifeless demeanor, reminded her of Gloria Zimmerman. She had been worried about Gloria, worried that Gloria was waiting, spending too much time on a dusty shelf with dead women poets. The poor girl had no friends and never did anything social. Was it time for Margo to intervene?

3.

Surprisingly, Henry's serendipitous plan had been working. And again he found himself engineering yet another opportunity to "accidentally run into" Gloria. It was the only way she would spend time with him. True, they lived in the same flat at St. Cross College. True, they were human and ostensibly both needed to eat on occasion, outside of the dreaded refectory. And true, they were both passionate about all things Van Morrison.

But patently and politely Gloria had refused Henry's many invitations to lunches, teas, dinners, pubs, clubs, concerts, and especially to listening to the extensive collection of Van Morrison vinyl he kept in his bedroom, only meters away from her bedroom.

Underneath his sloppy good looks, dirty wrinkled rock T-shirts, and cocky dimpled smile, Henry was incredibly insecure. No matter how kind or gentle she was, Gloria's many rejections stung. And for some reason, like an idiot, he kept coming back for more.

His psychologist know-it-all sister Claire suggested that Gloria's red, sore hands and nonstop cleaning demonstrated that she had some serious obsessive germ issues. She urged him to avoid taking

Gloria's refusals personally. But he couldn't help it. Whether he showed it or not, Henry took everything personally.

And it made perfect sense to him that a gorgeous and intelligent creature like Gloria would not want to spend time with him. He considered her disinterest a karmic sign, given the sorry state of his own psychological and physical health. He also had serious issues and was not entirely certain he could pursue Gloria no matter what his fantasies decreed.

The Rolling Stones were on the mark with their 1969 anthem "You Can't Always Get What You Want." It was a fitting anthem for Henry as well, summing up so much disappointment and missed opportunity in his brief but eventful twenty-five years.

He owned the Stones' album *Let It Bleed*, on which the song in question appeared, but his record collection also included covers by such diverse performers as Aretha Franklin and Def Leppard. He was especially keen on Def Leppard's acoustic version of the Stones' classic. Listening to the song made Henry feel like an old man at the end of a long, tiring, and entirely futile journey.

So after two weeks and fourteen no's in a row, a tired and weary Henry stopped asking Gloria and her blood-red hands to tea. Instead, he relegated her to the uncomplicated and often erotic world of his dreams and fantasies, where she always said yes.

And then, in real time and with a very real Gloria, an extraordinary thing happened. She said yes. *Yes. Yes. Yes.* Yes to spending time with him. Such a pleasant and unusual surprise; Henry felt like a teenage girl, vividly remembering the day and time and place and even what he was wearing—an old, ripped long-sleeve Doors T-shirt.

It was Wednesday, the 2nd of September at 17:01 GMT. He was walking through the courtyard adjacent to the Bodleian Library when by chance he saw Gloria sitting at an outside table with two very serious-looking women and a stack of serious-looking books, which he assumed were written by very serious and dead women poets.

Unlike her colleagues, who shot him nasty looks, Gloria appeared pleased, almost relieved, to see him. The longing in her large almond-shaped eyes reminded him of a dog he once saw at the pound when he was ten. The lab mix kept pushing the metal cage and barking, trying to get Henry's attention, desperately wanting to be adopted and loved and taken from that awful gray place. Gloria's sad blue eyes told him she wanted to be rescued. *From her dreary colleagues and dead women poets?*

Gloria's fellow research assistants packed their bags and scurried away as he approached their table. Gloria ignored them, even forgetting to say goodbye. With an encouraging smile, she motioned for Henry to sit down next to her.

As if bracing himself for another refusal, he cautiously asked, "Is it okay if I join you, Loomate?"

"Yes, I'd love to hang out with you, but the name is *Gloria*. Have a problem with that, Mr. Young? It is a classic Van Morrison song that he sang with his band Them. You must know it since you're the expert on all things Van Morrison."

Henry responded to her teasing with the first few lines of Van Morrison's classic.

> *Did I tell you about my baby?*
> *Well, she comes around.*
> *Five feet four*
> *From her head to the ground.*
> *Comes around here*
> *Just about midnight.*
> *Makes me feel so good.*
> *Makes me feel alright.*
> *And her name is G-L-O-R-I-A*

And together they sat at the table moving through some of the most famous covers of "Gloria" by Patti Smith, David Bowie, Jimi Hendrix, Bruce Springsteen, R.E.M., and Energy Orchard. They even dwelled on U2's "Gloria," though technically not a Morrison cover, along with Green Day's "Viva La Gloria."

Interestingly, one famous (or perhaps infamous) version, which they did not bring up, was by the Doors, as was written all over Henry's bloody Doors shirt. Henry thought the Doors' "Gloria" was much too steamy for this first foray.

But Gloria was on to his thoughts. She may have been a bit odd, but she was not ignorant, especially when it came to Van Morrison's music. She was staring at Henry's shirt with a naughty grin; of course, she knew the Doors' version of "Gloria."

But he refused to bring it up, giving her his own suspicious grin in return. He refused to say a word. He was grateful she was sitting at the same bloody table with him; he was not about to scare her away now. Their staring contest lasted a long and tense moment, after which they both burst out laughing, practically singing in unison the Doors' notorious version of "Gloria."

> Check me into your room.
> Show me your thing.
> Why'd you do it baby?
> Why'd you show me your thing?
> Can't stop now. Can't back out.
>
> Slow it down, gonna feel it down.
> Alright, OK, alright, hey-hey.
> Getting softer—slow it down.
> Now you show me your thing.
>
> Now why don't you wrap your lips around my cock, baby?
> Wrap your legs around my neck,
> Wrap your arms around my feet,
> Wrap your hair around my skin.

So, much to his astonishment, Henry found himself singing Jim Morrison's sexually provocative—some might say perverted, even pedophilic—definitely orgasmic version of "Gloria" with his American germophobic loomate who was scared to death of having tea with him or even entering his room. It made no sense. It was absurd. Arbitrary. Inconsistent. Random.

But Henry quickly learned that nothing with Gloria was random. Greenwich Mean Time personified, she adhered to a rigid and orderly schedule, her life and whereabouts always perfectly predictable. Before long it was second nature for him to predict where in Oxford she would be at any given moment on any given day.

He knew her bloody schedule better than his own. He didn't have a schedule. Fuck, before he started hanging out with Gloria, he couldn't find his bloody watch. The only predictable moments in his week were when he was stalking her, orchestrating opportunities to "accidentally" cross her path, or running late to his own stupid classes.

He found that if he worked around her strange requirements, she would gladly spend time with him. She seemed to want to spend time with him. As long as it did not involve off-campus food or much advanced planning, Gloria would most always say yes whenever Henry *happened upon her*. And he made sure he *happened upon her* as often as possible.

And when she said yes, despite her rigid manner, they would talk easily and freely about so many things—rock lyrics, writers and poets, and difficulties with their families. They covered all sorts of subjects, from the existential to the mundane. And they always ended up laughing about the most bizarre and stupid things. Henry liked making her laugh. They were bluesy souls who both, at bottom, were in need of a good laugh.

For the first time at Oxford, Henry had found more than an acquaintance; he had discovered a real friend. With Gloria, he was not a fuckup whose life achievements were all the products of nepotism. He was just Henry, fellow Van Morrison devotee and foil for dead women poets everywhere.

His life may have been as fucked up as the dead women poets she studied, but Gloria didn't need to know that. He couldn't bear the thought of scaring her away.

4.

Gloria used books by her favorite dead women poets—Sylvia Plath, Anne Sexton, and Sara Teasdale—to form a protective barrier around her own perfectly neat and organized lunch tray. Dangerous Henry sat opposite her, laughing wide with dimples blazing, as he purposefully and playfully knocked down her wall.

"Okay if I join you, Loomate?"

Oliver tried to protest.

How dare you let that disgusting germ-infested stranger, who doesn't even wash his hands after using the toilet, sit at your clean table? He's a strange stranger with strange germs, and how many days in a row has he been wearing that filthy Tom Petty shirt? Don't eat with strangers. Don't talk to strangers. Say no. No! No! No!

Gloria disagreed with Oliver's fallacious assumption; Henry was not a stranger. He was her friend and loomate. Oliver would have to deal.

She gave Henry a playful look. "What if I said no?"

He pushed aside her books, teasing, "I assure you, Sylvia, Sara, and Anne have no objections."

But Oliver had objections, and she couldn't dare tell Henry about Oliver. He would think she was fucked up, messed up, and totally over-the-top crazy. With Henry, she felt like a real person for once, almost normal.

She liked almost normal and smiled as she retorted, "Hard for them to object, Henry. They're dead."

His laugh was sultry as he commented, "So that's why they're so quiet?"

In spite of herself, she laughed with him, shaking her head at his inappropriate, some might say misogynistic, comments. She was a feminist poetry scholar, for Christ's sake, why did she find him so charming? *Dangerous as hell.*

Henry's smile turned a bit solemn as he opened his bag of potato chips, Walkers cheese and onion crisps, asking, "Seriously, Gloria. Don't all these dead women poets depress you?"

She shook her head and responded, "Not at all. Why?"

Henry shoved a handful of potato chips in his mouth as he continued this uncharacteristically serious line of inquiry. "I mean, didn't all three of our illustrious, albeit quiet, lunch guests commit suicide? Young, smart, beautiful, and dead. So sad. Tragic, really."

Gloria gave Henry an awkward laugh, listening to him talk about suicide with a mouth full of potato chips. The crumbs were falling from his lips like yellow snowflakes. He wiped his mouth with the long, deliberate fingers of a guitar player.

"The next time you call me inappropriate, Miss Zimmerman, I'm going to remind you that you were the one laughing about your dead women poets. Care to fill me in on the joke?" he asked.

"Sorry, Henry. Just the contrast struck me. Watching you eat potato chips, talking about suicide," she answered meekly.

Gloria looked down in embarrassment as she nervously started peeling yet another perfect orange with imperfect shaky red hands. Henry did not say a word, but he placed the bag of chips on his tray and displayed his devious Cheshire-cat grin. What was he thinking?

Glancing up tentatively, she knew he was thinking about something dangerous, something he did not want to share. Had he noticed she was looking at the crumbs that lingered on his lower lip? She had to focus before Oliver chastised her for these dangerous and dirty thoughts. She had to focus before Oliver made her leave the table. Leave the flat. Leave Oxford. *Focus. Focus. Focus.*

To calm herself down, she thought of one of her dead women poets. She thought of the stark contrast between this lunch on this autumn day and Anne Sexton's lunch in the autumn of 1974. At that lunch, Sexton was dining with fellow poet and dear friend Maxine Kumin to discuss Sexton's latest manuscript, *The Awful Rowing Toward God*, to be published the following spring.

Anne Sexton had written the brilliant and tortured work when she had been institutionalized. The poem Gloria liked most from that collection was "The Sickness Unto Death":

> *Someone brought me oranges in my despair*
> *But I could not eat a one for God was in that orange.*
> *I could not touch what did not belong to me.*

Maxine Kumin had not gone into great detail about what they discussed at lunch or even what they ate. Probably not oranges or potato chips. But what had happened after lunch was well known and publicized. By all accounts, Anne went home, put on her mother's fur coat, locked herself in the garage, and started the engine of her car.

On that autumn day, it seems she preferred carbon monoxide poisoning to Walkers cheese and onion crisps. Gloria straightened her back and stack of books, in defense of Anne Sexton and her dead women poets.

"Actually, Henry, I find their stories—their lives—fascinating, how Sylvia Plath, Sara Teasdale, and Anne Sexton understood and described their suffering. And besides, I am here to study with the foremost scholar on feminist poetry and a celebrated poet herself," she explained defensively.

It was very prestigious and a great honor to work with Dr. Margo Mitchell. She'd been chosen through an election open to all members of Oxford's Convocation. In addition to her other teaching duties, she delivered three distinguished lectures a year, including the acclaimed Creweian Oration. Professor Mitchell had published over six influential texts on feminist poetry and mental illness as well as four books of her own confessional poetry about her family's struggles with breast cancer.

She had been the recipient of a MacArthur Genius Grant in 2006 for her seminal treatise on Plath, Teasdale, and Sexton, which explored their suicides through the lens of mental illness in addition to the traditional critical feminist perspectives. Her most acclaimed book, *Love Letters to My Breasts*—composed of powerful poems reflecting on the loss of her mother and two sisters to breast cancer as well as her own battle with cancer, resulting in a double radical mastectomy—won the Pulitzer Prize in 2009.

"It's a very exciting honor to be chosen as Margo Mitchell's doctoral student and research assistant," Gloria insisted.

But Henry looked at her skeptically, all the potato chip crumbs having fallen away.

"Even with all the acclaim and prizes, they're still just dead women poets. Not very exciting, if you ask me."

She read from the stack of journals by his tray, which he had somehow magically retrieved from the dreaded library he never entered.

"No, Henry. Not nearly as exciting as *18th Century Views on Church Organ: Composition and Analysis*," she said, feigning a yawn.

He smiled wide, dangerous dimples on full display. "Don't you dare insult the church organ. Organs can be very exciting indeed, especially mine."

Even Henry's double entendres were dangerous as hell. She had to *focus*. She forced another serious turn in the conversation, addressing the disconnect between his dissertation topic and real musical interests.

"We both know the church organ, no matter how significant or powerful, is not the music you're really into, *sweet thing*."

"*You don't know how it feels*," he replied, a hint of challenge in his voice, "*to be me*."

Gloria was insulted—as if she didn't know her Tom Petty.

"Tom Petty, 1994. *I won't back down*, Henry," she countered.

"Tom Petty, 1989. *You can't always get what you want*, Gloria."

"Petty never covered that, unless he performed it live in concert. Have to go with classic Stones, 1969," she replied with a reluctant smile.

"Petty never recorded it, but he did perform it at Wembley with the Heartbreakers," Henry said in a sad voice that Gloria suspected had nothing to do with Tom Petty's Heartbreakers.

She moved closer to him, failing to notice that she was practically reaching over the table and touching his germ-infested tray.

"And what is it you want, Henry?" she asked with real interest.

"Did Tom Petty record that, Gloria? Haven't heard of that one," he responded, with a fake little laugh.

"Nope. Gloria Zimmerman, 2010," she said, holding his gaze, refusing to let go.

"I don't know what I want," he replied in a quiet voice.

He looked around the dining hall as if his words had run away and were hiding in the corner somewhere. Not knowing what to say, Henry took a bite of his sandwich and grimaced.

"A Big Mac? This chicken sandwich is disgusting," he said as the laughter returned to his voice.

Gloria laughed with him and scrunched her face as he spat the disgusting germ-infested food into a napkin like a three-year-old.

After wiping his mouth, he gently asked, "How about a piece of your orange? It must be perfect since you spent twenty minutes choosing it."

Extraordinarily, it was okay for Henry to talk, even laugh, about Gloria's "perfect" orange. He was not really mocking her, but at least he wasn't ignoring the peculiar way she ate or, rather, did not eat. There was a dichotomy in the way people usually responded to Gloria's idiosyncrasies. They either ignored them entirely, pretending everything was fine, according to the Frank Zimmerman model, or, like her mother, they gawked at her, the gorilla in the zoo, a crazy freak.

Both extremes made Gloria feel invisible, lost, and irrelevant. But when Henry laughed at her perfect orange in his gentle way, he seemed to be saying, "I know you have problems, but it's okay. I still think you're great. I still like spending time with you. I still like having lunch with you." At least that's how he made her feel.

Oliver was not as magnanimous, looking to ridicule Henry at every turn.

That disgusting overgrown adolescent rocker wearing a four-day-old vile, smelly shirt with three holes and countless germs is not worthy of your perfect orange. You're a winner, Superstar. He's a loser who listens to music and does not do a damn thing. Why is he even at Oxford? He never studies. He never reads. He does not do a damn thing but follow you around like a dirty, filthy, worm-infested puppy dog. And you want to encourage him, giving him a piece of your perfect orange? You know about Pavlovian conditioning. You're a smart girl, Superstar.

Gloria was not going to tolerate Oliver's irrational jealousy. Henry was her friend who accommodated her rules and oddities. Oliver could accept them as well. After taking a deep breath, Gloria took a large piece of orange and gave it to Henry with a shaky red hand. Henry smiled widely as he put the orange in his mouth in one large bite.

"Best damn orange I ever had. Stuff of poetry," he announced with his mouth full, juice squirting everywhere.

He was a mess. Gloria looked at him in astonishment as he wiped his mouth with the long sleeves of his dirty Tom Petty shirt, splattering juice on her poetry books. For once, she was not anxious about the mess. She was rational and calm, acknowledging to herself that he was the dirtiest, messiest eater she had ever known. It was a fact. And no matter what he said, his eating and her orange were not the "stuff of poetry"—more like comedy or farce.

But as she watched him carefully wipe off her books and pile his orange peel with hers, poetry did come to mind. She thought of poetry, her dead women poets, and Anne Sexton's gruesome suicide. As she watched Henry wipe his mouth with his long, delicate fingers, she felt sorry for Sexton. She felt sorry that at Sexton's last lunch she had not shared an orange with Henry Young.

5.

In keeping with Gloria's unyielding itinerary, Wednesday afternoon found Henry "accidentally" encountering her outside of the
Bodleian Library, surrounded by her militant lesbians and dead
women poets. As usual, it was the perfect moment for him to lighten
things up.

He did not agree with the common stereotypical assumptions
about feminist scholars, but when it came to Liz and Sam, they truly
despised men. Or maybe it was just Henry. When he came around,
they either ignored him altogether or glared at him with daggers in
their eyes, ready to castrate at a moment's notice.

They certainly did not understand or appreciate his sense of
humor. In fairness, he did have a tendency to provoke them. But
they made such easy targets, taking themselves so damn seriously.
And like Gloria, they needed to lighten up. He doubted they even
had a sense of humor and decided that henceforth, he would call
them "humorless militant lesbians."

Gloria did appreciate Henry's sense of humor. Henry could tell
she secretly enjoyed watching the repartee between him and her

research colleagues. When she noticed him approaching the table, she gave him a knowing wave, subtly warning Liz and Sam that it was past five and their favorite misogynist was accidentally running into them right on schedule.

Eager to eschew dead women poets in favor of a messed-up music student who was very much alive, Gloria started distributing books and papers to Liz and Sam with the speed and fluency of a blackjack dealer passing out cards.

"How about you guys work on Sexton, and I'll focus on Plath?" she suggested as she organized the last of the books, practically loading Liz and Sam's satchels for them.

When Henry reached the table, the humorless militant lesbians exchanged a frustrated look, glaring at him as if he'd just murdered their cat.

Unruffled, Henry grinned and said, "Hello, girls. Sam, Liz, Gloria. Are you beautiful girls enjoying this beautiful September day? Probably the last before the weather turns."

Sam ignored him, obviously preferring her dead women poets.

"Okay, I'll work on Anne Sexton's depression leading to suicide and how it influenced her later work on the architecture of alienation," Sam said as she finished packing her bag.

Henry remained undaunted.

"I'm enjoying the day very much, girls, thank you."

Sam continued to ignore him and said, "Liz will examine the classic feminist issues and their impact on cadence in the early period."

Liz nodded in agreement as she zippered her bag, saying, "Menstruation, abortion, masturbation, and burgeoning sexuality."

Henry saw Gloria suppress a smirk as her gaze shifted back and forth like a dignified Wimbledon spectator, avoiding any display of preference. But he figured his favorite American was an Andre Agassi fan, so he went for the ace at match point. "Isn't masturbation a man's issue as well, Liz? Definitely something I'm interested in."

He proceeded to move his hand up and down in a crass gesture. Gloria's chuckle broke free as Sam and Liz shared their revulsion, darting up from the table, eager to be far away from Henry and quite possibly the horrifying image of him masturbating.

"Well, it was great seeing you again, girls," Henry said.

Gloria buried her face behind her red hands, swallowing her laughter, pretending she had something stuck in her throat. They would have to work on that. Like most Americans, she was not very subtle.

After clearing her throat several times, she said, "Bye, Liz. Bye, Sam. See you tomorrow."

They solemnly bid Gloria farewell and "good luck," as if she were graduating from Oxford or dying of cancer or running away from home or befriending a dangerous misogynist arse like Henry.

Liz and Sam walked away hand in hand, without looking back. Engrossed in each other, they appeared to have quickly recovered from Henry's callous assault. To Henry's surprise, they stopped by a nearby Shakespeare statue and kissed tenderly, as if inspired by a love sonnet from a dead white man, of all things. Henry had not realized they were a couple, and he had to admit it was surprisingly refreshing to see them happy, their serious demeanors somewhat faded.

"Forget Sexton, I'm sensing they'll be studying the poetry of Sappho on the Isle of Lesbos," he said, trying to keep it light.

Gloria scolded through her own laughter, "You're a misogynist, Henry Young."

"Misogynist? At least I didn't call them carpet munchers."

"Lesbians would do, Henry. No need to be cross."

"Cross? I think lesbians are amazing. I fantasize about them on a regular basis."

"Liz and Sam?" she asked, laughing once again.

"No. They terrify me," he responded, lifting his brows in horror.

She was laughing hard now. Henry loved Gloria's laugh. He knew she didn't laugh often enough. The dead women poets and humorless militant lesbians were not exactly helping in that regard. He could listen to her laugh all afternoon, as she held her belly and crossed her legs.

It then occurred to him that she was probably resisting a desperate need to pee, and the laughing was only exacerbating her discomfort. Given her standard for impossibly clean toilets, he imagined that the poor girl had probably gone the whole day without using the loo. No matter how prestigious Bodleian was, its loo was not up to her stringent standards. He decided to be a bit more subdued to go easier on her bladder.

"In all seriousness, why do they hate me so much?" he asked.

"They don't hate you, Henry," Gloria reassured. "They hardly know you."

"Are you daft, Gloria?" he asked with incredulity. "They treat me like I'm the Antichrist."

"Not the Antichrist, Henry. But definitely antifeminist," she clarified.

"*Antifeminist?* That's rubbish," he retorted indignantly.

Gloria shook her head, laughing again.

"For one thing, you call them *girls*, which they perceive as your patriarchal way of establishing power and dominance."

"I have no power whatsoever. I'm scared to death of those humorless militant lesbians. They'd tear me to shreds," he protested.

She went on, "What about the fact that you call them *Liz* and *Sam*?"

"But that's what you call them! Those are their names," he offered, truly baffled by this point.

"Their nicknames. Their formal names are Elizabeth and Samantha. Only those who have been invited into what feminists call 'the realm of the familiar' should call them Liz and Sam. Surprise, surprise, Henry. You're a party crasher. You've not been invited into that realm, so you're intruding on their personal identities," she explained in a professorial tone with a chuckle lurking beneath.

"Unbelievable," Henry said, shaking his head, utterly perplexed.

She wore a mischievous grin to make her next point. "And you've committed the absolute worst crime possible in the world of feminist poetry..." She moved closer to whisper in his ear, "You. Have. A. Penis."

He wondered whether it was the first time she said the word *penis* out loud; she was giggling like a young schoolgirl in sex education class. Gloria needed to laugh. She looked so beautiful when she laughed. She needed to be able to use the loo in the library. She needed to stop cleaning so much. He wondered about the albatross she wore around her neck and on her red hands. Why all the cleaning? Why so scheduled? Why so sad?

But he did not dare ask these questions now. This was a precious moment, and he did not want his friend to stop laughing even if she did wet herself. God knows his own trousers were filthy, now that he'd worn them three days in a row.

So Henry looked at his loomate with an exaggerated expression of surprise and said, "A *penis*, Gloria? Did you say *penis*? Didn't realize I had one. Shocker!"

6.

Gloria's favorite class at Oxford was somewhat nontraditional with its renegade instructor. And she attended this class without the instructor even knowing she was there. Behind the mysterious loo door, she would listen intently to his wisdom and insights about one of her favorite poets, Van Morrison. Gloria thought Henry was one of the best teachers she ever had, rivaling anyone at Yale or Oxford.

Tonight's explication was *Tupelo Honey*, Van Morrison's gorgeous Woodstock album and song of the same name. She loved the title track, agreeing with Peter Mills that it was a "slow-dripping declaration of love."

> *She's as sweet as tupelo honey.*
> *She's an angel in the first degree.*
> *She's as sweet as tupelo honey.*
> *Just like honey baby.*
> *Well straight from the bee.*
> *They can't stop us from the road to freedom.*

Gloria always thought of "Tupelo Honey" as more of a country song, but tonight Henry was playing it as pure blues. This recent remake with Bobby "Blue" Bland was *a-fucking-mazing*. Rhythm and blues maestro Bland together with Van Morrison transformed the song into heartfelt blues with profound lyrical resonance, totally capturing the moment. At Bland's sultry pronunciation of "Tipelo" instead of "Tupelo," Gloria immersed her quivering body in the sultry water of her warm bath.

Every night, she would listen to Henry's illumination of the music as she lay in a warm, soothing bath. These were not Oliver's harsh scrubbing baths of morning ritual and prayer. Rather, these were Henry's late-night Van Morrison baths—soothing, sultry, and calming to the soul.

As she lay back and closed her eyes, allowing the water to frame her face, Gloria thought about tupelo trees; they too thrived in water, preferring the moist ground of riverbeds and creeks. Their blossoms were beautiful and fragrant but extremely delicate and vulnerable to the elements. One strong wind or harsh rain, and they were gone for good. That vulnerability and their short blossoming season made it a fucking miracle anytime one survived.

But when it did, the blossom produced sweet and delicious tupelo honey, which Gloria thought an incredible prize for the remarkable feat of holding on.

7.

As always, on Sunday afternoon, Henry found Gloria by the sundial in the middle of the St. Cross quad sitting on a favorite bench surrounded by loads of books. He decided it was time to push the boundaries a bit, given that they were spending more and more time together, talking about everything from dead women poets to penises.

He spied her from their loo window. She was reading one of her dead women poets, no doubt, and wearing a particularly tight navy blue jumper. Even from his second-story vantage point, her tits looked scrumptious, and her hard nipples told him she might be a bit cold.

It was the very end of September, and her dead women poets were not *that* exciting. The weather was starting to turn. With the chill in the air, he wondered whether he should bring her a coat. Would she think he was some kind of pervert, having noticed her nipples from the window?

According to her usual Sunday routine, she would finish her reading in a few hours and would then be happy to join him for dinner at the refectory, but he couldn't wait that long. He was anxious to see if she would leave her dead women poets aside to be with him off schedule, an impromptu experiment.

Wearing his black peacoat in case there was an opportunity to lend it to her, he skipped every other step as he ran down the creaking wooden staircase to join her in the quad. Her knockers were calling. A naughty schoolboy craving attention, he snatched her Sylvia Plath book as he sat down next to her, eyeing her navy blue jumper up close and personal.

She was taken by surprise and exclaimed, "Hey! Give me that, Henry!"

He started reading Sylvia Plath's *Ariel* with relish,

> *You do not do, you do not do*
> *Any more, black shoe*
> *In which I have lived like a foot*
> *For thirty years, poor and white,*
> *Barely daring to breathe or Achoo.*

> *Daddy, I have had to kill you.*

Gloria was not amused by his performance. Her almond-shaped eyes sternly let him know it was not time to be boisterous; he would have to wait until dinner.

Resigned, he gave her back the book and asked with all seriousness, "So why *this* poetry?"

She was thoughtful for a long minute before she replied, "Why music? This poetry is like listening to Van Morrison."

"But Van Morrison is not quite as hopeless as Sylvia Plath and the other members of your suicide club. Wanting to kill their fathers and themselves. Don't these dead women poets depress you?" he asked with an urgency that surprised him.

"It's the same, Henry. It's all about access to someone's soul. Raw emotion. I understand Sylvia's pain. And she understands mine," Gloria explained, crossing her arms and shivering a bit.

He took off his coat and put it over her shoulders. She smiled as she slid it on.

"But I actually listen to Van Morrison for more than understanding, Gloria. For optimism. Hope. Ultimately transcendence."

To his surprise, he actually believed what he was saying.

He kept going, "The famous rock journalist Lester Bangs talked about Van Morrison's music as having a *redemptive element in the blackness*. So it's not like your dead women poets at all. Van the Man points the way out."

Gloria looked at Henry in revelation, grinning wide now. It scared the living shit out of him.

"Now that should be the seed of your dissertation, Henry," she announced, her eyes lurching forward as if she'd been drinking too much Red Bull.

She was treating him like a fellow intellectual, and nothing good could come from that. It utterly terrified him. Once again, it was time to lighten things up and focus on her luscious breasts, which were covered up by his bloody coat. Damn, he was always engaging in self-sabotage.

"A proper feminist like you speaking of *planting* seeds? Admit it, deep down you want me," Henry said, forcing a laugh.

"I want you to be serious about this, Henry Young," Gloria insisted.

He looked away, uncomfortable. She was taking him and his passion for Van Morrison too seriously. His interest was amateur and did not matter. It was about his own amusement. It was not scholarship. Just ask the scholar of scholars, Nicholas Young.

"I don't really belong here, Gloria. I'm not a scholar like you. The only reason I was admitted was because my father is chair of the music department," he offered meekly.

But she met his meekness with loud confidence. "I listen to you play records. The way you group albums and songs. You separate and connect them according to their influences. Blues. Soul. Jazz. Celtic. Country. Chronologically or thematically or by connecting various singers and songwriters who were inspirations of Van Morrison, followers of Van Morrison, collaborators of Van Morrison, or foils of Van Morrison. That's critical scholarship whether you believe it or not, Henry Young."

"When do you listen to me play music?" he asked in amazement.

She looked away, embarrassed.

Quietly, she admitted, "I often take an extra bath late at night just so I can listen to your musical erudition, Professor Young." She gave a little laugh, looking at her red hands, and added, "And as you know, for me, taking another bath is a big deal."

Henry spoke very gently. "Come in my room next time. We can listen together. Easier on your hands."

Henry reached for her hands, but she quickly hid them in the pockets of his coat. Even though he didn't know what to say during the awkward silence that followed, he was pleased he had pushed the boundaries a bit. Gloria was pushing them as well. That sneaky girl had been listening to his music, and he had a plan.

8.

The rainiest day since she arrived at Oxford was also the worst day since she'd arrived at Oxford. Everything felt ruined. Gloria devastated, Oliver gloating, and Mitchell let down; it was too much for her to bear. There were so many deadlines and projects to complete before the end of the month. She was nervous about getting it all done and doing a good job. Not just a good job. A great job. A perfect job. Perfect. Everything had to be perfect.

Gloria was totally and utterly stressed out. And the disapproving email she received the previous night from Margo Mitchell only exacerbated her anxiety and stress. On the surface, it may not have been that severe, but Gloria was a perfectionist. She had difficulty accepting even the most mild and constructive feedback, especially in academia, where she held herself to the impossible standard of Superstar.

Gloria frantically rubbed her hands as she doused them with more Purell, finishing up the bottle. *I saw a man pursuing the horizon. Round and round they sped. I was disturbed at this. Disturbed. Disturbed. Disturbed.*

She read the email from Mitchell again for the hundredth time, and it still made her just as nauseous as it had when she first received it the night before.

Dear Gloria,

While your Plath outline was very compelling, it is missing the perspectives of two important works: Tracy Brain's *The Other Sylvia Plath* and specifically her essay "Dangerous Perspectives: The Problem of Reading Sylvia Plath Biographically," where she argues for an expansion of the traditional critical interpretations. And Dan Monaco's "When You're in Trouble, Go Into Your Dance: History, Culture, and Sylvia Plath," which thoughtfully examines "Lady Lazarus" in the context of 20th-century politics and culture.

I hope everything is well. You are usually so thorough. Nice to know you're human like the rest of us :-) I am thinking that maybe you've been working too hard and can use a bit of a holiday. Please know that my partner Patricia and I have a small flat in London and I would be delighted if you would borrow it for a weekend. Theatre, museums, dining, shopping. A great time of year to spend in town.

Again, if you need anything, please let me know. Anything at all.

Yours,
MM

Rationally, Gloria knew Mitchell was not angry or even mildly disappointed. Quite the contrary, Mitchell sounded quite relieved that Gloria was human. Mitchell was always so desirous of connecting with Gloria's more human side. But Gloria's reserved character was wary of Mitchell's many attempts at intimacy. They made her feel uncomfortable. Mitchell always had some strange agenda that Gloria could not quite decipher. She always felt like Mitchell was trying to save her like she was some messed-up charity case.

Well, no matter how powerful or resourceful the prestigious poet was, she couldn't possibly save Gloria from Oliver. The truth was that Gloria was more concerned about disappointing Oliver than Mitchell. Oliver was the real enraged scholar with unyielding standards.

Are you pleased with yourself, Superstar? Spending all this time laughing with that filthy, germ-infested overgrown adolescent who's more interested in your breasts than your mind. That lecherous, filthy, boob-ogling bum is going to have you kicked out of the program. He is tripping you up, causing you to make easy, careless mistakes. You're messing up.

What made matters worse was that Gloria had intended to look up the sources Mitchell recommended. She had written the citations on her to-do list. She did not want to admit it, but Oliver had a point. Henry had been distracting her. She was spending too much time with him or thinking about him. She was allowing him to take her off task and to bend the rules. Since she started hanging out with Henry, she had not been living up to her potential as Superstar.

Oliver did not mind admitting it. Oliver was jealous of the precious time Gloria was spending with Henry. Like a cheetah lying in wait, Oliver took this mess-up as an opportunity to pounce.

You're letting him distract you. He's causing you to mess up. The shame. The puking. The germs. The blood. Do you really want to go through that again? Are the dimples and dirty rock shirts and Van Morrison love fests worth it? If you mess up, you get sick.

She could not endure Oliver's ranting today, and she did not want to read the fucking email again. She had to get to Bodleian Library as quickly as possible to retrieve the books and articles and calm her anxious mind. Everything was too loud. She had to get to the library to quiet things down.

Gloria was speed-walking through the quad in a red raincoat, carrying a matching red umbrella. With her severe expression and ugly red hands, she looked like a giant angry lobster as she marched through the rainy courtyard on her way to Bodleian.

And of course, at the absolute wrong time, she nearly collided with a soaking-wet Henry who, impervious to the rain, was happy as a clam. A very wet clam. She tried to dodge him, but he shuffled from right to left, as if playing defensive basketball, blocking her path. And like Gene Kelly, sans raincoat and umbrella, happy Henry started singing in the rain,

> *She makes me feel so good Lord*
> *Makes me feel alright*
> *Her name is G-L-O-R-I-A*
> *Gloria, Gloria, Gloria*

Gloria stopped but was in no mood for song and dance, especially the kind that celebrated her name. She had messed up her assignment for Mitchell, and Oliver was on high alert. She had to get those articles as quickly as possible. She agreed with Oliver: Henry was dangerous. Once again, he was diverting her and ruining everything. She should have moved out of their flat weeks ago. It was impossible to stay in control with Henry in her peripheral vision.

"Henry, please let me pass. I am going to be late. I have to get to the library. I have a lot of work," she announced flatly, blinders on. She needed tunnel vision with him. *Focus. Focus. Focus.*

"Some things are more important than work," he said, trying to get her attention.

"For you, everything is more important than work," she replied with a weary grimace.

Henry took two tickets out of his pocket and announced, "What about these?"

Gloria looked confused. Trying to make out what the tickets were for and why ridiculous Henry would be letting them get soaked.

He put the tickets back in his wet pocket and explained with the widest smile she'd ever seen, "Two tickets to the Van Morrison *Astral Weeks* concert in Ireland the end of January. For us to go together. You and me, Gloria. His biggest fans."

Henry was glowing under the soaking-wet hair matted to his forehead. Gloria momentarily let her umbrella drop, losing all train of thought. She could not focus. Henry. Van Morrison. *Astral Weeks*.

"Van Morrison? *Astral Weeks* concert? Are you kidding? That's incredible. Oh my God, Henry," she muttered in shock, a bit delirious.

They had spent hours talking about Van Morrison's historic show at the Hollywood Bowl in 2008, where he played his 1968 album *Astral Weeks* with a hundred-piece orchestra.

Even at the age of sixty-three, people who attended the concert described Van Morrison's voice as "purer, stronger, heartier" than ever, "conjuring Muddy Waters and Howlin' Wolf." Gloria thought it would be incredible to see Van Morrison with Henry, her professor who knew even more about Van Morrison than she.

But going to the concert would be dangerous as well. Dangerous as hell. What was she thinking? She wasn't thinking. She couldn't think clearly in front of him. But she didn't know what to say. He was being so generous and thoughtful. And he looked so happy. True, he had been bending her rules, but she had been allowing and even encouraging him. She had to stay focused on why she came to Oxford. *Focus. Focus. Focus.*

But what should she tell Henry? She didn't want to hurt his feelings. Should she tell him the truth about Lollapalooza in Chicago, three summers ago, the one and only time she had seen Van Morrison in concert? The one and only time she had seen *anyone* in concert?

Should she tell him that in spite of the smells and germs from the cigarettes and beer and blue portable toilets and sweltering Chicago humidity, she stood there among the other Van Morrison devotees ready to worship, solemnly standing somewhere between familiar landmarks, Buckingham Fountain and the Sears Tower, in the vile, fetid dirt of Grant Park listening to Van Morrison inspire his flock?

It was filthy but wondrous listening to Van Morrison live as he captivated lost souls, bellowing the ascending staccato rhythms of "Beside You" with the reverence and devotion of a cantor on the high holidays. Mind you, he was not singing the more polished and tidy studio version of "Beside You" from his album *Astral Weeks*. No, it was the edgy, spontaneous, and utterly desperate wailing "Beside You" from *New York Sessions*. The song you sang when you wanted to be inscribed in the Book of Life. The song you sang when you wanted to live—really live.

Maybe it was the longing in the song or the blistering humidity or the fact that she had not had anything to drink for four hours in order to avoid the germ-infested portable toilets, but Gloria fainted on the field as she worshiped Van Morrison that day. She collapsed right there on the dirty, vile, fetid, heinous, germ-infested field at Grant Park, surrounded by dirty, germ-infested Van Morrison fans who offered her their drinks and their hands, which smelled of cigarettes and beer and Porta-Potties and weed.

Instead of allowing those friendly Van Morrison devotees to help her, Gloria started screaming, writhing, and shaking. Van Morrison even stopped singing for a minute as they called for an ambulance. The paramedics thought she had overdosed on hard drugs and was hallucinating.

Should she tell Henry that she ended up spending the weekend at Northwestern Hospital's Stone Institute of Psychiatry? And because the Stones went to her parents' synagogue and were members of her parents' club, she had been poked, prodded, and humiliated in the best room in the house with a private nurse and private toilet.

The pouring rain began to erode her smile as Oliver reminded her of that disaster.

Too risky. Too many people. Too many germs. Too many germs and you'll die or go to the hospital again. Do you miss the coziness of the restraints and implicit threat of electric shock? Do you miss them poking and prodding with their germ-infested instruments as they ask you all sorts of fun questions about suicide and toilet bowls?

Gloria finally spoke in a quiet voice. "Henry, I am so sorry. But I can't..."

He tried to reassure her, saying, "I will take care of everything. Bring your crazy equipment. A bag of perfect oranges and a mountain of antibacterial wipes. Whatever you need, Gloria."

He sounded desperate but she could not risk the germs or hospitalization or getting kicked out of the program. She had to stay focused. *Focus. Focus. Focus.*

She tried to explain, "Concerts. Traveling. People. Too many people. Not for me. I just can't, Henry. I had a panic attack at a Van Morrison concert before—and it was not good. It was a mess. I am a mess."

A soaking-wet Henry started to plead. "I will be there with you. I will take care of you. Gloria, Van Morrison is our god. We worship him. Please say yes. *Yes. Yes. Yes.*"

"I can't go with you, Henry. It's impossible. The germs. My work. I have to say no. But thank you so much for the invitation." She choked up at the sight of his melancholy eyes and the way he crossed his long wet arms.

It was raining harder now. She moved closer, trying to shield him with her umbrella.

He was wet and cold and devastated. "You're really saying no? That's it. No?"

"No," she responded gently.

Like flipping a switch, he suddenly became cold and distant, and he moved aside so she could pass. But she did not want to pass.

She knew that behind the confident swagger he was just as vulnerable and insecure as she. She knew he was hurt and angry.

"I am so sorry, Henry. I will pay you for the tickets," she offered.

"I don't want your money," he said bitterly, marching back toward their flat.

Was it still their flat? She had never seen him so cold. It wouldn't surprise her if he moved out of the flat or St. Cross altogether. And even if he stayed and they continued to share the loo, she knew they were no longer loomates. She had lost that right the moment she chose Oliver over Henry. She had lost that right for good.

9.

It had been several days since she rejected the Van Morrison tickets, and by no coincidence, Gloria had not run into Henry since. It was obvious that he was hurt and had been deliberately avoiding her. September was almost over, and everything seemed over. Gloria had spent the last hour staring at him in the courtyard through their bathroom window. She watched him laughing with other St. Cross students as he fell in muddy, wet grass after tossing a ball to the big black dog, who entertained students in the quad almost every afternoon.

She felt just as alienated from him as she did from everyone. But Henry's absence was getting to her. It struck her that she felt lonelier now than she had before she started spending time with him—before she even knew him.

She realized that the years leading up to Oxford, which she used to describe as *lonely*, would more accurately be described as *empty*. Loneliness was losing someone rather than never having him in the first place, and it was definitely more painful than emptiness.

All three of her dead women poets—Plath, Teasdale, and Sexton—had lost love of one sort or another. Their lives may have been isolated and empty before love, but they were definitely lonely and tragic having lost it. Gloria sat on the pristine toilet seat feeling sorry for her dead women poets and for herself.

Her lone companion, Oliver tried to reclaim her focus.

He's happier without you. He's happier living in a pigsty with other dirty, filthy, germ-infested pigs. News flash: You're not a pig. In addition to germs, you hate dirt. You hate mud. You hate germ-infested people.

Oliver was wrong; she didn't hate Henry. She missed him. But to appease Oliver, she went back to her cleaning rituals, stealing looks out the window at dirty, messy Henry whenever possible. She knew they could never be loomates, but she was hoping that eventually he would speak to her again. She missed the sound of his voice. Oliver's ranting was getting old.

10.

Henry came barging into the loo as Gloria was finishing her cleaning. He was still hurt and angry and did not care that he was tracking dirt and wet grass all over her perfect floor. She tried to wipe up the mud he trailed behind, but he purposefully skipped around, making it impossible for her to keep up. Ignoring her and refusing to even acknowledge her presence, he started running a bath.

She spoke with hesitation in her voice as she said, "Couldn't you have taken off your muddy shoes, Henry? I just finished cleaning the floor."

He knew his voice was cold as he said, "I *could* have."

Gloria sounded confused. "You could have, but you didn't?"

He kept his distance. "Obviously."

"You're not really answering my questions, Henry. You know what I mean. Please don't be so angry," she pleaded.

"What do you want me to say, Gloria? This is how students at university live. They enjoy the day. They play. They get dirty. They track dirt into their rooms and the loo. This is a university residence, not a royal palace."

Looking down, she responded in a quiet, timid voice, "It's not how I live."

"This is not living, Gloria."

He startled her, grabbing the cleaning products from her hands and throwing them into her bucket.

"Cleaning the loo every fucking five minutes is not being alive. You're worse than your dead women poets. I bet even fucked-up, depressed, suicidal Sylvia Plath had a better time at university than you."

He threw his coat on the loo floor with flourish.

"At least she and Ted Hughes were shagging at Cambridge," he added bitterly.

Henry was sick of trying to scale Gloria's fucking walls and defenses. He could not overcome the formidable army of humorless militant lesbians, dead women poets, and germophobic red hands that protected her or held her captive, depending on whom you asked.

His anger dissolved into regret when she flew into her room, slamming the door and locking it with fury. Was it crying he heard from the other side of the door? They were both so messed up. Too fucked up to be loomates, friends, or anything more.

He peeled off his remaining clothes, examining his tall, sweaty, naked body in the mirror. Would Gloria be appalled by this—the real Henry Young? Although he had years to get used to them, he was still shocked and traumatized by the visible and invisible scars he would wear for life.

Precious fleeting life. Was that the line on his mother's headstone? Was it from Van Morrison's "Precious Time"? He knew precious time was slipping away for him, as it was for everyone, and there was nothing more he could do. So Henry Young slid his weary body into the now lukewarm water of his bath, with its antiseptic lemon smell from being cleaned too bloody much.

PART THREE:
OCTOBER

Oxford Messed Up

Despair,
I don't like you very well.
You don't suit my clothes or cigarettes.

Anne Sexton, 1976
From "Despair"

When the dark clouds roll away
And the sun begins to shine

Van Morrison, 1970
From "Brand New Day"

1.

At six o'clock Saturday morning, Henry awoke with a raging headache and queasy belly. Had he been up all night vomiting, sick in the loo? His breath was absolutely rancid. He could not recount what had happened; he only knew he felt like shit. It had been so long since the last incident: four years, three months, fifteen days to be exact. He tried to reconstruct the events of the previous evening. Where, when, why and, most importantly, how many pints?

He would have to cull together his scattered memories before ringing up Amir. Green lantern lights. Women's crudely made-up faces with red lipstick. The hiss of tonic water poured into a glass. He dreaded talking with Amir. Most sponsors had the requisite drill-sergeant approach peppered with tough love, which Henry found familiar and reassuring.

What the hell happened, you weak, pathetic loser? I knew you would drink or use eventually. You know where drinking leads; you've been down the dangerous road of addiction before. Are you trying to get yourself killed? Wouldn't be the first time. That's to be expected

*when you skip meetings, neglect your work, and spend all your time
chasing a crazy American who doesn't even want to be with you. I'm
really not surprised at all—once a fuckup always a fuckup.*

But Amir was not tough. He was all love. Too much love for
Henry's liking. A tall, lanky Anglo-Indian man with copper skin and
a ravishingly white smile, he reminded Henry in both appearance
and demeanor of Barack Obama, always spouting cheery optimistic
clichés: *Yes, you can. Tomorrow's a new day. Together, we can
accomplish anything. There's greatness in you, Henry, if only you'd
believe. I believe.* Bollocks.

Amir was a medical doctor who led a project developing
innovative treatments for juvenile diabetes at Radcliffe Hospital,
where Claire was on staff. Henry always thought this was quite ironic
since both Amir's professional and Alcoholics Anonymous lives
involved vast quantities of sugar.

In fairness, Amir, who had been sober himself for over twenty-
two years, had always been a great supporter and ally of Henry's,
especially in the darkest days after his mother died.

No matter how fond he was of Amir, however, Henry decided to
ring him only after a much-needed pee, two aspirin, and maximum
quantities of black coffee.

He staggered out of bed, pulled on dirty shorts, and headed to
the loo. Bollocks! The fucking door was locked again. As usual, he
could hear crazy Gloria cleaning away. Given the recent cold war
that had developed between them, she ignored his knocking, which
quickly crescendoed into pounding. He was not about to let this
fanatical American, who'd been toying with his feelings and even
driving him to drink, impede him a moment longer. He would break
down the bloody door if need be.

But he did not have to break down the door. While Henry did
not learn much in school, he did learn how to pick locks, especially
the inexpensive, flimsy kind, retrofitted in old academic buildings.
This skill had come in quite handy since his main extracurricular
activity at school had involved using and dealing drugs. When he
was not inebriated himself, Henry had spent a lot of his time at
Hampton School helping other boys get high, which often involved
gaining access to places where he should not have been.

He retrieved a small Phillips screwdriver from his desk, which he
skillfully used to open the loo door. As he made his way through the

door, however, he slipped on the soaking wet floor, landing squarely on his arse right next to a startled Gloria, who was cleaning the toilet as she listened to music through headphones.

She smiled apologetically as she took off her headphones and offered him a hand up. He refused her assistance with an icy demeanor, preferring to stand on his own. He did notice renewed sadness in her eyes, and a part of him hoped she did not think that he had refused her red, sore hands because they appalled him. It was quite the opposite. He wanted to touch those hands. He felt sorry for those hands. That was the problem.

"Are you okay, Henry?" she asked with trepidation, hiding her hands in her pockets.

"Aside from the fact that I nearly broke my back, I'm fine. Didn't you hear me knocking?" he asked, uncontrollable hostility rising in his voice.

He did not want to be a bastard, but he couldn't help it. He felt pain everywhere: his head was pounding, his back was sore, his bladder was about to explode, and her perpetual rejections—especially in response to the Van Morrison tickets—still stung.

"Headphones. Van Morrison's *Tupelo Honey*. Got carried away. I'm sorry, Henry," she offered with remorse.

How dare she bring Van Morrison into this? Like the bastard he was, he looked out the window at the gray October day, ignoring her apology as well as her sad and searching eyes. She was a dangerous creature. He would make every effort to avoid her at all costs.

So what was this horrid guilt welling up in his gut? He didn't care, didn't want to care. She was crazy and dangerous and messed up. And all this cleaning was going to kill him one way or another. He would suffocate from the fumes of the strong cleaning products or end up paralyzed with a broken back from one too many slippery floors. He had to stay away. But right now, he had to pee.

Seemingly crestfallen, Gloria went back to scrubbing the toilet, which was treating her with a lot more respect. Henry suspected she was cleaning it more thoroughly than usual because he had been sick in the loo all through the night. He could not remember exactly what had happened, and this made him even angrier. He knew he had visited the Bird and Baby Pub on St. Giles, drank more than he should have, and even brought a few bottles back to his room.

This was not the behavior of someone who was supposed to be sober. And why was he still so angry with Gloria? *He* was the one who had soiled the toilet, which *she* was now cleaning, and *he* was being a bloody arse. But he couldn't help it, and fuck, he needed to pee.

With a voice louder than he intended, he growled, "I've got to pee, Gloria. Now. Badly!"

"Just a minute, Henry. I'm almost finished," she said, brushing the underside of the toilet rim with the care and thoroughness of a dentist performing a root canal on the Queen.

"Now, Gloria. I can't wait. I have to pee. Now. I. Have. To. Pee. Now!" His voice mounted; he could not hold it much longer.

"I said, one minute, Henry. Almost done. Please be patient," Gloria scolded with a polite but patronizing tone as if he were an unruly schoolboy with an attention disorder.

She did not look up as she squirted more liquid in the sparkling white bowl and started brushing the same area over again. He thought the bloody bowl looked clean enough to eat out of and could not take her madness one moment longer.

"Fine. I told you I had to pee," he announced with finality.

At the subtle sound of Henry relieving himself, Gloria dropped the scrubbing brush in the bowl and gasped, realizing at once what he had done. Her eerie demeanor alarmed Henry as she walked toward the bathtub with the hesitant but inevitable steps of a condemned inmate walking to execution. She peered over the edge of the tub, saw his shallow yellow puddle, and fell over the fucking edge of sanity.

A hysterical Gloria started screaming, "You peed in the tub! You dirty, vile, fetid, heinous, disgusting, filthy, sick, repulsive piece of shit! You fucking peed in the tub! You fucking peed in the tub! You fucking peed in the tub! You dirty, vile, fetid, heinous, disgusting, filthy, sick, repulsive piece of shit! I will be here all day cleaning this filthy tub because of you! This dirty, vile, fetid, heinous, disgusting, filthy, germ-infested tub! Your germs! Your germs! Your germs!"

It was a true provocation; he'd known it would make her angry. He had wanted to make her angry—for refusing him, for refusing to be his friend. His real friend. And she had been blocking access to the toilet and herself like a bloody football goalie. But he never anticipated this hysterical reaction. He had no idea how debilitating her germ issues were. Had he known, he would never have acted with such audacity, such cruelty.

He had no idea how to fix this. He had no idea how to help her. It was about so much more than peeing in a bathtub. Shrieking, she convulsed as she fell to the floor. And impotent Henry left her there, defensively clutching her blue bucket with her red, savaged hands.

As he fell back in bed, pulling the blanket overhead to block out her screeching pain, he thought her assessment of him was spot-on. He was a vile, fetid, heinous, disgusting, repulsive piece of shit. He prayed to God, Amir would agree. As he looked for his mobile to ring him up, he vowed that if offered even one positive cliché, he would shoot Amir, himself, or quite possibly the pair of them.

2.

Was the room shaking, or was she? Gloria sat in the corner of her bed clutching her knees with one hand and her empty bottle of Klonopin with the other. She was rocking back and forth as she internally repeated a mantra reserved for only the most somber of occasions. *Pills. Pills. Pills.* She had lost control and was willing to confess to a higher power or anyone who would listen that she needed those damn pills after all.

An adept researcher, Gloria knew that her Obsessive-Compulsive Disorder was a biological condition due to serotonin abnormalities in her anxious brain, which could then be triggered by stimuli in her environment. That is why Luvox, a serotonin reuptake inhibitor, was a powerful force against her OCD. But she hated her Luvox and therefore never took it, relying instead on the quick relief of Klonopin, and even then only when she absolutely needed it. Except she had last seen her precious Klonopins scattered on the filthy, germ-infested concrete outside O'Hare Airport.

A raging Oliver, who was somewhere primal beyond language now, was submerging her brain in images of Henry's urine. Klonopin would be her life preserver. If only she could get some. If she did not take some soon, she was afraid she would drown. But in her infinite wisdom and stubborn desire to say "fuck you" to Gladys, she never bothered refilling her prescription after the germ mishap at O'Hare back in August. What could she do?

While the OCD had taken over most of her anxious brain, there was at least 10 percent still capable of rational thought, of devising a much-needed *get drugs now* strategy. She knew, however, that what lucidity she had left was deteriorating quickly. She needed to act swiftly. Could she find an open pharmacy at six-thirty on Saturday morning in Oxford?

With its cobblestone streets and mom-and-pop storefronts, Oxford did not strike Gloria as a 24-hour pharmacy–food mart–strip mall–Walgreens kind of town. Gloria thought this was mostly a good thing, unless, of course, you were losing your mind. And assuming she found an open pharmacy, she doubted any licensed pharmacist would refill her Klonopin prescription based solely on an empty bottle from the United States.

Unfortunately, she did not have a proper copy of her prescription with her. Her mother had implored her to carry the prescription at all times in her Louis Vuitton monogrammed wallet. When she received the wallet from her mother for Hanukkah two years ago, Gladys included a $100 bill and prescription of Klonopin "for good luck." Gloria almost tossed the "gift" in the garbage. "You never know what can happen or where you'll be," Gladys had insisted.

Her mother had a way of making her feel like Hester Prynne with the scarlet letters *OCD* branded on her forehead, so Gloria refused to carry her prescription in the damn wallet. *Fuck you, Gladys.* But as always, when Gloria rebelled against her mother, she ended up screwing herself more.

As she saw it, she had two unappealing options. She could wake her judgmental, narcissistic, pill-pushing mother or go to the Student Health and Welfare Centre at Oxford Radcliffe Hospital and talk to some self-righteous, meddlesome British doctor who, though polite on the surface, actually thinks all Americans are freaks and Gloria especially so.

Moreover, she hardly knew if she could get out of bed, let alone make it over to Radcliffe. Most disturbingly, what if she went to the hospital and they wanted to keep her there for observation, even if it was only overnight? The thought of being hospitalized again, no matter how briefly, utterly terrified her. And if Mitchell found out, she would throw Gloria out of the program. She was always so concerned with Gloria's mental health.

Gloria did not need doctors or hospitals. She needed a drug dealer to help her get drugs, and quickly. *But who?* Henry would help, but there was no way she could ask him, even if he lived next door. She was mortified by her behavior in front of him and all her previous rejections of his generosity. Ashamed by her eruption, she never wanted to see him again. There was no way their friendship could bounce back from this. No, this time she had gone too far off the deep end.

She turned to her drug dealer of last resort. Gladys picked up the telephone on the second ring.

"Gloria, are you all right?" she asked with a tired but concerned voice.

"Mom, I need Klonopin," Gloria muttered.

"No problem, I'll call Dr. Weinberg first thing in the morning," Gladys responded enthusiastically, always eager to give her daughter drugs. "I will make sure you get your medication today."

"Totally out. Can't wait. Lost control," Gloria whispered, straining to make the last bit of sense.

Gladys must have detected crisis in her daughter's voice, because she reassured her with an unusual display of affection, "I'll get you some help right away, Gloria. Right now. Are you there, sweetheart?"

"Yea," she mumbled.

"Stay on the phone with me. Are you in bed? Pull the covers tight?" she asked.

"Yea," Gloria mumbled even more quietly.

"Okay, I'll call the university right now. They must have a medical emergency line or something. Just stay on the phone with me."

Gloria closed her eyes and listened as her mother walked from her bedroom to pick up another phone in another room, probably the study. She heard her talk to someone at Radcliffe in that bitchy, entitled voice that implied she would sue unless someone acted immediately to help her daughter. *She was Gladys Zimmerman and had paid a lot of money and her daughter was halfway across the world and hurting, goddamn it.*

Gloria was usually extremely embarrassed by that voice. But with Gladys as her only tether at the edge of sanity, it was remarkably reassuring. Her mother was caring for her and advocating for her. Like switching back to Dr. Jekyll from Mr. Hyde, Gladys' voice turned gentle again—even motherly—when she returned to her conversation with Gloria after having threatened to have some innocent Oxford employee fired.

"Sweetheart, I spoke to the supervising doctor on duty at Radcliffe Hospital, and they're sending someone to your room right away. I told them a nurse or assistant would not suffice. The doctor should be bringing you medication within thirty minutes. I am going to have your medical records and prescription faxed later today."

She tried to visualize her mother—this caring version of her mother. What was she wearing? The camel cashmere robe Gloria had bought her from Saks last year for her fiftieth birthday? Was she sitting at the Saarinen tulip table in the wood-paneled study with the Oxford website open on the computer?

That corner room had a majestic view of Lake Michigan and part of the Chicago skyline. Gloria especially loved when the view included a glorious Midwestern sky sprawling over the great lake, a patchwork Roger Brown quilt of white and blue. *White and blue. White and blue. White and blue.*

Dreaming about the predictable and endless pattern was comforting until Gloria remembered that it was one o'clock in the morning in Chicago. At this hour, all she would see out the grand window was emptiness, a vast unknown—lake and sky having disappeared. In the darkness of a long night, she wondered whether the lake and sky even existed at all. She was saddened at the possibility that the illuminated skyscrapers were merely skeletal remains.

But then Gloria remembered she could see Navy Pier from that window as well. She thought about the lights of the Ferris wheel pulsating through even the darkest Chicago night with the steady reliability of a beating heart, urging her to keep breathing until the lake and sky returned in the morning. They always returned in the morning.

3.

Gloria's Chicago reverie was interrupted by the sound of someone knocking at her front door. She had to praise her mother's ability to get things done quickly when she was determined. It seemed only minutes since they had hung up the phone, or maybe Gloria had lost track of time.

The loud, confident knocking was like a bugle call announcing the arrival of Gladys Zimmerman's personal cavalry. It was astounding how rapidly staff acted for the right price and under threat of litigation. Buoyed by the thought of imminent rescue, Gloria somehow made her way to the door.

Her savior was a tall woman with a starched white medical jacket and warm eyes. She spoke with a soothing Mary Poppins–like British accent, saying, "Hello, Gloria. I'm a psychologist from Oxford Radcliffe Student Health and Welfare Centre. I understand you may be in need of some assistance. May I come in? Shall I take off my shoes?"

Obviously, the doctor had experience with germ-related Obsessive-Compulsive Disorder. She did not attempt to enter the room or even shake Gloria's hand without permission, and she knew Gloria might be squeamish about foreign shoe germs. As far as Gloria was concerned, however, Henry's urine had irrevocably polluted her mind and world so shoe germs were fairly insubstantial at this point.

"Thanks—for coming so quickly," Gloria garbled with increasing incoherence. "Shoes okay."

Gloria offered the doctor the rocking chair by the bay window while she sat on the edge of her bed. With hardly any battery life left, Gloria's head felt heavy and tired, and she suddenly found herself lying down in front of the nice doctor. This was not classic psychoanalysis, but the scene reminded her of a photograph in Margo Mitchell's office of Sigmund Freud's treatment room in London. Freud was smoking a pipe as he sat in a walnut rocking chair with white hair and matching beard, red Oriental rug at his feet, and black chaise nearby covered in carpetlike blankets for the hysterical female patients.

Gloria was not quite hysterical at the moment, although she had certainly gone there with Henry. And while this psychologist did not smoke a pipe, Gloria smelled the faint odor of something smoky. Cigarettes? No battery life left. She found herself closing her eyes and curling into a fetal position. The kind shrink covered her with a blanket and pulled the rocking chair a bit closer to the bed so they could "have a nice chat about things," Gloria remembered her saying.

Even in her semicatatonic state, Gloria laughed to herself at the thought that while Americans tended toward hyperbole, Brits loved their euphemisms, even when treating psychotic graduate students. Gloria was not capable of determining whether they had a *nice chat* or what *things* they even chatted about. She seemed to recall a muddled discussion about OCD, medication, and how Radcliffe had psychologists who specialized in anxiety disorders like OCD and could provide her with a more intensive and comprehensive treatment in addition to the medication. Did she talk about how quickly Cognitive Behavior Therapy works to reduce obsessions by eliminating compulsions? Did she politely chastise Gloria for neglecting to take her Luvox?

Gloria struggled to hear. But as interesting as this conversation was, all Gloria could focus on was the Klonopin. *When would the damn doctor give her the damn pills?* God, she hoped she had not said that out loud. And this doctor was being so nice. So kind. As if reading her mind, the psychologist reached into her Mary Poppins carpetbag to take out a small bottle of medication and a bottle of water.

The doctor's voice was gentle, but she spoke a bit louder and more slowly, as if she could sense that Gloria was drifting. "Gloria, I have a few Klonopin tablets to get you through the next few days. As soon as you receive your prescriptions from home, bring them to Radcliffe, and we will fill them straight away. We would also be happy to chat about the supplemental Cognitive Behavior Therapy we discussed."

But wasn't her mother having the prescriptions faxed? Gloria was confused, but all she could do was nod feebly as the doctor handed her the holy pill. She put it on her tongue and swallowed with the hope, faith, and reverence of a devout Catholic receiving communion. *Thank God for Father, Son, Holy Ghost, and Klonopin. Amen.*

Before the doctor rose, she put a white business card with an embossed Oxford Radcliffe crest on Gloria's side table next to the shrine of the holy pharmaceutical gifts.

"Gloria, I am leaving you my contact information, including my mobile number. Please do not hesitate to contact me at any time, day or evening, if you need anything. Anything at all. I'm here for you," the earnest psychologist said. She cleared her throat and added, "I mean, we at Radcliffe are all here for you."

A drained Gloria smiled weakly in response. She wanted the doctor to know how grateful she was. For coming so quickly. For bringing the pills.

She used her last bit of energy to thank the kind doctor. "Thank you so much, Doctor. Responding so quickly to my mother's call. I hope she wasn't too pushy. She's just worried, being so far away. In Chicago. So far away."

The doctor crouched down, gently feeling Gloria's forehead. Gloria was sweaty but not feverish. It seemed like the doctor wanted to make sure she was stable before leaving. She wanted to make sure the medication was kicking in.

As the doctor stood, she spoke with what sounded like mild contrition. "I am happy to have responded, Gloria, but I must clarify. It was not to your mother's call. I do not think I properly introduced myself before. My name is Claire Young. I am a doctor at Radcliffe Hospital, and my brother Henry is your neighbor. I believe he said

you two are 'good friends and loomates.' I was responding to Henry.
He was the one who rang."

Gloria was not sure whether Dr. Claire Young stood there for a
moment or left right away. She had no recollection of Dr. Young saying
goodbye or walking to the door. She had no idea what happened to
her mother's call and whether someone else from Radcliffe would
respond as well. This information about the kind doctor's connection
with Henry was utterly and completely overwhelming. Gloria's brain
could not take it; she had to sleep.

But as sleep was washing over her, she tried to hold on to the
shame she had felt at losing control in front of him. She tried to
hold on to the humiliation, the mortification. But the medication was
taking effect and loosening her grip.

So with defenses down and the usual frenzied activity in her
brain temporarily suspended, the only feeling she was able to
muster as she drifted into unconsciousness was gratitude. Gratitude
he had called his sister. Gratitude he was her loomate. Gratitude he
still considered her his friend.

4.

mir was a renegade sponsor. He wanted to meet Henry at the very pub where Henry had lost control and started drinking. Amir believed in returning to the scene of the crime in order for Henry to take full responsibility for what he did and know that it was okay. *He could always start fresh. Tomorrow was a new day.* (Fill in favorite cliché here.)

The pub in question also happened to be one of Amir's favorite places for lunch, so as long as Amir was paying, Henry agreed to go. They met at the pub on St. Giles Street just down the road from St. Cross. The Eagle and Child, popularly known as the Bird and Baby, was a frequent haunt of some of Oxford's most distinguished literary dons, including C.S. Lewis and J.R.R. Tolkien.

Admittedly, Henry was not travelling through a wardrobe to a strange land called Narnia, nor was he leaving the comfort of his shire on a dangerous quest to Mordor's Mount Doom. But as he entered the seventeenth-century landmark watering hole, he did feel a creeping sense of dislocation and even fear.

And of course, with his dark oval face and deep-set brown eyes, Amir was holding court in his usual corner booth and waiting for Henry with a wise and self-satisfied smile, like a bloody Indian version of the wizard Gandalf. As Amir hopped down from the booth to give him an overly enthusiastic hug, Henry knew this meal was going to be painful—very painful indeed.

"Henry, good to see you, my boy. You're looking well," Amir sang in a voice entirely too cheerful for Henry's comfort, given the most recent events.

"Bloody brilliant, Amir," Henry responded, struggling free from Amir's tight embrace.

Henry took off his coat and sat opposite Amir, whose blinding white teeth showed through his relentless grin. Neither of them said anything for what seemed like ages. They just kept staring at one another, Amir smiling and Henry looking at him searchingly, as if he were the strangest man he had ever met. Amir finally broke the uncomfortable silence, reaching over to touch Henry's shaky hand.

"Things are not so bad, Henry," Amir said gently.

Henry pulled away, wanting no part of Amir's warmth today.

"No, things aren't so bad, Amir. It's been a bloody brilliant twenty-four hours. Last evening, in this very pub, I had a jolly good time undermining my many hard-earned years of sobriety drinking more pints than I can remember with random people I barely knew. After which, I spent the rest of my brilliant night being sick in the loo. And because things went so well, this morning was even more bloody brilliant. After picking the lock on the loo door, I thought it would be quite amusing to urinate in the bathtub, knowing full well it would drive my germophobic flatmate stark raving mad to the point where she had a nervous breakdown on the loo floor. And being the chivalrous English gentleman I am, I, of course, left her crying alone on that floor. Things just couldn't be any better. A smashing time was had by all. Bloody fucking brilliant."

After sitting silently for several minutes, Amir finally spoke. "Are you quite finished?"

"Yes," Henry replied, looking down, pretending to read his menu.

Of course, Henry knew exactly what he was going to order. He always ordered the same bloody thing, the breaded Whitby scampi, which he'd hardly touch. These drawn-out confessionals with Amir completely robbed him of his appetite. But he liked ordering one of the most expensive items on the menu; he wanted Amir to pay, quite literally, for the unwanted hugs and extreme psychological and emotional discomfort.

"If you're going to offer such a scathing diatribe, you need to at least be honest with yourself, Henry," Amir said, opening his own menu.

He pretended to read as well, but they both knew that he too always ordered the same bloody dish: the veggie shepherd's pie. Unlike Henry, Amir ate the whole thing. Bloody vegetarian. Amir was much too nice to both humans and animals. At least Amir's enthusiastic eating interrupted his enthusiastic lecturing. Henry loathed Amir's lecturing love fests. Why couldn't his sponsor be a cruel carnivore like his alcoholic father?

"Aside from the sarcasm, Amir, everything I said is true," Henry replied. "Even you, the most optimistic person I know, can't sugarcoat my appalling behavior last night and this morning. The disgusting mess I caused for Gloria, literally and figuratively."

"The mess *you* caused?" Amir asked with an edge in his voice. "Is it really *your* fault—*your* responsibility that this poor girl lost control?"

"Of course it was. I urinated in the tub, Amir, knowing full well she obsessively cleans the loo three hours a day to the point where her bloody skin is coming off."

"But yes or no, Henry—were *you* really the cause of her breakdown?"

"We've been through this. I fucking peed in the tub," Henry repeated in a loud voice, as if Amir were daft.

Patrons at the next table were glancing over, but Amir didn't care.

Amir was focused and uncharacteristically stern. "I said *yes* or *no*. Did you cause her breakdown?"

Henry responded quietly but with confidence, "Yes, I did."

"*You* caused this girl to suffer from Obsessive-Compulsive Disorder? *You* caused this girl to avoid taking her medication or seeking other medical treatment? *You* caused this girl to spend three hours a day obsessively cleaning the loo? *You* are the reason her hands are red and sore?"

"I don't care what you say, Amir. It was I who made a mess of things."

"And you've tried to clean your mess, my boy."

Henry laughed in disbelief, taking a sip of his water. "Everything's just peachy, Amir. I did a really great job taking care of things with Gloria."

"You called your sister, who came straight away to help Gloria. Isn't that right? Yes or no?" Amir asked authoritatively.

"Yes," Henry answered meekly.

"You spent the rest of the morning scouring the bathtub, knowing that Gloria would have a hard time facing a soiled tub when she awoke. Isn't that correct? Yes or no?"

"Yes," Henry responded quietly. "But what else can I do, Amir? I don't know what else to do," Henry pleaded, leaning across the table for guidance.

Amir grinned like a wizard whose underachieving apprentice finally grasped the point. But Henry hadn't grasped the point, and Amir's wide grin terrified him.

"Now you're asking the right question, Henry. What can *you* do? That is the only question that really matters. The only part you can control. The only mess you have responsibility for. You are not responsible for how messed up Gloria is, my boy. You are only responsible for your own actions and your own state, nothing less and nothing more."

Amir's charitable approach was making Henry feel sick again. He was letting Henry off so easy.

"Why can't you be tough on me? Beat me up for a change. You're my bloody AA sponsor, for Christ's sake," Henry reproached through a forced and half-hearted smile.

"You beat yourself up enough for the both of us, my boy. That is why you drank last night, and that is the real mess you need to address," Amir said authoritatively with a mouth full of bread. And then, pointing his knife toward the ceiling, he chanted, "God, grant me the serenity to accept the things I cannot change, the courage to change the things I can, and the wisdom to know the difference."

Of course Amir had to recite the bloody Serenity Prayer. No Alcoholics Anonymous meeting or meal with one's sponsor would be complete without it. Amir loved the bloody poem and probably had it tattooed on his dark chest or written in henna on his firm Indian arse.

But today Amir and his Serenity Prayer were off the mark. Henry knew perfectly well the differences between his mess and

Gloria's. But he absolutely could not accept these boundaries with serenity. He would not accept these boundaries with serenity. As wise a wizard as he was, Amir did not understand that Henry had deep feelings for Gloria, which undermined any ability or desire to accept what he could not control or change.

Amir was correct about one thing, however. There was a distinct possibility that Gloria was too messed up, in her own life with her own issues, to accept Henry's apology and desire to make amends. And this tragic prospect, no matter how reasonable and unrelated to his own actions, utterly and completely terrified him.

Messed-up Henry had fallen for messed-up Gloria, and no Serenity Prayer or optimistic Indian sponsor or pint of liquor was going to change that.

5.

It was late in the day when Margo Mitchell heard about Gloria. She and Patricia were taking a rare Saturday afternoon nap. Patty had been so exhausted, painting in her studio until late the previous evening. A sound sleeper, Patty snored away through Margo's entire telephone conversation with Dr. Claire Young.

Apparently, Gloria had experienced a mild breakdown, and Dr. Young was calling to inform her as Master of St. Cross and Gloria's faculty advisor. The doctor told her that she had checked on Gloria several times during the day and all seemed to be well. Gloria had taken Klonopin and was now "sleeping it off." The conscientious doctor promised to keep Margo updated on Gloria's status.

As she hung up the phone, Margo recalled that Claire Young was the psychologist who was heading the university commission on postgraduate mental health. This provided some relief. Gloria was receiving good care.

Still, Margo had to wonder whether being at Oxford was good for Gloria's mental health. Margo felt protective of Gloria in ways that went beyond her duties as Master of St. Cross and her faculty advisor. There was something about Gloria's sad eyes and red aching hands that reminded her of another young anxious poet. Herself. Or maybe her former self?

Was all their research about dead women poets exacerbating Gloria's anxiety and contributing to her obsessive-compulsive issues? Was Margo's email to Gloria about the missing citations too severe? She had tried to be gentle and even offer Gloria a respite in London.

There were so many questions, but Margo had two in particular. Would Rebecca Greenberg accuse Margo of ensnaring Gloria in a "web of sadness" or some other god-awful cliché? And was it time to contact the Zimmermans about their sick daughter, who indeed was tortured but not at all in a good way?

6.

Gloria awoke at eight o'clock that evening sealed inside the cocoon of her bedsheets. An unspoiled silence reigned in the room, a silence to which Gloria was unaccustomed, a silence unruffled by Oliver's nagging. But this rare silence was soon filled in with the gentle chords of Van Morrison's "Brand New Day" coming from the bathroom.

The music summoned her to return to the scene of her crime. She had a mess to clean. She walked through the bathroom door with cleaning products in hand, only to find that they were not necessary. Henry had thoroughly cleaned the bathroom from top to bottom, leaving behind a sparkling bathtub and a note written with dry-erase marker on the mirror—

> G.,
> I am so sorry. Didn't realise how difficult things were for you. Can we start over, Loomate? Brand new day?
>   H.

Listening to the music, Gloria knew she had another mess to clean. She was nervous as she opened Henry's bedroom door with an ugly red hand.

The music was blaring and rushed to fill the open space like a gas expanding to fill a room of any size. As if in Mozart's *Magic Flute*, she was completely transfixed by the lure of Van Morrison's expansive music as well as her loomate's promise of a brand new day.

> *When all the dark clouds roll away*
> *And the sun begins to shine*

Although it was risky, it was time.

7.

Dr. Claire Young twirled a cigarette in her hand as she nervously read the draft report.

At approximately 6:40 am, I received an emergency telephone call from Henry Young (my brother), a doctoral student and St. Cross resident, regarding his fellow student and flatmate, Gloria Zimmerman. He said that he had provoked her by purposefully urinating in their shared bathtub, which triggered a breakdown since he believes Ms. Zimmerman has serious germ issues, possibly Obsessive-Compulsive Disorder. He called me to come help straight away and informed me that he had on several occasions observed a bottle of Luvox medication in their shared bathroom but that it appeared she was not taking the pills. He also noticed an empty bottle of Klonopin. Around 7:00 am, I visited Ms. Zimmerman in her room and gave her a brief examination. She displayed all the symptoms of OCD. She also made

it clear that she is supposed to take Luvox but
does not like the pills and does not take them.
She is also supposed to take Klonopin for immediate
relief of symptoms but had run out of pills. Based
on the bottle with the US prescription, I brought
four Klonopin tablets to her and administered one.
I told her to follow up at Radcliffe when her
prescriptions come from America and to also follow up
regarding supplemental Cognitive Behavior Therapy.
I checked on Gloria twice today and she was sleeping
peacefully. I informed St. Cross College Master
Dr. Margo Mitchell of Ms. Zimmerman's status.
I intend to recuse myself on this matter since
there is a conflict of interest, given my brother's
personal involvement with Ms. Zimmerman.

Claire felt ill. There was so much wrong with this report and this
situation. Henry's involvement and relationship with Gloria. Claire
medicating Gloria without a prescription. Claire chairing a committee
about appropriate policies to assist postgraduate students with
mental-health issues. Claire knew it would be disastrous if any of
her resentful colleagues or Alfred read this report.

This complicated and uncomfortable situation was way beyond
the power of the *Wednesday Worry List*. So Claire got out a red pen
and started making changes.

At approximately 6:40 am, I received an emergency
telephone call from ~~Henry Young (my brother),~~ a
~~doctoral student and~~ St. Cross resident, regarding
his fellow student ~~and flatmate,~~ Gloria Zimmerman.
He said that he ~~had provoked her by purposefully
urinating in their shared bathtub, which triggered
a breakdown since he~~ believes Ms. Zimmerman has
serious germ issues, possibly Obsessive-Compulsive
Disorder. ~~He called me to come help straight away
and informed me that he had on several occasions
observed a bottle of Luvox medication in their
shared bathroom but that it appeared she was not
taking the pills. He also noticed an empty bottle of
Klonopin.~~ Around 7:00 am, I visited Ms. Zimmerman

in her room and gave her a brief examination. She
displayed all the symptoms of OCD. She also made
it clear that she is supposed to take Luvox but
does not like the pills and does not take them.
She is also supposed to take Klonopin for immediate
relief of symptoms but had run out of pills. Based
on the ~~bottle with the~~ US prescription, I brought
four Klonopin tablets to her and administered one.
I told her to follow up at Radcliffe ~~when her~~
~~prescriptions come from America and to also follow up~~
~~regarding supplemental Cognitive Behavior Therapy~~.
I checked on Gloria twice today and she was sleeping
peacefully. I informed St. Cross College Master
Dr. Margo Mitchell of Ms. Zimmerman's status.
~~I intend to recuse myself on this matter since~~
~~there is a conflict of interest, given my brother's~~
~~personal involvement with Ms. Zimmerman.~~

After rewriting history and smoking a nervous cigarette, Claire
vomited into her rubbish bin.

She felt ashamed; she thought her supervisors should rescind
her license and take away her degrees. She was an unethical,
insecure fraud. She had no idea how she was going to be able to
look at her chair, Dr. Alfred Mars, tonight, let alone sleep with him.

8.

Gloria carefully sat in the rocking chair next to Henry's bed, and he was surprised she did not seem to notice or care that it was covered in dust. If he had known she was really coming into his bedroom, he certainly would have tidied up in advance. But for once, Gloria was not put off by mess. Her sights were set on other things.

"Henry, I am so sorry for everything."

"No, Gloria. What I did was unforgivable. I'm the one who should be sorry. I didn't realize...I would have never..." He was not about to let her take responsibility for his impudence. My God, he was the one who had pushed her over the edge, peeing in the bloody tub.

"You were hurt. I wasn't being a good friend. Those Van Morrison tickets were so thoughtful. I wanted—I want—to go with you so badly, but I just can't," she said, looking away from him.

"Not a problem. I've already put them up on eBay. Some other crazy, obsessed Van Morrison fan will overpay," he laughed, trying to lighten the mood and put her at ease. Oh fuck, why did he have to use the word *obsessed*?

"Obsessive-Compulsive Disorder. Had it since I was thirteen," she whispered as if revealing a dirty family secret.

"It's okay," he went on, contemplating his own dirty family secrets and how she would run from his room if she knew everything.

She shook her head and rubbed her hands in agitation. "No. I am truly, royally, totally fucked up, Henry."

"No, you're not. You're beautiful inside and out," he said with an unexpected fervor he didn't recognize.

She put her hands in her pockets and looked away again. She rocked back and forth, gazing around his room with an expression of confusion and wonder, reminiscent of Dorothy crashing into Oz.

He wanted to touch her soft cheeks and turn her toward him again. He wanted to look into her eyes to explain and show her how sorry he was and how he felt about her. But he had to tread carefully. Very, very carefully.

Entering his dirty room and sitting on his dusty furniture were outside the boundaries of her tight and structured comfort zone, especially after her meltdown. If he pushed too far or too hard in word or deed, he could instantly scare her away, maybe even out of St. Cross, out of Oxford, and maybe even back to Chicago.

So he sat quietly with her for a long while as they listened with rapt attention to side one of Van Morrison's tour de force, *Moondance*.

Moondance, Van Morrison's third solo album, was considered by many to be among his best. Its mind-blowing songs were pure genius: "And It Stoned Me," "Moondance," "Crazy Love," "Caravan," "Into the Mystic," "Come Running," "These Dreams of You," "Brand New Day," "Everyone," and "Glad Tidings."

One of his most famous and commercially successful albums, it appeared on many best-album lists, including UK Albums Chart, Billboard's Pop Album Chart, as well as *Rolling Stone* magazine's Greatest Albums of All Time.

But true Van Morrison aficionados like Henry did not care about other people's lists, the populist dictates and prescriptions of mass culture. True Van Morrison devotees appreciated *Moondance* for its eclectic blend of R&B, folk rock, country rock, and jazz. True Van Morrison believers agreed with critic Ralph Gleason, who said of Van Morrison on *Moondance*: "He wails as the jazz musicians speak of wailing, as the gypsies, as the Gaels and the old folks in every culture speak of it. He gets a quality of intensity in that wail which really hooks your mind, carries you along with his voice as it rises and falls in long soaring lines."

True Van Morrison disciples marvel at the fact that those long, soaring lines in the musical arrangements were only in Van Morrison's head when he entered the recording studio in the summer of 1969. And so many of the vocals were recorded live.

Thus, for Henry, *Moondance* captured the ultimate living, breathing life experience, with its unknown outcomes and limitless possibilities, so different from his own life.

They were almost finished with side one and were listening to one of Henry's favorite songs, "Caravan." Henry wanted to ask Gloria whether she had read Nick Hornby's *Songbook*, about his favorite songs of all time, which included "Caravan." Hornby expressed the wish that "Caravan" be played at his funeral because Van Morrison so perfectly "isolate[s] a moment somewhere between life and its aftermath."

Henry had thought about this quite a lot and, with a nod to Hornby, had asked Claire to have "Caravan" played at his funeral as well. Claire always dismissed this request with a laugh, but he knew she was taking notes and would honor it if need be.

Henry did not bring any of this up to Gloria. He didn't dare speak. Her eyes were closed as she rocked in the chair and listened to "Caravan" with the serenity and singular focus of a Zen Buddhist in meditation. *I long to hold you tight so I can feel you. Sweet lady of the night your eyes shall reveal you.* But Gloria's eyes were still closed.

After side one finished, Henry broke the silence. "*Moondance* is genius."

"Pure genius," Gloria agreed with the reverence of a fellow disciple. "Again and again, I'm reminded why I adore Van Morrison."

"But second to your dead women poets, no doubt. For me, Van Morrison trumps all else. My religion," he bragged.

She laughed. "You're so competitive, Henry Young. God forbid that I'm as devoted a fan as you. Can't Van Morrison be my religion too?"

He smiled, nodding his head. "Okay, but you're second in command. I'm the gentleman, so I get to be the patriarch. As such, you have to denounce your loyalty to poetry and kiss my feet."

He laughed as he wiggled his hairy toes in her direction.

Gloria responded with the mock seriousness of a barrister. "I reject all your erroneous misogynistic assumptions, Mr. Young, and want to clarify a few points for the record. One: Van Morrison, being the enlightened genius that he is, would not condone a religion that was patriarchal or hierarchical; Two: My disability precludes me from kissing feet; Three: Van Morrison is not just a brilliant musician but also the most inspiring, profound poet I know; and Four: You are *not* a gentleman."

He laughed. "And I thought I was the most inspiring, profound poet you know, aside from your dead women poets, that is."

She was laughing with him now as she continued rocking in the chair. "Well, if I'm on equal footing with you as co-Pope and do not have to kiss your feet, then you're on equal footing with my dead women poets. And in many ways, you've got an important advantage."

Henry looked puzzled.

Gloria smiled. "You've a much better collection of vinyl poetry than they ever produced. Can we listen to more?"

Henry leaped from his bed to grab another Van Morrison album, eager for her to stay in his room.

9.

It was getting late as they sat quietly listening to *Astral Weeks*, lost in their own thoughts. Again, it was Henry who broke the silence. "This album got me through some tough times when I was utterly fucked up." He smirked, "Even more so than I am now."

He slowly lifted the right sleeve of his Led Zeppelin shirt to reveal extensive track marks up and down his arm. He had no idea how Gloria would respond and whether his scars from years of intravenous drug use would scare her away. She slowly stood up. But instead of heading toward the door as he expected, she came to his bed.

Gloria sat down on the edge of his bed and stared at his track marks for a long few moments. He didn't know what to make of her silence. And then without uttering a word, she reached to touch his scars with her rough, red index finger. She traced the jagged patterns up and down his arm. His whole body shuddered under the gentle touch of her rough, red finger.

"So that's why the long-sleeved concert T-shirts?" she asked compassionately.

"Seven years since rehab. Van the Man got me through," he responded with a slight lump in his throat.

"Van Morrison's the only voice in my head that can drown out my OCD and encourage me to keep trying. 'Brand New Day' and all the rest. I'm glad he was there for you too, Henry," she said quietly.

He couldn't tell her everything just yet. Her OCD paled in comparison to all of his fucked-up problems.

"Van Morrison gave me hope during my darkest days and still does," he admitted.

"You need to write about that, Henry. The hopeful transcendent qualities of Van Morrison's inspiring poetry. It's who you are. Your dissertation should connect with your passion. It needs to be your calling, why you're here. Not just at Oxford, but on this planet," she said with real urgency.

He couldn't help but think this adorable creature was completely delusional and out of her mind. How could he explain that, unlike her, he was messed up everywhere—a fuckup in life and in school? No one would take his dissertation on Van Morrison or anything else seriously. He couldn't take it seriously. But he had to be careful in responding. Those beautiful delusional eyes were so earnest and hopeful.

He spoke with gentle laughter in his voice. "Invite my dissertation committee onto my messy bed? So we can listen to *Moondance* and *Astral Weeks* as I drone on about my dead mother and heroin addiction?" He gave her a playful shove. "Silly girl. And besides, you know hanging around libraries is torturous—unless, of course, I'm teasing humorless militant lesbians."

There was still purpose and mission in her eyes as she said, "The library's easy, Henry. I can help you with research. Anyway, the library comes second. You first need to visit your musical landmarks."

He rolled his eyes, muttering, "Musical landmarks?"

Gloria kept at it. "You know, the places that have shaped your feelings about music, about Van Morrison and why his music means so much to you."

"Sounds cliché and scary," he said. "Precisely why I dread dining with my wonderful but utterly intrusive maternalistic psychologist sister and why I am ill every time I hear positive clichés from my AA sponsor who spews enough to fill all the greeting-card shops in Oxford."

Gloria's smile waned ever so slightly. Was she disappointed? Bollocks, he didn't want to ruin this unexpectedly brilliant night.

"Gloria, I appreciate your faith in me. But I can't. I have no idea how to write a dissertation about Van Morrison. I'm just a former drug addict who listens to a lot of his music. I'm not a Van Morrison scholar. I wouldn't have the support of my chair or department or arrogant wanker of a father. If I wrote about Van Morrison, I would be totally out there on my own and would surely fail. Believe me, it's happened before."

"You wouldn't be alone, Henry. You have Van Morrison and me," she said. Her eyes lit up, and she took his hand. "Although, he's the messiah. I'm not nearly as genius, only a minor co-Pope."

"But you're holding my hand," he said, interlacing her rough red fingers through his own.

10.

Even the best parties have to end sometime; and so it was. In the pale morning light of a brisk October Sunday, Oliver came back.

Gloria awoke with Oliver breathing down her neck, which felt tight and tense.

Good morning, Sleeping Beauty. Rest well? I'm sure you slept like a baby, especially because I was gagged and tied up and hidden in the closet. Or bloody wardrobe, as your new best friend says. The bathroom is filthy, and you're wasting the day and your life away with your vile, fetid, pushy new best friend. He's such a peach. Exactly why you came here. Are you getting a doctorate in wasting your life away too? Is your lazy loser new best friend your new tutor? He's the fucking expert in wasting his life away.

Oliver's ranting was interrupted by a jovial Henry, who sashayed into her room humming "Reveille" and carrying a breakfast tray, which included all her favorites: unpeeled orange, Special K in an unopened box, black coffee, and a Luvox pill. He put the tray on her side table and drew the blinds before sitting on the edge of her bed.

Oliver reacted as if Gloria and Henry had spent the previous night making love instead of listening to Van Morrison.

Anything your neighbor...I mean, tutor...I mean, lover...shoves down your throat, you'll gladly swallow? Are we living in a parallel Oxford dropout–Van Morrison–germ-infested universe now? Might as well lick the germs from inside the bloody toilet bowl. Please, lock me in the closet. I can't stand this. He's a dirty, filthy loser feeding you germs. I wouldn't trust him to feed the bloody germ-infested dog that, by the way, he French kisses on a regular basis.

Unaware of his jealous rival, Henry cheerfully said, "Good morning, Loomate. I wanted to knock you up earlier, but you were sleeping so peacefully."

"Please tell me 'knocked up' has a different meaning here."

"Here it means 'wake up,' but what you have in mind is much more interesting," he replied, adding with a mischievous grin, "especially to my friend John Thomas."

"English major, remember? I have read *Lady Chatterley's Lover*, and I know what your John Thomas is," Gloria giggled. "I don't know if it's the Big Ben clock tower or Sigmund Freud's London roots, but you Brits have penis issues. So many euphemisms...knob, pecker, plonker, todger, willie."

For once, Henry was blushing. "Now I'm embarrassed."

"I'm glad something embarrasses you, Henry Young. God knows I've seen you in the bathroom enough times with barely a blush."

She swallowed the Luvox pill, relieved that they were laughing and making inappropriate jokes. They were back on track. It had only been a week or so, but Gloria had missed him during their silence.

"Shut up, and eat your delectable breakfast. We have a busy day ahead of us," he announced, handing her the coffee mug.

Gloria tried to hide her concern. "Busy day?"

He responded matter-of-factly, "Thanks to you, I have a new dissertation topic I care about, and I am taking you up on your offer to *tour my musical landmarks*. An eloquent cliché *you* coined, remember?"

Oliver's concerns were creeping back.

Gloria could not possibly write off another day wasted. Not that being with Henry was a waste. Quite the contrary. It was just that she was off schedule. Totally off schedule. The whole weekend had been off schedule. *Off. Off. Off.*

In agitation, she started rubbing her hands with hand sanitizer in frantic circles. *I saw a man pursuing the horizon. Round and round they sped.* She needed her hand sanitizer. She needed to be in control. She needed her schedule. But she also needed the company of her loomate. She hated having to choose between activities equally desirable and dangerous.

She tried to let Henry down gently. "But I am totally off my schedule, Henry. Yesterday, I was completely...Well, you know about yesterday. Can we do it next weekend? I really want..."

He was insistent. "Your idea—touring my musical landmarks. Remember? You're coming, Loomate." He laughed his throaty, soulful laugh, "I will take you by force if need be."

"Are you threatening to kidnap me, Henry Young?" she asked in a playful way that surprised her.

He took her iPhone out of his pocket. "Yes, and I kidnapped your taskmaster last night. Excellent taste in music, by the way."

She tried to sound angrier than she felt. "Hey, what if I kidnapped your precious record player? Aside from being angry that I'd scratched all your records, I'm sure you'd feel somewhat violated."

"I did it for your own good. You needed some unstructured rest, for once. Please come with me, Gloria?" he pleaded.

"I don't know. I have to study, I have to clean—" she explained, trying to avoid his sad puppy dog eyes.

He smiled wide and said, "You can bring your antibacterial wipes. And besides, it's bloody wrong to clean the bathroom on Sunday, the Sabbath. Day of rest."

Gloria smiled back. "My Sabbath was yesterday, Henry. I'm Jewish. Remember?"

"Jesus was Jewish, and trust me, he'd want you to sleep in, relax, and let me show you my musical landmarks in Oxford," he said triumphantly, knowing full well his enthusiasm and charm were infectious.

"Well, I wouldn't want to offend your lord," she sighed, as she peeled the imperfect orange.

"Just like you, my one true god is Van Morrison," he said as he helped himself to a bite of orange.

Gloria was surprised and pleased that Oliver did not protest Henry's unauthorized bite or the intended musical pilgrimage.

But thinking about it, it made sense. Oliver knew that protesting this day would be as futile as pursuing the elusive horizon.

Luvox, Henry, and Van Morrison were indeed a powerful combination. While Oliver couldn't compete today, Gloria knew he would be waiting in the wings for the right moment. The perfect moment. *Perfect. Perfect. Perfect.*

11.

Jesus College felt farther away than it really was. The college, founded in 1571 by Queen Elizabeth, occupied a large site in the city center with a sense of grandeur and regal entitlement. Jesus was comprised of picturesque old buildings arranged around three quadrangles and handsomely kept up due to the college's large endowment from generous benefactors and prestigious alumni.

The chapel at Jesus College was particularly striking and was especially so today as Henry watched Gloria wander about, illuminated by a rare October afternoon sun streaming through its large stained-glass windows. She seemed to be impressed with the seventeenth-century chapel and its intricate woodwork, original tiling, elaborate screen, and marble ornamentation.

But her blue eyes truly lit up when she noticed the majestic organ. She appeared awestruck by the hundreds of organ pipes that filled the chapel and came together, angels returning to Heaven, in a magnificent gold-leaf case.

But Jesus College Chapel was overcrowded with both angels and demons. For Henry, the elaborate ornamentation was weighed

down with dark connotations. He sat down at the organ, remembering his father slapping the side of his head every time he played the
wrong chord rehearsing for the dreaded Jesus College Christmas
concert. Although the slapping did nothing to improve Henry's performance, the Pavlovian conditioning did work. He hated the chapel
almost as much as he hated Christmas.

But it was refreshing to look at the organ and chapel anew through
Gloria's unbiased, obsessive, and utterly beautiful eyes. When she
heard him start to play an organ rendition of Van Morrison's "Bright
Side of the Road," she slyly wiped off the rosewood bench before
sitting next to him.

"So what do you think of my pipes?" he asked with a grin. "Would
you like to give them a try?"

> Little darling, come with me
> Won't you help me share my load
> From the dark end of the street
> To the bright side of the road

"Very large and impressive pipes, but I'm not sure I know how
to play. And I'm slightly intimidated by their majestic size and sound.
And won't this get me kicked off the campus of the very prestigious
and snooty Jesus College? Jewish girl making phallic jokes in church
on Sunday," she laughed.

"I have good connections here. As my loomate, you'll never be
kicked out. Just sneered at an awful lot like me," Henry said, his
smile waning ever so slightly.

"But I thought Jesus College was your second home," Gloria said.

"It is," he replied matter-of-factly. "Just as cold and alienating as
Equanimity."

"Equanimity?"

"My first home. Didn't I mention that my family home is called
Equanimity? We name our houses and our horses over here. I've never
felt comfortable at Equanimity or at Jesus. And both names are quite
misleading. My father's on the faculty here, a don and department
chair in music. Expert on the scintillating topic of nineteenth-century
organ. He, my mum who died, my sister Claire, and even my grandfather
studied and read for their degrees at Jesus. I was supposed to keep
the tradition going but got sidetracked. So to speak."

He suddenly struck up an organ version of "Rehab" by Amy Winehouse.

Gloria grabbed his fingers, halting the self-flagellation, and said, "Anyone with brains and talent can graduate from Jesus College, Henry, but it takes much more to graduate from rehab. Courage, guts, tenacity."

She started playing chopsticks with two chafed fingers. Henry took over, adding nuanced chords and trills.

Gloria smiled at him. "So competitive! But see? You have brains and talent too. No looking back, Henry. You are here at Oxford, unscathed."

The sweet delusional girl had no idea how irrevocably damaged he was.

He looked at her with a sad smile and said, "Not unscathed, Gloria. You saw my scars."

"Proof of life. You won the war, Henry. Your scars are awesome."

Mimicking her American accent he said, "You're awesome."

"Are you mocking me in church, Henry Young? On the Sabbath?"

"Never," he said in his stylized accent.

"I am serious, Henry," she pleaded through her smile.

"As am I. Gloria Zimmerman, you're bloody fucking awesome."

He started playing and singing his new favorite Van Morrison song.

> *Like to tell you about my baby*
> *You know she comes around*
> *She's about five feet four*
> *From her head to the ground.*
>
> *You know she comes around here*
> *At just about midnight.*
> *She make ya feel so good, Lord*
> *She make ya feel all right.*
> *And her name is G-L-O-R-I-A*

Gloria was laughing again as he and the organ sang out her name, completely unaware of how bloody fucking serious they both were. *And her name is G-L-O-R-I-A.*

12.

The next musical landmark on Henry's itinerary was even more holy than Jesus College Chapel. Oxford Dusty Vinyl was a vintage record shop packed with albums from floor to ceiling. A large sign by the cash register warned, DON'T ASK STUPID QUESTIONS, AND KEEP RECORDS ORGANISED! While the sign and serious atmosphere intimidated most new customers, they were very much appreciated by the regulars like Henry.

The shop was filled with people of diverse ages and backgrounds who were frequent patrons and knew a lot about music. Henry did not think Gloria would feel intimidated even though she was new to the shop. She knew a lot about music as well and could comfortably hold her own with music experts of all ages and genres.

Henry knew his way around the shop well. He deftly made his way to a section in the back underneath an old photograph of a young Van Morrison in his twenties. Even outside the realm of stained glass and organ pipes, Gloria followed Henry in reverence, looking around the musical mecca in awe. She was impressed, but her American enthusiasm caused her to speak in a voice that was a little too loud, given the devout worshipers silently perusing the inventory.

"Oh, Henry," she said. "This is just like Reckless Records in Chicago. Do you know *High Fidelity*? The John Cusack movie? It has that same feel: music, knowledge, attitude. I love it here. I bet they have everything and know so much."

Henry cleared his throat and spoke quietly. "*High Fidelity* was originally a novel by Nick Hornby—Jesus College graduate, by the way—who spent a great deal of time in this very record shop."

Gloria smiled. "Always so competitive. You Brits take credit for everything. There are some great things that originated in Chicago. Van Morrison, for example, was highly influenced by Chicago blues. Think Muddy Waters."

Gloria pointed out a photograph of Muddy Waters on a nearby wall.

"Fair enough. I give you Chicago blues. Muddy Waters. Bo Diddley. Willie Dixon. Otis Rush. Buddy Guy. Very influential. I also give you McDonald's. I enjoy Big Macs almost as much as perfect Zimmerman oranges."

Gloria shook her head and then continued to take in the ambience as Henry focused on the stack of Van Morrison records in front of him. He was determined to find what he was looking for. He desperately wanted to show it to Gloria and hoped it had not been sold since the last time he checked on it. He was greatly relieved when he found his treasure, a messed-up old album with a frayed and torn cover.

"Here it is. Gloria, have a look at this," he said with urgency.

Henry handed her the dusty and damaged record. He saw that she was reluctant to touch it, so he wiped it off with a long sleeve.

"Take it, Gloria. I refuse to use baby wipes in this shop. It will destroy my impeccable reputation." Softening, he added, "And this is one of the few places in Oxford where I have a decent reputation."

Gloria carefully took the album, a Van Morrison *Moondance* album from 1970. She inspected it and seemed impressed.

"*Moondance* from 1970. It's not in the best condition. Most collectors prefer no marks. No scratches. The more pristine, the more valuable. But I like the marks," he said in a trance. "And this utterly intrigues me," he added as he pointed to the back cover. "Read it, Gloria."

Gloria read from the back cover,

To Sally,
Please believe in our Crazy Love.
                    N.

She uttered, "Wow" as she traced the words with a red finger.

Henry had been obsessed with this album for months. No one had bought it, and in all likelihood, no one ever would. It had too many scratches and too much writing on the jacket. He didn't want to buy it either, but he was so curious about its cryptic origins.

In a craze, he took the album back from her, asking, "Did Sally and N. get together? Did they stay together? Did they break each other's hearts? And why would something so special between them, like *Moondance*, end up in this dusty old shop, thrown away for losers like me to find?"

A strident Gloria took the album back, saying, "Hey, Mr. Doom and Gloom, finding this album does not mean that Sally and N. had an unhappy ending. You're jumping to some very pessimistic conclusions. Isn't that against our Van Morrison creed?"

She gestured in the direction of an older couple in their mid-seventies. If it weren't for the matching Burberry raincoats, they'd look like hippies from the sixties. As if on cue, they held hands and gave each other a little kiss under a photograph of Jimi Hendrix, taken at Woodstock, no doubt. Maybe they had been there.

Gloria's voice was melodic as if she were telling him a bedtime story or reading a poem. "When their kids moved out, Sally and N. downsized, and this record got lost in the shuffle as they were packing various boxes for charity."

Henry followed Gloria's gaze to Lucy, the punk cashier with a streak of blue hair who was wearing a Ramones "Pet Sematary" shirt and about ten earrings in her face, distributed democratically in various painful locations.

"Some music-store guru snatched it up, knowing that Oxford was filled with messed-up Van Morrison fans like us, in need of his inspiring optimistic poetry. 'Crazy Love' is still Sally and N.'s favorite song, but they listen to it on mp3 or CD or on the iPod their grown children gave them last Christmas. They've been making love to this song for years. It was the song they first made love to in the early 1970s, the song she got knocked up to—in the American sense—and it will always be their song."

Gloria bowed to Henry's applause.

Still applauding, he said, "Unusually cheerful for a woman who spends most of her time with dead women poets."

"As a Van Morrison devotee, my religion requires that I believe in happy endings," she replied as her smile faded ever so slightly. "Don't you believe in happy endings, Henry?"

He returned her smile, but it was forced.

The best he could offer was a meager, "In theory."

His life was too messed up, and he was too sick for happy endings and a long life together, but he couldn't tell her that. To hell with happy endings, he was grateful to be having such a happy day.

13.

Thirst, a popular nightclub located in historic Oxford City Centre near Carfax Tower and the Church of St. Mary, was Henry's final musical landmark. The October sun was setting when they arrived, and it illuminated the surrounding limestone buildings in a warm sepia glow. It had truly been a miraculous day, but Gloria was nervous about going into a nightclub. Henry had told her that people at Thirst cared more about the music than the drinking and carrying on. But her anxiety persisted.

Apparently, Thirst played different musical genres each evening. Like satellite radio, there was always something for everyone. Indie, alternative, pop, punk, disco, hip-hop, classic rock, electric, Latin party, and many other kinds of music. They even had a night dedicated to gay dancing.

Henry promised that Thirst was a great deal quieter on Sunday evenings than on Fridays and Saturdays, when it was packed. No matter what night or genre, it was just the sort of place Gloria would always avoid. Just the sort of place Oliver always warned her about.

Can't you see how dangerous this is? Crowd. Food. Cigarettes. Beer. Germs. Dangerous as hell. This is asking for trouble. You know the story of Icarus. You're going too far, flying too high, Superstar.

As Henry pulled open the door, the sepia glow was fading fast. Suddenly it was evening. Nervously, Gloria grabbed Henry's arm, steering him back toward the sidewalk. How could she explain that while it had been a wonderful day, this was too much? Oliver would not let her go clubbing. It was far too dangerous for someone with her baggage.

She spoke gently, not wanting to hurt Henry again. "I'm going to head back now, Henry, but it has been a wonderful—an amazing—a truly fabulous day. Thank you so much for sharing your special places. I learned so much and have so many ideas for your candidacy paper."

With dangerous dimples on full display, his enthusiasm would not ebb. "You haven't been to Thirst, the most important landmark of all. Best music and dinner in Oxford. I know you'll enjoy it," he said.

"I'm really tired out. Another time, I promise," she said, trying to sound sincere.

"You slept until noon, Gloria. On alternate Sunday evenings, they play all the music you—we—love: Van Morrison, Bob Dylan, Neil Young, Doors, Tom Petty, Grateful Dead, Rolling Stones, the Who, Rush, Cream."

"It's not the music. Too many people. Germs. I just can't..." she tried to explain.

Henry's dimples were taking their toll.

He begged, "A little while? Before it gets too crowded? It's never that bad on Sundays this early. Please, my final musical landmark."

She couldn't say no and risk hurting him again. And she wanted to make good on her promise to tour all of his musical landmarks to help him with his new dissertation topic. He was going out on a limb; why shouldn't she?

Moreover, she wanted to be normal for once. She wanted to be able to listen to music in public with her friend and loomate. How could such an innocuous act be dangerous?

So, ignoring Oliver, her own sordid history, and the vile, fetid smells emanating from beyond the door, a terrified Gloria followed a delighted Henry into the sprawling two-story nightclub.

Two disc jockeys sat in a second-floor balcony overlooking the dance floor. Even though the club was somewhat crowded and loud, Gloria had to admit she liked the music. Fittingly, she walked with a slight beat in her step to Pete Townsend's "Let My Love Open the Door." Henry led her to a high table. It was off to the side in a relatively private corner with a great view of the massive bar and enormous dance floor.

While Henry was away getting drinks, Gloria took a close look at the table, daring herself to explore its surface with her finger without cleaning it off first. She smiled as she followed the big outline of the *T* inlaid in the wood.

Moments later, Henry returned with two Diet Cokes. Understanding and accepting what Nana Zimmerman had called her *mishagas*, he wiped both bottles with an antibacterial wipe before opening them. She smiled at the fact that he understood and accommodated her mishagas so well.

They clinked their drinks as Henry toasted, "To Pete Townsend, the Who, and antibacterial wipes."

As she drank her Diet Coke, Gloria was surprised that she felt fine—better than fine. She was awesome. *Bloody fucking awesome*, as Henry would say. They laughed and sang as they listened to the familiar music. Henry had French fries and Gloria ate potato chips from a factory-sealed bag, of course. They relaxed as they enjoyed their refreshments and listened to the music.

They stayed at Thirst much longer than the negotiated thirty minutes. After Henry finished his third drink, he went upstairs in search of the loo, leaving a surprisingly happy and comfortable Gloria at the table alone, feeling almost normal for once.

When Van Morrison's "Wild Night" started playing, Gloria herself felt better than normal. She felt wild. She beamed, wondering if Henry had requested it on his way to the restroom. They both loved that song, and Henry had played it in their flat that very morning, as they were getting ready for their musical pilgrimage. Together they had danced around the flat to Van Morrison's infectious melody.

> *As you brush your shoes*
> *Stand before the mirror*
> *And you comb your hair*
> *Grab your coat and hat*

And you walk, wet streets
Tryin' to remember
All the wild night breezes
In your mem'ry ever

Without realizing it, Gloria found herself, Diet Coke in hand, having danced from their table to the perimeter of the dance floor. Like a child tired of sitting at the edge of a pool waiting for her parents' supervision, she decided to wade further toward the center of the dance floor, alone.

And ev'rything looks so complete
When you're walkin' out on the street
And the wind catches your feet
Sends you flyin', cryin'

Ooo-woo-wee!
Wild night is calling, alright
Oooo-ooo-wee!
Wild night is calling

And that's when it happened, almost in slow motion. A large man on Gloria's right accidentally knocked her Diet Coke, spilling it all over her legs.

"I'm so sorry. Let me help," he said in apology.

"No. No. It's okay," she responded a bit panic-stricken.

But when the large man started wiping off her legs with his bare filthy germ-infested hands, she fell over the edge once again.

Gloria screamed, "Don't touch me! Don't touch me! Get away from me, you dirty, vile, germ-infested piece of shit! Get away from me! Get your vile, fetid, filthy, germ-infested hands away from me!"

Realizing she had lost control, Gloria ran from the dance floor like she was on fire.

Awake now, Oliver commanded her to run and put out the fire.

Party is over, Cinderella. It's not just your carriage that's turning into a pumpkin. You're turning into a pumpkin—a rotted-out, disgusting, vile, fetid, heinous, germ-infested pumpkin. Leave while you can. Run. Run. Run.

An unhappy and mortified Gloria ran as Van Morrison's joyous song continued to play.

> *And the people, passin' by*
> *Stare in wild wonder*
> *And the inside jukebox*
> *Roars out just like thunder*
>
> *And ev'rything looks so complete*
> *When you walk out on the street*
> *And the wind catches your feet*
> *And sends you flyin', cryin'*

14.

Henry was walking down the stairs when he saw Gloria dash across the dance floor and through the bar with her hands on her head, hysterical. He followed her, running across the dance floor himself as he called her name. When he caught up with her outside on the pavement, she was frantically flagging a taxi. He ran to join her in the taxi, but she practically closed the door in his face with an expression of remorse and inevitability. For a brief moment, their eyes met, and her lips formed the words "I'm sorry" before the taxi pulled away.

When he arrived back at their flat out of breath, he found her in the loo, frenetically scrubbing the bathtub with her bare hands.

She did not notice him, as she was cleaning and chanting in an almost cultlike stupor: "Clean the tub. Clean the tub. Clean the tub. Clean the tub."

Trying not to startle her, he gently put his hands on her back and said, "Gloria, I am so sorry. We should have left earlier. I want to make it better. How can I help?"

When she did not respond, he slowly tried to take the cleaning products out of her already raw hands.

He spoke very gently as he carefully took a tattered sponge from her withered hands, as if disarming someone with a dangerous weapon. "Please talk to me, Gloria. I am here for you. I want to help."

She covered her eyes with her red hands and answered, "You can't help me, Henry. I'm tortured when I venture out too far, trying to be normal. I'm a fucking mess. You deserve normal."

"I'm far from normal. I'm messed up. You're messed up. Come on, Gloria. You were the one who said scars are proof that we survived. War wounds," he responded.

She put her hands right in front of his face, screeching, "Look at these hands, Henry. I haven't survived. I'm not over it. I haven't graduated from rehab. I'm still addicted to my compulsions and haunted by my obsessions. I'll be scrubbing this bathroom all night, and my ugly red hands will be even more red and chapped and bleeding in the morning. I don't have war wounds. I'm still fighting the fucking war, and I'm losing. These hands are a warning for you to stay away. I'm too messed up for you. Look at my ugly red hands, Henry. Really look at them. Don't you see? These are my landmarks."

He gently took her hands in his. "I see the hands of a beautiful woman who, in spite of a difficult and challenging illness, works hard every day not just cleaning her own shit but her loomate's as well." He paused to kiss her hands and then added, "These hands are bloody fucking awesome."

Gloria started crying as Henry continued to kiss her ugly red hands again and again.

PART FOUR:
NOVEMBER

Real Real Gone

Unless I learn to ask no help
From any other soul but mine,
To seek no strength in waving reeds.

Sara Teasdale, 1917
From "Lessons"

Real real gone.
I can't stand up by myself.
Don't you know I need your help?
And I'm real real gone.

Van Morrison, 1990
From "Real Real Gone"

1.

Henry was real real gone, and whether Gloria liked it or not, he was going to find a way to help her. This became his candidacy paper. This was his dissertation. This was his calling. He had finally heard his calling. If he did nothing else in his messed-up life, he would find a way to help her.

He would help her even if it meant negotiating with his loving-but-know-it-all-fix-everyone-and-everything-psychologist sister. Claire had previously mentioned that she had some "boundary issues" with respect to helping Gloria, but he was sure she could be persuaded and prevailed upon.

Given the sorry state of Claire's own love life, it would be extremely hypocritical for her to complain about boundary issues with Gloria. But he did not think he would have to play that card. After all, he had other potent bargaining chips that would give him leverage in their delicate brother-sister negotiations.

Soft-hearted Claire had been desperately trying to forge reconciliation between Henry and their father, who Henry had been deftly avoiding since August, even though he was chair of the music department and lived less than thirty kilometers from St. Cross.

Claire had been nagging Henry about seeing their father for a brief meal. Apparently, the pompous arse actually missed his son but was too proud to admit it to him directly and instead put pressure on Claire to organize such a reunion. Claire always insisted that underneath their father's icy exterior, he really did care. Bollocks! He manipulated Claire as he did everyone. And obedient Claire was pleading on their father's behalf as she and Henry walked through the busy mental-health (or lack thereof) corridor at Radcliffe on their way to her office.

Twisting the red visitor's pass he wore around his neck, Henry was agitated as Claire spoke. "It's been almost four months, Henry. I'm not talking about moving back to *Equanimity*. Just one meal—you, Dad, and me. How difficult could that be?"

He stopped and looked at Claire as if she were mad.

"How difficult? Maybe you should move in here, Claire, because you're bloody crazy," Henry responded in a voice so loud that patients and staff passing by turned their heads. "And I am here to talk about Gloria, not the pompous arse," he added more quietly.

"Bring Gloria to dinner?" Claire asked with forced cheer, as they resumed their walking.

"Why would I do that, Claire? I care about her," he said, trying to contain his frustration. He softened his tone, as it was his turn to plead. "Listen, Claire, I will dine with you and Dad every bloody week if you do something for me. If you help me help Gloria fight her OCD. That's why I'm here. I need your assistance. I need your expertise. Will you help me? I'm desperate here."

Claire did not respond, but from the way she was chewing on her fingernails, Henry could tell she was taking his plea seriously. When they reached her office, he fell into a brown leather sofa as she nervously straightened papers on her desk.

After several minutes and four very perfect ninety-degree angles on her stack of paper, she took a deep breath and sat next to him. He knew that expression well—the *I wish I could but can't* expression—and he did not like it one bit. As he learned from his experience with Amir, rejection coated in sugar was still rejection.

"Henry, it is obvious you care for this girl very much..." Claire started.

"We are just flatmates, Claire," Henry said defensively as he edged away from her toward the end of the sofa.

Claire spoke with the remorse of a sister balanced with the condescension of a young psychologist, saying, "But even so, you are emotionally attached. At the very least, she is a friend for whom you deeply care. And that is precisely why I cannot treat her. When I brought Gloria the medication the other day, it was only on an emergency basis, as I was the only doctor on staff that morning and you were frantic. You were so worried about her being alone in such a state and your role in pushing her over the edge. And besides, there are so many good doctors at Radcliffe. I would gladly introduce her..."

Henry petulantly interrupted. "She has a fear of hospitals and doctors. Some very bad things happened, Claire. I'm sure you can understand. And I don't need you to treat her directly if it would get you into trouble or you don't feel comfortable. Just tell me what to do, and I can try to tutor her a bit on my own. I'll take whatever I can get. The poor girl is going to rub her bloody skin off."

Claire looked at him soberly as if he were one of her psychotic patients and probed, "Why is this so important to you, Henry? Why do you feel compelled to save this girl? This is not *Catcher in the Rye*, and you're not bloody Holden Caulfield. You're a doctoral student who should be concerned about your candidacy paper as well as your own health issues. The energy you're focusing on her, you should be focusing on yourself."

"Just stop, Claire!" he yelled louder than he intended. Regrouping, he added, "There is nothing for me to focus on. My candidacy paper is a fait accompli and a bloody fraud. The only reason I'm in the program is because of Dad, and he has given me all the research I need to write a perfunctory meaningless paper that will pass and be utterly worthless. Worthless to me, the academic field, and even to the rubbish bin. I've been taking my medication twice a day every day, and hopefully, it will give me more years on this planet than I deserve. But as we both know, I'm sick, and I can either do stupid, meaningless things waiting to die or, for once in my life, I can feel useful helping someone I care about live a normal life with normal fucking hands."

He knew his dramatic outburst had pierced her armor when she went to the bottom drawer of her desk and pulled out a cigarette. She only smoked when highly stressed and reeling with guilt. Moreover, Claire was a stickler for rules, and he knew there was no smoking allowed in Radcliffe.

He despised himself for using his illness as collateral to push her to such a point of distress. But this was the only way to save Gloria. He did not have to be Holden Caulfield to know she needed to be saved from falling off the edge of the cliff again and onto the bloody loo floor. She spent way too much time on that bloody floor.

"And what if I do like her?" he peered down at his wonderfully ordinary hands. "What's wrong with me putting myself out there for someone I care about?"

Claire looked wistful. "It's lovely, Henry. I wish the person I cared about would be willing to put himself out there for me."

They both knew who she had in mind, but Claire clearly did not want to talk about her own hopeless love affair with her department chair. No matter how good the sex was, married men could be even more disappointing than cruel fathers.

As Claire lit her cigarette, she refocused on Henry's own hopeless love life, speaking to him in the hushed whispers of a criminal. "You know I can be severely reprimanded or even fired or lose my license for treating Gloria directly or indirectly through you, especially if I do not disclose the potential conflict and there are no official medical records of a treatment plan. This is serious business, Henry."

"I would never say a word to anyone, Claire. I swear on Mum's grave. Our secret," he vowed with solemnity.

"Okay, Henry. I will help you help Gloria, but only because you're a manipulative bastard who I dearly love more than anything," she replied as she blew smoke in his direction with mock hostility.

She put down her cigarette and quickly gave him a stack of books with titles like *Talking Back to OCD*, *Freeing Yourself from Obsessive-Compulsive Disorder*, and *Strategies and Solutions for OCD*. Henry was finally ready to be a scholar and read his research. He was grateful his expert sister was willing to oversee his studies and be his guide.

"You know I feel the same for you, Claire," he said in appreciation.

"Liar," she scolded. "I imagine I'm third on your list. Gloria, Van Morrison record collection, and then me," she laughed and took a deep drag of her cigarette.

Henry's blush betrayed him. Indeed, he loved his wise and perceptive sister very much. He smiled back at her, took out his mobile, and dutifully rang their father, inviting him to tea.

2.

It was an unusually bright November day, and the sun awoke Gloria as it came streaming in her room. She was groggy but could see that Henry had already opened the blinds, placed a breakfast tray on her side table, and was now sitting on the edge of her bed.

"Good morning, Loomate," he grinned.

Gloria yawned, "What time is it anyway?"

"Eight o'clock in the morning, first Monday of November. I'm calling it the Zimmerman Effect. The weather has been much less gloomy than usual since you arrived in England. Another beautiful autumn day in Oxford. Cold, but not a cloud in a perfectly blue sky," he sang with the contrived cheer of a television meteorologist.

Startled, she sat up and looked at her watch. She was in no mood to celebrate the weather. He was making her late again, taking her off schedule.

Careful not to offend him, she spoke to him in a measured tone. "Eight o'clock? Henry, did you take my iPhone again? I thought we agreed, not during the week. It is Monday. My schedule. I need to clean..."

He interrupted, "You have plenty of time before your ten o'clock research meeting. And besides, I already cleaned the loo this morning."

She looked at him skeptically. "You barely wash your hands after using the toilet."

"We're going to try to do things a little differently around here. From now on, I promise to wash my hands," he vowed. With a devious smile, he added, "Occasionally, I will even use soap."

Gloria was not amused by his cleanliness jokes; nor did she appreciate his dangerous dimples. Didn't he know she had to contend with Oliver, especially on an off-schedule Monday morning? She had not taken her Luvox and could not seem to find her hand sanitizer.

Of course, her mounting anxiety triggered Oliver.

Who does he think he is? This is your room, your breakfast, your Monday morning. Is he moving in now? Is he fucking Mr. Rogers, making himself at home? It's a beautiful day in the neighborhood. Is that a Van Morrison cover I don't know about? Because Van Morrison is so happy and cheerful like fucking Mr. Rogers. Let's waste another day, boys and girls, while the germs dance around the potty and Mr. Rogers feeds them to you for breakfast. Yum. Yum. Yum.

Gloria was increasingly agitated as she reached for the hand sanitizer on the side table. It wasn't there. She examined the breakfast tray. It had all the requisite components—orange, Special K, and coffee, but something was wrong. Very wrong.

With what Oliver would call "audacity" and "impertinence," Henry had actually cut the orange into wedges himself as well as opened the box of cereal with his germ-infested hands, placing it in a germ-infested bowl. From Oliver's perspective, this was "outrageous" and "dangerous." Gloria always did the cutting and opening with her disinfected hands and disinfected utensils to defend her food and herself from contamination.

Oliver seized the opportunity to excoriate.

Wonderful. Why don't you let Mr. Rogers use his feces-encrusted hands to infect your breakfast with germs. What's he doing? What's his plan? That's not what you usually eat for breakfast. Not the way you usually like it. Don't eat the apple, Snow White, unless you like poison. Unless you like germs.

Holding back what felt like anger mixed with panic and a strong desire to not alienate Henry again, Gloria said firmly and quietly, "This is not the way I like my breakfast, Henry."

He gently corrected her, "It is not the way your OCD likes it, Gloria. Which has nothing to do with your preferences at all. I did my research. I know there is a voice in your head that is holding you hostage." He moved the tray to her lap as he added, "But this tray is close to your OCD's oppressive routine. All your favorites but in a slightly different form."

For Oliver, this meant war.

Slightly different form, my ass! What does he mean? Slightly different form because everything is soaked in germs? Easy for him to say; he barely washes his hands after using the toilet. Don't eat the apple, Snow White.

Henry knew about Oliver? This could be dangerous for everyone. Especially for Oliver.

You believe him? That overgrown, filthy adolescent fraud? Overnight, he has turned into an expert about what you eat? What you need? Maybe he is a germ expert, all right. An expert about getting germs all over your food. I'm the one on your side. He's conspiring with germs. He's assembling them. He's feeding them. He's watching them grow. Germs. Germs. Germs. Is that what you want? What is this about?

"What is this about?" Gloria asked, trying to contain Oliver as well as her own agitation, now at fever pitch.

"Shh. Shh. Just take a bite of this piece of orange," Henry said in a calm voice, holding the orange wedge up to her mouth, as if he were soothing a colicky newborn with a pacifier.

Oliver would not be soothed.

Snow White's evil stepmother said the same thing. Don't do it. Don't do it. Don't trust him. Vile, fetid, unrefined oaf. He's a filthy pig with an agenda and another fucking dirty rock shirt. Dirty, vile, germ-infested, contaminated orange. He's giving you germs. Dangerous germs. Where has that orange been? Who's touched it? Has he touched it with his feces-encrusted hands? Has he used a feces-encrusted, filthy, germ-infested knife?

As if responding to Oliver's protestations, Henry said, "I promise I washed my hands with soap before using the knife and even wiped the bloody knife with an antibacterial wipe. One small bite," he announced as if he were Neil fucking Armstrong landing on the fucking moon. *One small step.* But his face was gentle and warm as he pleaded, "Come on, Gloria. I am on your side, Loomate. Trust me."

This was it. Henry was forcing her to choose. She hated choosing between Henry and Oliver. They were both comforting and threatening and cared about her in their own ways. Oliver and Gloria had a history. She was not sure whether that meant Oliver actually knew her better.

But who the fuck was she anyway? Her dead women poets wrote reams and reams, won prizes, and touched scores of generations, asking themselves who the fuck they were. What a load of good it did them.

In some ways, she felt more herself with Henry than she did with Oliver or anyone else, for that matter. Since she had been at Oxford, Oliver's dictates felt more and more like the confines of a jail than the safety of a cocoon.

Henry may have been an unrefined oaf who she just met, but she felt free with him and treasured their friendship, even when it involved things that were dirty, like inappropriate phallic jokes and germ-infested fruit.

And he took such good care of her in a way that did not make her hands rough and red. It was incredible how tender he was after her meltdown at Thirst, not to mention the time he had called his sister to the flat when she most needed help.

She liked Henry. She really liked Henry, germs and all. She more than liked Henry. Was *more than like* the same thing as *love*? She couldn't face this question quite yet. She was confused and overwhelmed. Thoughts of *like* and *love* were more scary and succulent and delicious than Henry's precut fruit. In spite of how frightening they were, Gloria chose Henry and his precut fruit.

But as a small consolation to Oliver, she grimaced as she ate the contaminated orange, as if Henry had been forcing poison.

"Good girl. Good job. See, not so bad," Henry said as he patted her on the head like his prized poodle.

"Don't talk to me like I'm some dog you're training," answered Gloria with suspicion in her voice.

She knew he was hiding something, even beyond track marks up the long sleeves of his stained Led Zeppelin shirt. And now that she had chosen him over Oliver, she was terrified of finding out what it was.

3.

It was a good sign that in spite of her grousing, Gloria was actually eating the orange wedge he had cut. Henry had to build on this positive momentum. *Strike while the iron is hot* or, in this case, cold.

"Come to the loo with me," he said as Gloria looked at him skeptically. "Please?" he added with all the charm he could muster.

"You know you're definitely more insane than I am," Gloria said.

She looked past her confusion, got out of bed, and followed him into the loo.

"Most certainly," he agreed as he started cuffing up the bottom of his trousers.

He turned on the water, filling the bathtub halfway. His dirty and wrinkled khaki trousers were rolled to his knees as he stepped in the water.

"Come on. Into the water, Loomate," he ordered with a seriousness that belied the ridiculous image of him standing in a bathtub fully clothed.

A confused Gloria was looking at him in disbelief, but then, to his surprise and great relief, she pulled up her leggings and joined him in the water.

She jumped out of the bathtub as quickly as she entered, bellowing, "That water's fucking freezing, Henry!"

"Come hold my hands and just put your toes in. Just the toes on your right foot if you like," he urged in a kind but persistent voice.

Reluctantly, she took his outstretched hands and put the toes of her right foot in the frigid water as she tried to balance on her left foot. He held her steady.

"Oooh. That's cold," she shivered as she rocked back and forth a bit.

"But not fucking freezing, right?" he asked, his eyes lighting up like a Christmas tree. "And in a few minutes it won't even feel that cold at all." He waited a few minutes as he held her red, chapped hands with a firm and stable grip and then asked, "Are you there yet? Is it feeling any better?"

"Not too bad anymore," she admitted after another minute.

"Excellent. Now place your whole foot in the water," he instructed.

She gave him a curious look but trustingly put her whole foot in the water. He guided her through a gradual and systematic process as she put her left toes, left foot, and finally both legs in the cold water. After a protracted ten minutes, Henry and Gloria were sitting in the bathtub in their clothes, facing one another. Although they made a ridiculous sight, they were both strangely quiet and serious.

Henry finally spoke. "This is how we fight your Obsessive-Compulsive Disorder, Gloria. Cognitive Behavior Therapy. CBT. Exposure and Response Prevention. Habituation. Research shows that CBT is often very effective and efficient in battling OCD. We could see dramatic changes straight away in a very short time. Coupled with your Luvox, CBT can be very powerful in eliminating your compulsions altogether. Quieting the OCD voice in your head. Extinguishing your fear. But to overcome your fear, you must face your fear gradually. The exposures need to be gradual, like getting used to cold water or climbing a stepladder. One toe at a time. One step at a time."

"*Cognitive Behavior Therapy? Exposure? Habituation?* When did you become an OCD expert? Where'd you pick up such big words? Research? I thought you hated libraries." Gloria asked in astonishment.

"When a wonderful but troubled girl moved in next door and captivated me with her knowledge of music and poetry, keen interest in my musical landmarks, and extensive supply of loo paper. And I talked to my psychologist sister who shared her expertise in a general sense, of course. But you probably have seen experts in Chicago? I know you mentioned you were in hospital," he said hesitantly.

"Yes and no. I have a psychiatrist who supervises the medication. But my parents had a difficult time with the Cognitive Behavior Therapy. I was obsessed with being perfect, compelled to succeed and be the best in school. When the psychologist wanted me to purposefully not check my homework and limit my study time for exams for therapeutic reasons and I started getting Bs instead of all As, my father kind of freaked out and fired her. I am Frank Zimmerman's Superstar, almost on par with his Mercedes and powerboat."

"And your mum?" he asked quietly.

"For her, my OCD is a major embarrassment. But it's all about shoving the pills down my throat and hiding my ugly red hands. She never wanted to do the real work it would take to make me better. Although, I have to admit that the pills do help. I'm so grateful you called your sister to bring me Klonopin the other morning. And again, it was so thoughtful of you to help me after my meltdown at Thirst. I just can't believe how much you're helping me, Henry, in spite of how I treated you."

"You've been nothing but a great friend to me, Gloria. I always want to help you," he said softly.

"Why, Henry? What's in it for you?" she asked, shivering.

Why was she shivering? The water no longer felt cold. It couldn't have been that cold, because when Henry looked in her searching eyes as they sat with their legs tangled in the small bathtub, he felt himself getting aroused.

As he subtly tried to adjust his trousers, he wondered whether this was the time and place to tell her how much he cared for her. That helping her made him feel useful and worthy and gave his messed-up life some purpose for once. That he wanted to help her because she was one of the kindest and most beautiful people he knew, and because she actually had faith in him.

But the thought of telling her these things scared the living shit out him and would certainly scare her as well. And in spite of his feelings, there were certain limitations and constraints that made it difficult for him to care as much as he wanted. He needed time to figure things out. He needed to talk with Claire about devising a way for them to be together, if they could be together. If there was any possibility, he would try.

But it was complicated and risky. He was complicated and risky. So with his hopes and erection now deflated, he decided to use his candidacy paper as his pretext. A true academic, Gloria could not resist a challenging research project. And all the people in his life would agree that if nothing else, Henry Young was a challenging research project of one sort or another.

"You promised to help me research and write a revised candidacy paper on Van Morrison, remember? I propose an even exchange. For the rest of the calendar year, you are my dissertation tutor, helping me with my candidacy paper, and I, in turn, am your OCD tutor. We both get to improve each other's lives by making each other miserable. Of course, we can take long study breaks listening to great Van Morrison music. Sound amusing?" he asked playfully.

But he was dead serious. Of course, he did not care about the meaningless candidacy paper, but he knew it was the only way she would accept his assistance. It had to be reciprocal. For Gloria, the perception of mutual gain was key. She contemplated his proposal for a thoughtful few minutes and then nodded her head in assent.

Delighted she had accepted his proposal, Henry said, "And besides, the question should be what's in it for *you*? Part of Cognitive Behavior Therapy is to give you a big heaping reward when you reach the top of your ladder. And you will—being such a snobby and showy Oxford overachiever."

"Would you give me one of your precious Van Morrison records?" she asked with a daring grin.

"Anything," he said, giving her a little splash. He then added, "And I will throw in the turntable if you kiss the German shepherd by Christmas."

Gloria splashed him back, getting water on the floor.

"I will let you be my OCD tutor, Henry Young. But there is no way I am kissing that vile, fetid, heinous, germ-infested Nazi dog."

"His name is Fritz, and it is ungenerous of you to blame him for the sins of his grandparents," Henry said through a smile. "And you better wipe this floor. I spent a long time cleaning it," he scolded as he splashed her some more.

The floor was getting soaked.

"News flash, Henry. The floor is still dirty," she giggled as she splashed him back.

"I will have you eating off this dirty wet floor by New Year's, Miss Zimmerman. And that is a promise," he declared.

Henry suddenly had to stop splashing and force himself to look away from her and out the window. He was trying to be a gentleman and not stare. But it was already too late. Gloria's shirt was soaking wet, revealing beautiful large breasts and hard nipples protruding. His trousers were tight as he felt his erection once more. God, he hoped the CBT worked. It was already too late, and he was real real gone.

4.

Although she had been sleeping much better, mornings could still be startling and uncomfortable. Gloria awoke at six o'clock to the sound of Van Morrison's "Real Real Gone" blasting from her iPhone. Had Henry been adjusting it again without her permission? Right on schedule, drill sergeant Oliver piped up to remind Gloria of her responsibilities.

You're sleeping too much and working too little. It's time to clean and get back on track. Time to clean the vile, fetid, heinous, germ-infested bathroom instead of splashing water all over the floor. Playtime is over, Superstar. Mr. Rogers doesn't live here anymore.

Obediently, she got out of bed and gathered the cleaning products in her blue bucket. Opening the bathroom door, she was stunned to find Mr. Rogers mopping the floor. And of course, cheery Henry was singing Van Morrison.

> *I'm real real gone*
> *I can't stand up by myself*
> *Don't you know I need your help*

Gloria stared at Henry; today, he was the gorilla in the zoo. A freak, an alien, and totally out of his mind. She had no idea what he was doing or why he was doing it. From his sloppy mopping, it was clear he didn't know what he was doing any more than she did.

The bathtub was filthy, there were floor tiles and grout he was skipping over, and Gloria was certain he had avoided the underside of the toilet rim like the plague. He probably did not even know it existed. Only relatively recently had he started putting the toilet seat down, for Christ's sake.

No doubt handsome Henry was a vile, fetid, heinous, germ-infested oaf. Gloria would not want him cleaning a doghouse, let alone a real house, especially one that she lived in. He was not getting rid of germs; he was merely moving them around and around, helping them grow.

Oliver noticed this and started to protest.

Your germ expert is doing a fabulous job. By the time he finishes, this will certainly be the most disgusting, filthy, germ-infested bathroom in all of Oxford.

And then Gloria's rational brain remembered the OCD training as Henry pointed to the cleaning schedule taped to the mirror that he and Gloria had developed and agreed upon together. Gloria nervously rubbed her hands, examining the schedule as if for the first time. But they both knew it was not the first time she had seen the schedule. They had been preparing for its implementation for a few days now. Gloria knew the drill. She had agreed to the drill. It was for her own good.

Still, Oliver lamented her making the deal and wanted her to refuse to honor it. Oliver wanted her to go back on her word to Henry and to herself. Oliver wanted her to rip up the fucking schedule and throw it away for good.

This is your mop. Your life. Your bathroom. For Christ's sake, wake up and smell the cesspool that is this bathroom. He says he's helping, but he's wrong. He does not care about you the way I do. Take back the mop. Take back your life. He's as dangerous as he is charming. And his mopping skills suck shit.

Gloria paused, and for the briefest moment she was tempted by Oliver's entreaty. Sensing her hesitation, Henry put aside the mop and approached her.

His hands on her shoulders, he spoke deliberately with the encouraging but disciplined voice of an AA sponsor. "Please don't listen to your OCD. Stay in the water with me, Loomate. It won't be so cold in a few minutes. You can tolerate the discomfort. I know you can. You've done it before. Please. *Stay. Stay. Stay.*"

She closed her eyes, trying to block out the dirty tile, dirty tub, dirty toilet, and dirty thoughts. She replaced them with Henry's throaty, soulful voice. It was strong but soothing. *Stay. Stay. Stay.* The discomfort was starting to subside as she breathed deeply, walked to the sink, and took her Luvox pill.

Henry's face told her he was proud. For some strange reason, his regard at this small step meant more than graduating Phi Beta Kappa from Yale. She smiled back at him but felt weary and tired.

He cheerfully resumed his ineffective, ridiculous mopping. He didn't care or probably didn't know that he was merely pushing the dirt around. *Round and round. Round and round.* But he sang Van Morrison in triumph, as if doing a victory lap at the Olympics.

> *Real real gone*
> *I got hit by a bow and arrow*
> *Got me down to the very marrow*
> *And I'm real real gone*
> *I can't stand up by myself*
> *Don't you know I need your help*
> *And I'm real real gone*

A desperate Oliver told her it was not too late. Oliver begged her to grab the mop from Henry's hands and reclaim her disciplined life.

Real real clean. Real real clean. Only you can make the bathroom real real clean. I'm the only one who really knows and really cares. I'm the only one who can protect you from evil germs. This is how I get treated for my years of service? Just because everything is new with him? Hope you enjoy his lovely germs.

Gloria went back into her room and used her headphones to fill her brain with Van Morrison and crowd out Oliver's ranting. Oliver's disciplined life was not a life. She rocked in her chair with urgency, listening to "Real Real Gone" on a repetitive loop, waiting for her medication to kick in.

Finally, at six forty-two Gloria took off her lifeline headphones, curled up in her bed, and fell back to sleep, knowing that Oliver was real real gone and Henry was in the bathroom trying to mop the floor.

5.

odleian Library's adjacent building, formally known as Radcliffe Camera, was designed by James Gibbs in 1737 in the English Palladian style. It was one of the earliest examples of a circular library with its famous celebratory dome. Its grand reading room was the perfect place for the celebration Gloria had in mind.

She felt like a little girl throwing a Van Morrison–themed birthday party and waiting for her best friend to arrive. Giddy and impatient, she kept staring at the clock on the wall in the private reading room off the main dome, hoping that the minute hand would move more quickly. Being a credentialed expert at the rare-book archive had never been this exciting.

Oxford's rare-manuscript collection was one of the most extensive and valuable in the world, so there were very tight controls to make sure all its precious documents were secure. Only credentialed faculty, staff, and graduate students who understood how to handle these valuable documents and who could be accountable for them were allowed access. Even then, they were only permitted use under the supervision of one of the assistant curators. Gloria had such credentials and was authorized to have rare documents pulled and set up in one of the private reading rooms in Radder.

The clock in the private reading room was still ticking too slowly. She could not wait for Henry to arrive. He was her special guest—the guest of honor at her party. Really, it was his party. It was only a few minutes past four, and Henry was not expected until five. Gloria did not know what to do with herself.

She bounced around the room impatiently, trying to contain her excitement. She was so happy to tutor Henry, help him with his candidacy paper, and finally reciprocate for all he had done and was doing for her. Research and writing were her strengths, and she was delighted to use them to help her loomate and great friend, whom she more than liked.

Like a proud party planner, she was pleased how she had set up the reading room so that Henry would feel inspired by his paper topic and might even conquer his psychosomatic "allergies" to research and libraries. She had organized the Van Morrison albums and a turntable with dual headphones on one table.

On another table, she had placed a special cloth to arrange rare vintage Van Morrison manuscripts and journals, which included original musical arrangements, draft lyrics, and personal notes. She handled these valuable and rare documents carefully, putting her white cotton gloves to good use. She also brought a pair of white gloves for Henry. Straightening out his white gloves on the table, she felt embarrassed when she recalled her fantasy of fitting the tight gloves on his long slender fingers as if placing a condom. She had been fantasizing about Henry a lot lately, which kind of freaked her out. At the very least, it was confusing.

For Christ's sake, she was a germophobe and should not be thinking about putting condoms on Henry. It was disgusting. *Or was it disgusting?* She should think it was disgusting. *Shouldn't she?* With Oliver dormant, she did not know what to think anymore, but she vowed that when Henry arrived, she would be focused and disciplined. *Focus. Focus. Focus.*

And looking at the rare books, Gloria thought she was being presumptuous fantasizing about Henry. She didn't belong with him. She belonged here. She was an immaculate artifact, an untouched antique. She wasn't meant for living, breathing, vibrant people like

Henry. He deserved someone who could party at clubs and not just in rare-book rooms.

And besides they had a lot of work to do. His candidacy paper was due in less than a month, and he would need to pass in order to be cleared for writing his dissertation. Even though the paper was only a fifty-page proposal, it had to provide a rigorous grounding of his research topic both in the relevant literature and within the appropriate theoretical frameworks. Thus, they had a lot of research and writing to accomplish in a short period of time.

The remaining table was filled with the secondary source material Gloria had spent the previous few days tracking down—various books and academic journal articles about Van Morrison and the impact of his body of work and its relationship to transcendental poetry. She arranged these sources thematically and then alphabetically.

Finally, she hoped Henry would not think she was overreaching or being too pushy, but she had taken the initiative to prepare an annotated bibliography and comprehensive index, maps to make it easier for him to navigate this new terrain, which she knew he found intimidating. She even left these resources for him the night before, sliding them under his bedroom door, so that he would feel comfortable and reassured about their research today.

She wanted the experience of writing this paper to be as much of a pleasure for him as it was for her as his guide. She wanted him to feel as inspired writing about Van Morrison as he was listening to Van Morrison's music.

At ten minutes to five, Gloria was bouncing out of her chair and around the small reading room like Tigger from A.A. Milne's Winnie-the-Pooh books. A.A. Milne went to Cambridge and not Oxford, but that was okay. He probably crafted Pooh in a similar reading room, albeit at England's second-oldest university.

When the appointed time came, Gloria was positively giddy that Henry would finally arrive. But five o'clock came and went without a sign of him. At five-thirty, she checked her iPhone, but there was no voice mail, no text, and no email.

She waited and waited and waited. Six, six thirty, seven, seven thirty. Still, no Henry. No voice mail, no text, no email. And he was not responding to her calls, texts, and emails. Gloria was worried. Had something happened? Holding back tears, she truly was the little girl all dressed up with nowhere to go and no one coming to her party. In light of her new relationship with Henry and Oliver at bay, her imaginary friends were not nearly as satisfying as they used to be. Where was he? Was he okay? Was he blowing her off? She didn't know what to think.

Her excitement had morphed into disappointment and then frustration as the hours passed. Feeling like a schmuck, Gloria was still waiting for him in her decorated study room. She was waiting for the guest of honor who had blown her off and treated her like a piece of shit.

But then she felt guilty. Maybe something happened. Was he okay? Should she call his sister? She had already started searching her wallet for Dr. Claire Young's business card when Henry showed up. The schmuck showed up. The clock's hands pointed to eight seventeen. He was over three hours late without having gotten in touch to explain. Gloria was livid.

With a guilty and contrite voice, he stammered, "Gloria, I am s-s-so s-s-sorry..."

Gloria interrupted, her voice flat and stripped of all emotion. "Let's get to work."

He looked nervous and sweaty in the cold study room as he spoke with mild desperation in his voice. "You see. I went in to London thinking I could do some research in advance of our meeting. And...I found this old record shop in the Charing Cross Road. I could not make it to the library and the tube..."

"Your excuses insult both of us, Henry," Gloria interrupted, appearing unruffled.

"I'm an arse, Gloria," he said, shaking his head in shame.

Gloria refused to indulge and enable this pitiful self-sabotage. He was better than that—the goddamn fucking vile, fetid piece of shit was better than that. They were having her goddamn fucking party whether he liked it or not—whether he felt worthy or not—whether he was a competent scholar or not.

But she kept all expression of her emotions in check; it was easier to talk to him as if she were a robot. "These are some of Van Morrison's personal journals with original lyrics and notes. The only reason I have access to them tonight is because Julian, the assistant curator in rare books, is my friend and has agreed to stay late. We do not have a lot of time. Let's get to work."

"Gloria, I am an arse," he wailed as if trying to provoke an angry response from her.

"We established that, Henry. You are a lying, lazy ass who is wasting my time and who is scared shitless of being successful and who fucks everything up. Same scratched broken record. Blah. Blah. Blah." She threw the white gloves at him and commanded, "Now take off your jacket, put these gloves on, and get to work. These manuscripts are due in four hours. You have already wasted enough of my time and your time. We both deserve better."

A remorseful and unusually subdued Henry took off his jacket, put on the white gloves, and started reading. Gloria, his angry tutor, felt a mixture of disappointment and rage. But mostly rage. Her party had been a bust, and they both felt like schmucks.

6.

He hated himself even more than he hated the blasted library. He felt absolutely dreadful. Gloria had spent hours and hours planning for him, setting up for him, organizing for him, and in turn, once again, he had treated her like rubbish. Worse than rubbish. And she had assembled the most incredible collection of Van Morrison documents. No, they were more like relics—sacred artifacts from their one and only true god. Henry did not deserve to be in their divine presence, let alone hers. Why was he such a blasphemous, wankerous arse?

The night before, Gloria had left him a copy of a bibliography that was so detailed, so well written and researched, that he thought it was good enough to be considered a bloody dissertation on its own. She was much too hardworking and clever for the likes of him. He meant to call her, but his modus operandi was self-sabotage, especially when it came to academics where he was Nicholas Young's messed-up son.

Gloria's Herculean efforts on his behalf both moved and terrified him. He was frightened she would find out he was a fraud. He was an uneducated, stupid, lazy dolt who was completely incompetent, the furthest thing from a scholar.

He did not know a bloody thing about libraries or research. But instead of acting like the enlightened man he wanted to be and sharing these feelings of vulnerability with her, he had behaved like a wanker, making her wait over three hours without ringing her up. Inexcusable. Bloody arse!

And even though he was a fucking bloody arse, she was still there. Anyone else would have left him and the organized reading room hours before. His father would have called him a failure and done the bloody schoolwork for him. His sister would have run around doing whatever she could to prop him up and give him false compliments because she had little faith in his ability to stand on his own. And Amir's smiles and clichés would have bypassed all the ugliness in his life on his sugar-paved high road.

Gloria was different. Like Van Morrison, she was honest about the good, the bad, and the possible. He needed to be kicked in the arse as well as patted on the back. He needed someone who believed he could do things instead of just having them done for him. Gloria did not let him make excuses. She believed he had an internal locus of control, and he was trying to prove her wrong. Bloody arse!

He felt terrible. It was long after midnight when he finished. Poor Gloria looked so tired as she handed the rare manuscripts back to the assistant curator. At least she was able to do some of her own research as she babysat Henry.

Julian—a short, stocky graduate student with black, curly hair— received the precious documents with a wide smile in spite of the late hour. Henry was convinced the bloke was shamelessly flirting with Gloria. Why else would someone look so pleased to be staying at the library so late to collect books for someone else's project?

Gloria looked in the hopeful bloke's eyes, speaking with a sweet kindness, which as Henry knew from experience, could be quite deadly. "I am so sorry, Julian, to keep you waiting so late. You're always so kind and helpful. Thank you so much for staying."

"Not a bother," he said, touching her arm as he reached for the last manuscript.

"These were tremendously helpful," she replied with a smile, subtly moving her arm away.

"Anything for you, Gloria. Always," the curly haired wanker said with a wink. He reminded Henry of a sleazy married insurance salesman trying to pick up young women on holiday. Henry was glad to be away from him.

Henry and Gloria were walking back to St. Cross in the dim light of November's crescent moon. He was contrite, and she was quiet. He could not tell if he had been forgiven. Was she still angry? Tired? Or both?

He decided to test the waters a bit, reaching out to carry her heavy bag brimming with books. But when he went to take it from her, she placed it on her other arm, letting him know he had more penance to do.

After a few more silent blocks, he said, "You know he likes you."

"Who?" she asked, without stopping.

"That bloke at Radder. Curly hair."

"The assistant curator? Julian?" she asked, laughing now.

At least she was laughing again; Henry turned to look at her smiling face and nodded with a grin.

"Oh, please. Julian and I are just friends. Just *good mates* as you say," she said, waving away his comment.

"Mates do not wait up this late for a bunch of old books. You're worth staying up late for. That means something," Henry replied quietly, hoping he did not sound too jealous, just a little jealous.

"Are you calling the original writings of Van Morrison *a bunch of old books*? How dare you insult the Holy Grail?" she scolded, mild laughter coming through again.

"Our Holy Grail. Not Julian's. That's all I meant," he said, unexpectedly serious.

"And *did* you learn anything from our Holy Grail?" she asked with a bit more friendliness than before; her cold demeanor seemed to be thawing.

"I learned a lot. I didn't deserve it, but having direct contact with Van Morrison's holy relics was extraordinary. Of course, the manuscripts you pulled were spot-on. Amazing. Belfast, 1966. Van Morrison wrote of visiting Cezil McCartney, a painter, who had drawings on astral projections—out-of-body experiences. He talked about seeing a light at the end of the tunnel, which inspired *Astral Weeks*. In my dissertation, I want to argue that this actually inspired his whole career and can be encapsulated by what I am calling Van Morrison's *fatalistic optimism*. The idea that there is always the possibility of transcendence, no matter how fucked up things are."

Henry panicked when Gloria stopped walking and stared at him with the most odd expression. Did she think his idea was ridiculous? Did she consider him an ungrateful idiot? She had never looked at him like that before. He was worried. Had he made things worse? He was terrified.

With concern, he asked, "Something wrong? Am I a total idiot? Am I still in trouble?"

She smiled as if taking mild pleasure in his paranoia and then said with her usual warmth, "Quite the contrary. Actually, I'm just impressed. You sound like a real scholar, Henry Young."

"So am I worth staying up late for?" he asked, his flirtatious grin returning.

He may not have been as smart, courteous, or accomplished as Julian, but damn, he knew he was more handsome and charming.

"Don't get greedy. I may just be having an out-of-body experience, you know. It is one o'clock in the morning," Gloria laughed as she passed him her heavy bag.

7.

Miraculously, Henry had worked his way back into Gloria's good graces. It appeared that she had forgiven him, and he was doing his utmost to show her he was finally serious about his paper and appreciated her efforts on his behalf. He had spent more time at the library in the past week than he had spent at the library in the past three years.

Every day, he proudly displayed his outline, which was growing both in its detail and analytical depth. Even he was impressed with his academic and intellectual progress under Gloria's obsessive and watchful eyes. He started thinking his paper might actually turn into something. Something real. Something more than a mere ruse for Gloria's OCD training.

But the OCD training was his priority. He regularly met with Claire to make sure they were adhering to the CBT plan correctly. While Gloria had been making meaningful progress, Henry was concerned because tomorrow was the dreaded day when Gloria would be forced to part from her most beloved drug: hand sanitizer. A former addict himself, Henry knew how difficult that could be.

"I don't know if she can do this, Claire. Reducing the hand sanitizer each couple of days has been hard enough."

"She can and she will, Henry," Claire insisted in between sips of black coffee from the hospital refectory. "The fact that she is so dependent on hand sanitizer shows how badly she needs to quit it entirely. She will not enjoy giving it up, but it will help her tremendously. You need to be persistent. She will listen to you because she trusts you. You're her boyfriend, after all."

"Boyfriend? Where did you get that idea?" Henry asked with affected incredulity.

"Come on, Henry. You're hopelessly in love with that girl, and from my vantage point, I would say she feels the same. Haven't you talked about it yet? Declared your affection by now? Kissed her at least?" Claire inquired, mildly teasing.

"Bollocks, Claire. How can I declare my affection or kiss the poor girl when she doesn't even see the whole picture, doesn't know the story that comes with the scars?" he replied, not at all amused.

"She trusts you, Henry. You need to trust her as well. Talk to her," Claire urged, in all seriousness.

"She has germ issues, Claire. She is going through so much right now with the CBT. Like you always say, we just need to take it one step at a time," he responded meekly.

How could he tell Gloria about his illness? An illness that threatened his life and might threaten hers. He felt guilty and perverse hoping it would threaten hers. He was an arse. It was selfish to love Gloria and hope for love back.

"But are you even taking any steps at all in that regard? You seem pretty stagnant, brother, if you ask me."

"Says the sister whose love life is a fucking treadmill. Talk about going nowhere very slowly indeed. Tell me who is more out of reach, Claire, an American germophobe or a married Catholic doctor with six children?" Henry said with a cutting cruelty he immediately regretted.

Claire reached for a cigarette from her purse, and indeed Henry felt like an arse. As she lit her cigarette and started smoking, they did not say a word. There was nothing to say. They were both in screwed-up, messed-up, utterly futile relationships. And once again thoughts turned to their dear father and his bloody idea of equanimity.

8.

She was always anxious in the morning but especially so today. Ready to leave for class, Gloria was rubbing her hands in a desperate search for hand sanitizer. *I saw a man pursuing the horizon. Round and round they sped. Round and round. Round and round.* Once again the elusive horizon was denying her all comfort, denying her all hand sanitizer. Every last bottle gone. For good.

In accordance with the Cognitive Behavior Therapy plan, Gloria had begrudgingly allowed Henry to gradually reduce her consumption of hand sanitizer, and this was the dreaded day when she was supposed to eliminate it altogether.

But she was not ready to dive off the platform. *I saw a man pursuing the horizon. Round and round they sped. Round and round. Round and round.* While she had been a good soldier and faithful student of Henry's strict and sometimes painful OCD tutoring, she had known this milestone was going to be difficult if not impossible, requiring extreme and devious measures.

Gloria had never cheated on tests or borrowed sources from the Internet for academic papers. She never stole or sold any of the rare manuscripts and other documents with which she came into contact. She was the one who found the missing Teasdale manuscript, worth tens of thousands of dollars, and called Oxford immediately. She was extremely honest and forthright in just about all of her dealings. But she knew she would lie, cheat, steal, and murder today, when it came to giving up her most prized comfort and dangerous drug, hand sanitizer.

A mother bear defending her cubs, Gloria would do almost anything to protect her beloved hand sanitizer. As coconspirator, Oliver had convinced her to stash emergency bottles of hand sanitizer around her room in case she needed them after Henry confiscated the official supply. She frantically searched for this emergency stash in her safety pouch and tote bag, where she had hidden away bottles in zippered compartments like buried treasure. But the loot was nowhere to be found.

An island castaway rubbing flint to make fire, Gloria kept rubbing her hands faster and faster in quiet desperation. *I saw a man pursuing the horizon. Round and round they sped. Round and round. Round and round.* But there was no fire. No heat. No warmth. No calm. No hand sanitizer. The only yield from her hands' friction was Oliver's wrath.

It's your life. It's your oxygen. You like breathing, don't you? Do you really want to die so young? I thought you'd outlive your dead women poets. You're too young and pretty to die.

Obeying Oliver, she searched under her bed, in her closet, and in various other bags and pockets for her stash. *I saw a man pursuing the horizon. Round and round they sped. Round and round. Round and round.* Her survival quest was as elusive as the fucking horizon. She was not going to make it. She was not going to survive without her hand sanitizer.

And then she saw him. Oliver saw him.

The culprit. The perpetrator. Treason. He betrayed you. Fucking bloody treason. The guilty party. Vile, fetid, heinous, pushy, overgrown adolescent, filthy, dirty, neighbor. He's not your friend. He's the enemy. He's a traitor. He's on the side of germs.

Henry had been staring at her from behind the bathroom door with a knowing and utterly detestable smugness in his traitorous green eyes. He probably was enjoying her frenzied and futile attempt to survive, the way a child tortures an insect, enjoying its last attempt at flight before it suffocates to death in a cleaned-out peanut butter jar.

Flightless and dead, Gloria noticed that Henry had a garbage can containing at least fifty bottles of hand sanitizer. *That bastard. That fucking bastard.* Apparently, he had sneaked around her room, confiscating her emergency stash. Why did they leave their doors unlocked these days? Why did she agree to this OCD torture, this OCD hell?

Why didn't she move out of this fucking flat when she had the chance? Didn't he know he was violating her Fourth Amendment rights against unreasonable search and seizure? She was a United States citizen, and this fucking British asshole was violating her constitutional rights under the guise of being her OCD tutor and friend. She hated him.

Henry put the garbage can down and spoke to her cautiously, putting both hands in the air as if she were threatening him with a gun. "For your own good, Gloria. Like we agreed, following the treatment plan. We have been working up to it. You're ready. You did agree, Loomate."

But Oliver did not agree, and she was no longer his loomate.

Smug British adolescent with his ripped shirt and self-righteous authority. Who the fuck does he think he is? You need to clean your hands. You need hand sanitizer. You need it now. Need it now. Emergency. Emergency. Emergency. Traitor. Fucking vile traitor. He is not your loomate.

"How about some lotion, Loomate?" Henry asked in a compassionate voice.

As he slowly moved closer, she felt like a feral animal being trapped by a hunter. Now, he was the one with the gun. Without her permission or consent, he pumped lotion on her ugly red hands. Like him, the lotion felt foreign—cold, smooth, and slippery.

As she rubbed her hands with the lotion, her anger was falling a notch or two. But she did not want to admit that to vile, fetid Henry. She hated him, but she loved him; and she hated the fact that she loved him in spite of how she hated him.

So she refused to tell him how soothing the lotion felt on her coarse, rough hands. She would not permit him any victory laps today. If she had to suffer, so did he. To make her point, she tried to leave her room in a huff. Her plan was foiled—not by Henry, but because she could not open the goddamn fucking door with her goddamn fucking greasy hands.

Henry smiled widely as he opened the door for her and said, "I know you want to be better, and I am just trying to help. I am on your side, Loomate."

"Fuck off, Henry," she flipped him the finger as she stomped down the hall for effect, refusing to acknowledge that both he and the lotion were helping her get better. Much, much better.

9.

His Van Morrison record collection was good for many things, but as it turns out, it was not very conducive for writing a candidacy paper on Van Morrison. Henry was supposed to be working on his paper, but instead he was listening to records and playing along on his guitar. The evening had been fairly peaceful until he noticed a stealthy Gloria hiding in the corner of his room with a wicked glare.

He knew she would be angry that he was procrastinating again. He also knew that she was especially irritable, given the recent hand sanitizer raid. As a recovering alcoholic and former drug addict, he knew withdrawal was miserable for both the addict and the addict's loved ones who had to enforce rigid and painful policies.

A fuming Gloria turned off his record player, indelicately as usual, scratching the needle across the record. No matter what a fuckup he was, his turntable and vinyl records deserved more respect.

"How dare you scratch my *Tupelo Honey*?" he rebuked.

She was not acting like an *angel in the first degree* no matter what the bloody song said.

"How dare you procrastinate again? Your hearing is just weeks away, Henry. Have you forgotten our deal?" she asked with more acid than sarcasm.

Before he could answer, the cow was nicking his record player, handling it carelessly as if it were a sack of potatoes. It was the main way he communicated to his god; he would protect his precious turntable at all costs. In his zeal, he found himself grabbing the infidel by her slight shoulders.

"Hey!" Gloria yelled, pulling herself free.

Henry was embarrassed that he had touched Gloria under such panicked circumstances. While he did not and would not ever hurt her, he knew it must have been slightly intimidating given their disproportionate sizes. But he was desperate to keep his turntable, his only salvation.

"I'll give you one bottle of hand sanitizer if you let me keep it. Please, Gloria!"

He could not believe he was willing to break their deal. Amir had been right; he needed to go to AA meetings more regularly. *Once an addict, always an addict.*

"You sound like a junkie, Henry. I'm taking the fucking record player. And if you don't make adequate progress on your paper tonight, the guitar is mine in the morning. Now get out of my way and get back to work," she scolded with confidence and contempt brimming from her curvy, slight frame.

"If I hear you scratching my records, I will bloody kill you— metaphorically, of course," he called to the snake as she slithered back through the loo to her evil lair.

10.

Oliver hated food and strangers, especially in combination. Gloria knew this social meal was a bad idea. Henry had some bad ideas. Her legs were noticeably shaking as she walked with him down the communal stairs from their flat. He tried to hold her hand to reassure her, but she pushed it away, putting her somewhat improved hands in her pockets to suppress a fleeting urge for hand sanitizer. As they walked through the quad, there was a strong, gusting wind, which unsteadied her further, as nervousness solidified like a stone in her stomach.

She noticed two senior Oxford dons, ignoring the *Keep Off the Grass* signs and arrogantly strolling across the lawn, lost in conversation, with their black academic gowns flapping behind them. The Great Christ Church bell was tolling. Its sonorous notes intensified Gloria's dread at having once again to face the terrifying combination of food and strangers.

This menacing combination is what originally triggered her OCD in the seventh grade, and she had not been able to have a normal meal with normal people ever since. For Gloria, that was the worst time. The time of the Great Flood and when she first received commandments from both her religion and Oliver.

Back in the seventh grade, Gloria had taken her bat mitzvah seriously, as she was to become a "daughter of the commandments." For months, she had been practicing at the synagogue, diligently chanting *Noah*, her assigned Torah portion. The conservative synagogue to which her family belonged was called Beit Emet, which meant "House of Truth." Gloria was not exactly sure whose house and whose truth. Certainly it was not referring to Gloria's house or truth. But maybe Gladys and Frank's. They were what the synagogue referred to as $25,000-a-year *Book of Life* donors after all.

Machers held in the highest regard, Gladys and Frank wanted Gloria to "hit it out of the ballpark" at her bat mitzvah. Even though they claimed to be community-minded, they secretly (or not so secretly) wanted everything about their daughter's bat mitzvah weekend, from the Saturday morning service to the Saturday evening shrimp and lobster buffet at the Standard Club, to be the best—better than anything anyone had seen or done or eaten before.

Like Gladys' wardrobe for the weekend, the Torah portion was divided into six important sections. The bat mitzvah girl would usually chant two or, if ambitious, three of the sections, and other family members would chant the rest. The original plan was that Gloria would chant three parts. Her strong linguistic intelligence made her a Hebrew maven of sorts. The rabbi had even called her his "Hebrew superstar." She had looked at him quizzically, but he said it was a compliment and that she was giving her parents and the congregation great *nachas*.

Three weeks before the Hebrew superstar was to perform, there was a crisis on par with Noah's Great Flood. Gloria was an only child, and there were no cousins who were able to chant the other sections of her Torah portion. And when Gladys found out that the rabbi had asked a *stranger*—a visiting rabbinic student from Jewish Theological Seminary in New York—to chant the other sections at *her* daughter's bat mitzvah, she threw a fit. No interloper schlep would take the spotlight from her Hebrew superstar.

Without even asking Gloria, Gladys told the rabbi that Gloria would chant all six sections herself. The rabbi was hesitant; even though she was talented and worked hard, it would be impossible to learn so much in such a short time. But as always, Gladys used the power of her purse to purchase her way.

So instead of experiencing the usual combination of excitement and nerves in the weeks before her bat mitzvah, Gloria was panicked and terrified having to learn three more sections of Hebrew. The pressure was maddening, as even the smallest mistake would be corrected on the bimah in front of 300 of the most judgmental, hungry, and tired people you could imagine.

And then the dreaded day came. Of course, it was that line from Genesis 6:17: "For My part, I am about to bring the Flood—waters upon the earth—to destroy all flesh under the sky in which there is breath of life; everything on earth shall perish."

And it was Gloria who would perish, for she had made a fatal mistake. She had pronounced the Hebrew word *ba-sar* as *ba-sed*. It was common to transpose the Hebrew letter *resh* for *dalet*. They looked so similar, and yet the meaning was so different. Instead of saying "to destroy all flesh" Gloria had said "to destroy every breast." And as she inserted her unwanted breast into the Torah portion and listened with shame as the rabbi laughed as he was correcting her, she felt something gush between her legs.

Her first menstrual period. The rabbi was oblivious, but Gladys saw. *Drip. Drip. Drip.* Three drips. It wasn't much, but it felt like a flood. Gloria thought about Edna St. Vincent Millay's poem "Menses," her very own version of Noah.

> *I felt it. Down my side*
> *Innocent as oil I see the ugly venom slide:*
> *Poison enough to stiffen us both, and all our friends.*

And after the Torah was blessed and dressed and returned to its hermetically sealed ark, Gladys pulled Gloria into a little room off to the side of the bimah to deal with her ugly, venomous flood. The little room was as unholy as the bimah was holy. Crackers. Empty water bottles. Various colored satin yarmulkes strewn all over a stained carpet, like cheap stripper clothes in a three-star Vegas hotel room.

Gladys acted swiftly, practically ripping Gloria's sheer white hose off her body. Her mother started rubbing between her legs with antibacterial wipes, which were unexpectedly coarse like Brillo pads and stung like Bactine.

Of course, her mother made no remark about how well Gloria was chanting. No, "Hang in there, Sweetheart" or, "We're so proud of you." No, "How do you feel?" or, "What a big day." All Gladys kept saying in that cheap, disgusting room was, "Vile, fetid blood" or was it, "Vile, fetid flood?" Unlike the Torah, the precise wording did not really matter. They both worked equally well to effectuate Gloria's complete and utter mortification.

"Why didn't you tell me you hadn't had your first period?" Gladys asked, rhetorically.

Why don't you know your own daughter? I'm not a fucking superstar. I'm a person.

"Vile, fetid blood!" Gladys shrieked as she kept rubbing and rubbing Gloria's bloodstained thighs. "This won't do. These hose are disgusting; they're covered in vile, fetid blood, and we have no backup. Bare legs it is. Remember, don't bend too much during *Aleinu.*"

And Gloria went back on the bimah with bare legs to lead the congregation in prayer. Her seventh-grade friends may not have noticed the blood, but they noticed the bare legs. What else would thirteen-year-old boys think about during a three-hour service in Hebrew?

At the Kiddush lunch, after she was congratulated and kissed and handed secret envelopes (no money can be exchanged on Shabbat or other holy days, unless of course you wanted to be inscribed in the *Book of Life* on Yom Kippur), Gloria went to the table to join her friends, who immediately hurled questions at her about her bare legs.

What happened? Was she trying to give the congregation all hardons? Was she humping the rabbi in the back room? Did she finally get her period? And when Gloria froze, they knew the truth. And they said, "Flood." *You had a flood. You're worse than Noah with your flood. Your flood of blood.*

She had a hard time eating in front of peers or anyone from that point on. She remembered that the last piece of challah she ate at that lunch tasted doughy and dry, like an absorbent tampon.

11.

Henry had no problem dining with peers. And so now they were to dine at the refectory with Henry's closest cadre of St. Cross acquaintances. Although he had only recently moved to St. Cross, Henry seemed to know everyone. It took him so long to walk even the shortest distance because he would constantly stop to chat with students in the quad or the corridor or in the small private St. Cross library.

With a superficial but utterly charming sincerity, he would ask about their exams, favorite football teams, and whether they missed wherever they hailed from. He knew how to say, "How's it going?" in three different languages. Henry reassured Gloria that she was his only close friend who really knew him. However, he was comfortable in superficial social venues where he didn't know the people very well and there was no pressure to perform.

Gloria knew that the students at St. Cross were curious about them, staring and whispering when they passed, wondering whether they were a couple and why they spent so much time together. Wondering why someone as outgoing and handsome as Henry would want to be with someone as introverted and weird as that American with the strange white gloves, obsession with oranges, and ugly red hands.

Henry had claimed he was just as weird as she. He tried to convince her that the staring was because she was more beautiful than she realized and a lot of his male colleagues were attracted to her, having commented on her unusually large eyes and breasts on several occasions. Intending to use his logic against him, Gloria had asked about the women who also stared.

And without missing a beat, with his dangerous dimpled grin he had replied, "There are a few lesbians and bisexuals at Oxford, Gloria. Didn't you know? I hope you're not a homophobic antifeminist feminist poetry scholar. What would Elizabeth and Samantha say? And it is quite misogynistic of you to assume that a woman cannot admire the breasts of another woman without wanting to sleep with her. I really thought you were more enlightened than that."

So Gloria found herself at a dreaded meal with enlightened Henry and his gawking friends. A jovial and dutiful OCD tutor, Henry tried hard to involve Gloria in the conversation at the dinner table, but she was utterly distracted by the vile, fetid, heinous, germ-infested food on her plate. To anyone else, the bland meal would look like chicken and peas, but all she could see was a dirty, filthy chicken running around in maggot-infested mud, eating its own feces. She brought her napkin to her mouth, afraid she might be sick.

Oliver was the only acquaintance at the table to whom she was listening and, of course, Oliver's observations only exacerbated her queasiness.

Why are you sitting here with these boring, stupid losers and this vile, fetid, heinous, disgusting, germ-infested chicken? These vapid people know nothing about music, and Henry is just pandering to them like a shallow politician. He's introducing you to losers. Losers with germs. Losers who will laugh at you and hurt you.

Gloria tried to focus on Henry's handsome, animated face. She pretended to eat, playing with the unappealing food on her plate, cutting it and moving it around in various shapes and geometric patterns. She discreetly put some of the food in her napkin, giving the illusion of progress.

"Can I show them the playlist on your iPhone, Gloria? The one with Van Morrison's *New York Sessions* from 1967?" Henry asked in what she read as a futile attempt to convince the others at the table that she wasn't a catatonic loser.

But Gloria and Oliver knew the truth. In spite of the Cognitive Behavior Therapy and her charming loomate's adroit social skills, this meal was a disaster.

Wouldn't you rather be getting a root canal than pretending to enjoy this meaningless conversation with these idiotic, pretentious Oxford graduate students who think you're a freak and are laughing at you? Of course, they're wondering why charming Henry Young sits with you, spends all his time with you. They probably think you're really great in bed. Bloody sex goddess! You could only wish.

"Sure," Gloria said meekly, taking out her iPhone.

With nothing to lose, she obediently searched for the requested Van Morrison playlist. When she handed the iPhone to Henry, she noticed that he was removing the chicken from her plate and patterning the remaining green peas in the shape of a heart.

The peas made her want to try. For him, she would try. She reminded herself to breathe as she finally settled into the conversation, sharing with the group some well-received insights about Van Morrison's early recordings in 1967. Gloria was a good researcher and teacher; it was obvious that Henry was playing to her strengths.

He seemed happy she was conversing more easily now but disappointed she was not eating her peas. He kept nudging the plate in her direction as if hoping she would get the message that her OCD tutor was not yet satisfied.

If they had been alone, she would have explained that the peas looked fine—innocuous enough. The Cognitive Behavior Therapy was working; she no longer considered them vile. But putting aside sustenance or OCD training, she did not want to mess up the heart. She was hoping it meant something. She was hoping it meant that he wanted to be more than her OCD tutor, but she just wasn't sure.

12.

Henry was suffering from performance anxiety as Gloria examined the first full draft of his candidacy paper with her meticulous and critical obsessive eyes. Every time she marked his paper with her thick red pen it felt like a punch in his gut; he had to look away. He gazed longingly at his kidnapped record player, a fellow hostage in her cruel feminine room. When the beating was done, she handed him the bloody paper smeared with loads of red marks for revision. It was a mess.

"Good start, Henry. But it still needs a lot of work," she said with the tentative encouragement of a doctor trying to reassure in the wake of a medical emergency.

He was not reassured. A defeated Henry took the draft from her improving hands, went back to his music-free room, and nervously began reading her comments. After several arduous hours, he was ready to give her a revised draft. Again, he swallowed hard as she took out her lethal red pen. She seemed to sense his anxiety and softened her demeanor as she invited him to sit next to her on the bed.

Sitting cross-legged with their knees touching, she spoke with a measured, hopeful voice. "Much better, Henry. Really good work. But that second section still does not make sense to me. You seem to argue that the spirit of place evokes the poetry, which then evokes the spirit of place. That seems a bit tautological. What are you trying to argue here?"

Henry cleared his throat, nervous as he spoke, and said, "I am trying to say that for Van Morrison, place is not just geographical. It is also where we travel in our minds, like James Joyce's stream of consciousness."

Gloria rubbed his arms with her noticeably softer hands. "Very insightful, Henry. Say it just like that. You're almost there. Keep going."

Although she tried to encourage him, he felt just the opposite. Van Morrison's fatalistic optimism was hopeless, after all. Perhaps he should have studied dead women poets. Suicide was sounding pretty sensible at the moment.

13.

It was four o'clock in the morning when Henry woke Gloria to give her his latest draft. He looked exhausted and emotionally spent. She was impressed by his tenacity, writing all through the night. She invited him to stay on her bed like before as she reviewed his paper. He declined, shaking his head and pointing his index finger to his temple as if shooting himself.

She released his record player and beamed as she said, "Sleep well, Henry. You did great work today. And tonight. And early this morning. Go rest. You deserve it."

He disappeared through the bathroom as Gloria started reading. She was surprised to find that she had no need of her red pen. His candidacy paper was good. Excellent, even. She read it a second time through, now more awake, fearing she might have been too tired to be constructive on her first pass. No, the paper was truly outstanding.

She read it a third time curled up in her bed. Reading Henry's insights and thoughts about Van Morrison and poetry transported her, like reading a good book or listening to a hopeful Van Morrison song.

She was much too excited to go back to sleep. He did it. He really did it. She wanted to wake him up and congratulate him on his incredible accomplishment. She wanted to wake him and congratulate him and kiss him. She was in love with him, and that too was an amazing accomplishment. But when she reached his bedroom door, an amusing sign delayed and somewhat changed her plans:

Can't take any more red marks until morning.
Too knackered and insecure.
Hope you showed me mercy, Loomate.

14.

Disheveled and exhausted the next morning, Henry stumbled into the loo. He had done more writing in the last week than he had done in all his previous years in school combined. He needed to pee, drink coffee, and listen to records—in that order. He was a bit surprised and worried that Gloria had not slipped the draft under his door. He hoped it was not a bad sign. He prayed the red marks were few. He really thought this draft was decent, but Gloria and her impossibly high standards could be so demanding.

After he emptied his bladder, he washed his hands with soap, a relatively new habit developed under the influence of his germophobic loomate. Looking at his tired face in the mirror, he was stunned to find Gloria's red marks written on the sparkling clean glass.

Henry Young is an awesome scholar
and totally worth staying up late for!!!

He stared at the message for a long while. He examined his unshaven, ruddy complexion in the mirror behind the words. He laughed, thinking that he had only agreed to the bloody Van Morrison paper so Gloria would allow him to help her fight her OCD. But this surreal and glorious moment was not about her OCD. It was about his paper. It was about him.

For the first time in three years as an Oxford student, he felt he might actually belong. Irrespective of his father or Professor Cook or the police officer who had called him a "privileged piece of shit" when he had been arrested. He had finally earned his place.

This breakthrough may not have been about Gloria, but it was because of her. Looking at the unkempt, bewildered face staring back, he had to be honest with himself: he was in love. He had no idea when, how, and if he could declare this love so he could act on it. So *they* could act on it. Both he and Gloria were only part of the way up their respective ladders. And they were both so messed up.

He was writing about fatalistic optimism, but he wished he could buy into his own theory. There was only one truth he knew for certain. With the absolute certainty and empirical proof of a scholar, Oxford doctoral candidate Henry Young knew that it was love. And he was real real gone.

PART FIVE:
DECEMBER

Hanukkah Miracles

I was a weaver deaf and blind;
A miracle was wrought for me,
But I have lost my skill to weave
Since I can see.

Sara Teasdale, 1917
From "The Song Maker"

Don't it gratify when you see it materialize
Right in front of your eyes
That surprise.

Van Morrison, 1970
From "Glad Tidings"

1.

Gloria was either in a trance, or this moment with Henry was a fucking miracle. Although she did not really believe in miracles, she had been working through her treatment plan more easily than anticipated, and there was no denying the miraculous fact that she was actually spending a cold and brisk December afternoon with a handsome Van Morrison fan and a germ-infested German shepherd.

She knew she still had a ways to go. Overcoming her most destructive obsessions and compulsions was only the first step on a long road to recovery. She would need to keep following her treatment plan, stay on her medication, and even seek out professional help at Oxford. She had placed a call to Henry's sister asking for a recommendation. Henry had done his time as her OCD therapist; and besides, she was ready for him to serve a different role in her life.

Henry had been playing with Fritz in the St. Cross quad and had gestured for Gloria, bundled up on their favorite bench with a book, to come over. She approached Henry and the dog with a curiosity that rivaled her hesitancy.

"Come on. Fritz just wants to say hello," Henry said in a doggy voice as if he were talking to a three-year-old.

He held Fritz in place while she hesitantly pet the dark fur with a gloved hand.

As diligent OCD tutor, Henry ordered, "Off with those gloves, Loomate. Fritz just wants to be friends. *Don't you, Boy?*"

Oliver had been sleeping more and more these days and was practically in hibernation. But Oliver was aroused by the germ-infested dog and Henry's increasing influence over Gloria.

Filthy Henry and filthy dogs. What, are you a zookeeper now? When you fell in love with Henry, did you fall in love with germs? Vile, fetid, heinous, germ-infested, worm-carrying beast with so many germs.

The OCD training and Cognitive Behavior Therapy had been going well, and Gloria was growing accustomed to tuning out Oliver's ranting, especially when Henry was around.

"Okay, okay. Nice dog. Nice...dog," she mumbled, trying to mask her apprehension.

She slowly pulled off her gloves, petting Fritz's silky black coat with her distinctly improved hands. Since it seemed to be going fairly well for both Gloria and Fritz, Henry let go. A part of her actually enjoyed this physical exchange of affection between man and beast. She liked the jubilant display of fondness as the dog wagged his tail in larger and larger arcs, responsive to her touch.

But the honeymoon was quickly over when the vile, fetid beast unabashedly started licking her hands, cheek, and even gently swiped her lips. Oliver was wide awake and outraged.

May I remind you that you didn't come all the way to Oxford to French kiss dogs. Might as well eat and swallow dirty fucking dog feces. Dirty, vile dog. Disgusting dog germs. Dirty, vile dog germs. Disgusting dog worms. Heartworms, whipworms, hookworms, round-worms, and tapeworms.

Gloria spat on the ground, removing contraband emergency hand sanitizer from her coat pocket as she started running away from the vile, fetid, heinous, germ-infested, worm-carrying beast. She was dousing her hands with hand sanitizer as she ran. *I saw a man pursuing the horizon. Round and round they sped. Round and round. Round and round.* Henry and Fritz were fast runners and easily caught up with her; apparently she was not as elusive as the horizon.

"I'll take that. Thank you very much," Henry said, winded as he knocked the hand sanitizer from her hands.

As "punishment" for owning and using illegal hand sanitizer, Henry, who had actually kissed the vile dog, licked Gloria's hands and cheeks himself. She gently pushed him away. When she slapped him, they both started laughing. After frisking her to make sure he had retrieved her entire stash of emergency hand sanitizer, they walked back through the empty courtyard toward their flat.

"I have to admit it, Henry Young. Not even New Year's yet, and it's pretty awesome that I can pet that vile, fetid beast and even survive being accosted by his tongue," Gloria admitted as she showed Henry her pink tongue.

"I wanted to tell you something—I mean, to ask you something. No pressure whatsoever," Henry said nervously.

Gloria was surprised that he did not pick up on her tongue remark. He always caught and contributed to their double entendres. Why was he so nervous?

"What is it, Henry?" she asked with concern and maybe a dash of hope.

"I don't know how to say this," he started with trepidation.

She stopped walking to face him. Perhaps this was the moment. *The* moment. She told herself that even if he had some residue dog germs on his mouth, it would be okay. It would be worth it. This moment would be worth it. She had been waiting and hoping for this moment.

"Anything, Henry, you can ask me anything," she said, looking in his green eyes, hoping this was *the* moment. Even with germ-infested dog saliva, it would be worth it.

She noticed he was trembling. He said, "I don't know how to say this, Gloria."

Putting her improved hands on his shoulders, she tried to reassure. "I'm your loomate. You can ask me anything. No judgment. No fear."

He looked away uncomfortably. "Well, I was hoping that perhaps you would have dinner with me and Claire at my family's house with my father? If it's too daunting, I can tell Claire to postpone it for another time. *Equanimity* is not going anywhere."

Gloria was relieved and maybe a drop disappointed, having hoped for a different turn in their conversation. As much as she wanted to kiss Henry, she had been hoping it would be after they brushed their teeth and not right after he had kissed a dog.

She laughed, "Too daunting, Henry?"

"I don't want to rush you, Gloria. My father can be a vicious beast. Much worse than Fritz, I'm afraid," he explained with real worry in his eyes.

"Kissing dogs, eating vile chicken, letting you clean the bathroom and cut my fruit. Those are daunting...or rather, were daunting. Arrogant professors who act like vicious beasts? Piece of cake. What is it you say over here? *Easy peasy lemon squeezy*," she said as she stroked Fritz with her soft bare hands, wondering whether Henry would ever make a move.

2.

They were all dining at *Equanimity*. Henry found it surreal sitting at the rosewood dining table at his family home with Gloria, Nicholas, and Claire. He felt confused and a bit scattered because they each knew him in a different way, and he, in turn, was different with each of them.

His father glared at him through a half-empty bottle of scotch; Claire nervously bit her fingernails, eyeing the pack of cigarettes in her purse under the table; and Gloria meticulously cut her meat into perfectly proportioned pieces, moving them around on her plate in various geometric patterns as if turning a kaleidoscope.

Henry wondered which one of these brilliant but utterly insane people knew him best and how he could reconcile that version of himself with the other versions. He always felt an odd dissonance when he was back at *Equanimity*, which was only exacerbated having Gloria by his side. He wanted to protect both her and the version of Henry he was with her, which he hoped was his most authentic self.

Nicholas sat at the head of the table with Claire on one side and Gloria and Henry on the other side, facing the large marble fireplace. Nicholas had been drinking scotch steadily through cocktails and into dinner. Unfortunately, he was not a charming and happy drunk like his son or Amir had been. The more he drank, the nastier he became. For most of the evening, Nicholas had been fairly restrained, but Henry could see the alcohol was taking its effect. His father was now staring at Gloria with a dangerous combination of derision and curiosity.

"So, Gloria, I hear you are a Rhodes Scholar for Professor Margo Mitchell. Quite an accomplishment for an American," Nicholas remarked in a condescending tone.

Undaunted, Gloria continued cutting her food as she replied, "All Rhodes Scholars are international students, and it's an accomplishment for anyone to study at Oxford, Professor Young."

Henry gave Gloria an apologetic grin, and she covertly winked at him, probably not wanting Nicholas to see her sweet side. In front of his father, she was all business—formal, detached, and cooler than the chilly December air.

"And you and Henry share a flat at St. Cross College?" Nicholas asked, knowing full well they did.

"I told you, Dad. We share a toilet. First time I met Gloria I had my arse on the bog," Henry said crudely, hoping to embarrass his father just as he had been trying to embarrass Gloria.

Nicholas put his knife and fork down and said with a stage whisper that could've been heard at the back of Royal Albert Hall, "They certainly do things differently at St. Cross."

"St. Cross has only postgraduate students, so there are more flexible living arrangements," Gloria replied matter-of-factly, totally ignoring the judgment and disdain behind his father's words and the cruel relish with which he'd pronounced *differently*.

"Also a lot of *foreign* students, I hear. Where is your family originally from, Gloria? I cannot quite place *Zimmerman*," Nicholas inquired with the friendliness of an Inquisition panelist.

Claire spat her food in her napkin and looked away. Henry was livid. But Gloria, completely unfazed, continued cutting and arranging.

"The motto of St. Cross is *ad quattuor cardines mundi. To the four corners of the Earth.* Over half of the students come from outside the UK. Unlike some other places in Oxford, Professor Young, St. Cross is very welcoming to international students, especially those with Jewish last names," Gloria replied coolly.

"And haven't you heard, Dad? Biodiversity strengthens the gene pool," Henry growled through clenched teeth, wanting to rip his father's bloody tongue out.

"Gloria has been a great friend to Henry, Dad. I think it is delightful how they've been able to collaborate on many things, including Henry's exciting new dissertation topic," Claire offered in a feeble attempt to let Nicholas know he should not be attacking someone who had been so good to his messed-up son.

Henry wondered why Claire continually missed the point. Nicholas did not want Henry to have friends who helped him feel good about himself. For an accomplished psychologist, she could be so daft when it came to their own father.

"New dissertation topic? Why am I not surprised?" Nicholas said with scorn as he pointed his knife at Gloria. "New college. New people. New research. If you're helping Henry with this new paper, Gloria, do not be disappointed if he gives up and doesn't follow through. He has always had trouble following through."

Claire exuded guilt at having begged Henry to arrange this meal, only to be attacked by full-frontal blows. She was obviously counting the seconds for an opportunity to leave the table, cigarettes in hand, to retreat to the garden for a smoke.

Nicholas took a triumphant sip of scotch, but his victory was short-lived. While he may not have intimidated Gloria, it was certainly perceptible that his father's cruelty toward Henry infuriated her. She put down her utensils, placed a hand of support on Henry's leg, and stared at Nicholas with stern, angry eyes.

She spoke with a steely tone. "This time it is impossible for Henry to give up or fail, Professor Young. He finally has the support, respect, and encouragement he needs to study something he feels passionately about, reflecting his true interests and marvelous talents. He's examining the intersection between Van Morrison's music and the transcendental poetry of optimism. In the spirit of Blake, Joyce, and Yeats. It is exciting, important work, and you should be proud."

Nicholas ignored Gloria and focused on Henry, who made easier prey.

He laughed coldly as he said, "So, Henry, you found use for that crazy record collection, after all?"

"It must be surprising to you, Dad, that my love of music has any scholarly value," Henry replied bitterly.

"Have you talked to Professor Cook about this preposterous connection between music and poetry?" Nicholas questioned, rubbing the rim of his scotch glass with his linen napkin.

"Come on, Professor Young, you of all people understand the connection between music and poetry," Gloria taunted as if challenging him to a duel to defend Henry's honor.

"Do I?" Nicholas replied, trying to contain furious curiosity.

Unruffled, Gloria continued eating her chicken very slowly, taking her time to draw out each bite. She was making Nicholas wait for an answer, which only made his anger mount. Henry and Claire watched with rapt attention, as the anticipation of Gloria's response tied their father in knots.

When she finally spoke it was with the authority, certainty, and detachment of a doctoral candidate defending her dissertation. "For example, Professor Young, I particularly enjoyed your article on Elizabeth Stirling, the nineteenth-century female organist, and how she was revered and denigrated in much the same way as female Victorian poets of that time, such as Elizabeth Browning and Christina Rossetti. Your paper has been cited by many feminist scholars as a seminal work illustrating the important connection between female persecution in both Victorian music and poetry."

Henry and Claire looked at each other as their respect for Gloria grew. She was a bloody research goddess, having read Nicholas' curriculum vitae and significant writings before coming to dinner. This Oxford overachiever had done her homework. In every way possible, Henry thought she was utterly brilliant. On paper, his father may have been the more formidable opponent, but at this dinner, she was crushing him.

Preying once more on Henry because Gloria was too intelligent, Nicholas said condescendingly, "For your edification, Henry, Elizabeth Stirling was educated at the Royal Academy in the 1800s on piano and organ..."

"I do know who she is, Dad. I am getting my doctorate in music at Oxford," Henry interrupted acerbically.

"Gloria seems quite clever, Henry. Showing us all up," Nicholas remarked as he sat back in his chair and took another sip of scotch from his almost empty glass.

"But not that clever. Right, Dad? If she is spending time with me? And you do not need to talk about her in the third person when she is sitting right next to you," Henry replied, trying to contain his own fury and remain Gloria's version of himself when it was so tempting to revert to Nicholas' version.

Nicholas grinned, clearly pleased he could still rile Henry at least.

His father looked at Gloria with an expression of false contrition and said, "I apologize, Gloria. I did not mean to offend you by not addressing you directly. I would very much like to hear about your research."

Gloria took a sip of her water and let it linger in her mouth before swallowing, as if she too were drinking scotch as a weapon.

Again, Gloria addressed Nicholas in a flat tone with no emotion, staring directly into his arrogant eyes. "I am exploring a variant on the Sylvia Plath Effect—the relationship between creativity and mental illness. I am examining a recent variant in the literature about destructive parenting. Specifically, I am discussing how a parent's derision can undermine one's accomplishments and sense of equanimity. But there is probably no need for me to go into great detail, Professor Young. You are undoubtedly an expert."

Henry and Claire shared a conspiratorial smile. Gloria was fucking brilliant! And she was right on point, referring to equanimity. Instead of scoring on her own, she passed Henry the ball.

"For your edification, Dad, *equanimity* means calmness and composure," Henry said in a patronizing tone with a hint of a wicked smile.

Nicholas could no longer contain his calmness and composure. "I know what *equanimity* means, Henry, for God's sake!"

"And do you also know it is Claire's and my code word for *fuck you*?" Henry said victoriously, finally scoring his goal.

Nicholas ignored Henry, examining his empty glass and bottle of scotch as if they had abandoned him. Henry thought his father's most recent thirst for scotch was particularly acute. After all, Nicholas had just been defeated by his sick drug addict incompetent son and the smarty-pants Jewish-American with whom he shared a toilet.

3.

They were eating breakfast at St. Cross Refectory, and Gloria thought Henry looked particularly handsome in his formal academic robe. He was reminiscent of a love interest in a nineteenth-century Jane Austen novel. Tall and soulful like Mr. Darcy, perhaps, but with lighter hair, a less brooding disposition, and track marks. But this was the day of Henry's candidacy hearing, and he was brooding and nervous, a total wreck. His father's appalling behavior at dinner the other night only exacerbated Henry's stress.

As his dedicated dissertation coach and loomate, Gloria had insisted he eat a good breakfast at St. Cross before they made their way to the intimidating examination room at Jesus College. Gloria's own breakfast repertoire had expanded significantly under Henry's tutelage. She was eating a toasted bagel with cream cheese, while he kept stabbing cold scrambled eggs with his fork.

"Henry, please eat something," she pleaded.

"I feel quite ill," he said in a gloomy voice.

"We don't want you passing out in the middle of your hearing. Please," she begged, handing him a piece of her bagel.

He took a reluctant bite, and when she wiped some stray cream cheese from his lips, he gave her a weary smile.

"I have a good feeling about today," she started to say encouragingly. "You are going to pass with..."

"I am going to make a fool of myself, Gloria," he groaned.

"By showing your committee—your father—how smart and original your thinking is?" she asked.

"It would take a miracle to impress those arrogant arseholes," he sighed. "You know firsthand how cruel my father can be."

"Tonight is the first night of Hanukkah. It's all about miracles," she said, taking a bite of bagel. "If the Maccabees can win against the oppressive Syrians, you will triumph against your father, Cook, or whoever else gets in your way. I'm a *chutzpadik* Jew from Chicago. I know these things."

"*Hootzpa* what?" he asked with cream cheese still smeared on his lips.

"*Chutz-pa-dik*," she pronounced slowly, articulating each syllable as she wiped his mouth again like a smothering Jewish mother. "Someone who does whatever it takes, no matter how bold. We Jews do not wait for miracles; we make them happen."

"So you're my Hanukkah hoots-pa-*DICK* miracle?" he asked, laughing now.

"In the flesh," she said, handing her Mr. Darcy a distracting double entendre and another piece of bagel.

4.

They were nervously waiting in the imposing examination room for Henry's candidacy hearing to begin. Henry sat at a large table in the front of the room facing a massive stained-glass window with the Jesus College coat of arms—three golden stags against a vibrant green background. Five intimidating dons, including the chair of his committee, Professor Cook, and his father, sat facing Henry on a raised platform wearing academic robes that signified the origins of their advanced degrees and were more ornately decorated than the simple black robe Henry had borrowed from the student center.

If Henry felt small before entering the room, he felt invisible once inside it. Everything about the arrangement of the hearing—where the professors sat, how they were dressed, and the glaring faces in the gallery—was designed to make him feel like he did not belong. Henry thought it quite ironic that the word *educate* came from the Latin *educere*, which meant *to lead out*. As this room reminded him, his Oxford education had been more about pushing him down than leading him out.

He turned around to face his only friends in the room, Gloria and Claire, who were sitting together in the front row of the spectator gallery. Claire was nervously chewing on a thumbnail while Gloria was going over a highlighted and annotated copy of his paper so she could follow along like a script supervisor.

She was his ever-diligent dissertation tutor, friend, loomate, and *chutzpadik* Hanukkah miracle, and he was grateful she was there. As the hearing was about to begin, he prayed to god (whether Jewish, Christian, or Van Morrison) that he did not let her down. She had invested so much in helping him prepare.

Putting on half-moon reading glasses, Professor Cook began the proceedings, "Good morning, Mr. Young. Thank you for coming on time for once."

Professor Cook was the only one amused at the barb. Henry could not even look at Cook and did not care about his ribbing today. He was nervously focused on his father. Their eyes locked. This public humiliation reminded him of the last time his father had sat in a position of judgment.

Professor Cook continued speaking as Henry sat immobile. "Distinguished faculty colleagues, doctoral students, and guests. Today, this doctoral committee will determine whether Mr. Young's candidacy paper, *Heading Toward the Bright Side of the Road: Van Morrison's Fatalistic Optimism and the Poetry of Transcendence*, is sufficient so that he may proceed to write his dissertation. Mr. Young, are you ready for your opening remarks?"

Henry did not respond. He sat frozen. In a stupor, he was still staring at his cold and distant father, who looked embarrassed, nervously fondling his Mont Blanc pen.

"Mr. Young?" Professor Cook asked in a confused voice.

Nothing. Henry was in a daze. He could not respond. He could not speak.

"Mr. Young, are you ready? Are you well?" Cook asked in a louder voice, hoping to get Henry's attention.

An eerie silence filled the large, cold room. Students were turning their heads. Faculty members were whispering. Nicholas was embarrassed. Gloria and Claire exchanged frantic looks. And Henry was real real gone.

5.

He had left his hearing and had been transported to another hearing at another time and place. Henry was a young teenager when his mother died of breast cancer and he had been expelled from school for dealing drugs. His father had banished him from *Equanimity*, telling him he was "a shame and disgrace to the family, was not worthy of the family name, let alone the family home" and that his "disgusting behavior had sealed Mum's grave."

When Claire's pleas for mercy were rebuffed, she secretly hid Henry in her university dormitory room at Jesus College, giving him most of her monthly allowance money, which he used for Walkers cheese and onion crisps and drugs. Unfortunately, it had not been enough to support his addiction. So he ran away again, this time to the streets of London, where he lived with other dodgy addicts, dealing drugs to feed his dreadful habit.

Like all his failings in life, Henry was not a very good drug dealer, especially in London, where large sophisticated syndicates controlled the drug market and dangerous turf battles would often ensue. He fell prey to one such vicious gang that took advantage of his naïveté and privileged background. They turned on him, beating and robbing him senseless.

Henry was arrested within weeks of moving to London, which was probably fortunate because he could have easily died if he stayed any longer. If not from the gangs, then most certainly from the drugs.

At his sentencing hearing in juvenile court, the magistrate, Honorable Richard Anderson, a Jesus College graduate and chum of his father, was keen on "rehabilitation" for "poor Henry." He thought Henry "had been punished enough with the death of his mother" as well as the "life sentence of an illness" he suffered.

All Magistrate Anderson required was for Henry's father to attest under oath that he would "take Henry back home and provide him the care and rehabilitation he needed to recover emotionally and physically to the greatest extent possible."

Henry had been surprised that Nicholas showed up at the sentencing hearing at all. He had always been ashamed of Henry, and the arrest only made the mortification worse. Claire was clutching Nicholas' arm with unusual force, which suggested that she had figuratively and literally dragged their father to the hearing. When it was finally his father's turn to testify on Henry's behalf, Nicholas took the stand, swore under oath, but was silent for what seemed like the longest ten minutes of Henry's life.

His father was totally, completely, and utterly silent when his chum the magistrate asked, "Are you here to speak on your son's behalf?"

Everyone at the hearing was stunned. Nicholas was frozen. He would not speak. He would not say, "I will provide for my son." He would not say, "I will take care of my son." He would not say, "My son can come home with me." He would not even admit that he had a bloody son.

And during those ten minutes, when Henry turned around to see Claire crying in the spectator gallery, he knew he had no one. She was powerless. His mother was dead. And his legal guardian, his mother's sperm donor, the fucking arsehole he called "father," would not even claim him. Nobody was there to fucking claim him. He was alone.

And then he heard a voice he did not recognize. The strange voice was getting louder and louder. The person attached to the voice was rubbing his shoulder, handing him a glass of water, and placing a sheet of paper in front of him. It was Gloria. Gloria had come to claim him.

6.

She was frantically punching the keys on her iPhone as she stood up and started speaking out of turn. "Excuse me, Professor Cook. I believe Mr. Young may be waiting for my faculty—"

"And you are?" Professor Cook asked in disapproval.

"Gloria Zimmerman. Special graduate assistant to Dr. Margo Mitchell, Lucille S. Baird Professor of Poetry and Women Studies," Gloria explained, seating herself next to Henry as she patted his shoulder, handed him a glass of water, and pointed to his outline, trying to jar him from his stupor.

"I know Professor Mitchell quite well," Professor Cook responded, clearly insulted by Gloria's impertinence and long-winded explanation.

A true *chutzpadik* at the moment, Gloria didn't give a damn for decorum; she needed to help Henry. Professor Mitchell had always made it very clear to Gloria that she would help her with anything. *Anything at all.* Well, it was time to see if that offer was real.

"She's on her way. She should be here any minute," Gloria said nonchalantly as she subtly glanced at her iPhone, delirious that Mitchell was actually coming to the rescue.

"And how is she relevant to this hearing? And why are you interrupting proceedings that do not concern you?" Professor Cook demanded in a voice with undercurrents of confusion and hostility.

Undaunted by the perplexed and angry glares, Gloria explained, "Actually, Mr. Young's hearing is related to work Professor Mitchell and I are doing for the next book she is editing. You see, Professor Mitchell has been a de facto member of Mr. Young's committee. Mr. Young's candidacy paper is a precursor to a chapter, 'Feminist Despair Versus Fatalistic Optimism,' which he will be contributing on feminist poetry and mental health. She's been very impressed by his cross-disciplinary research in the areas of music, poetry, feminist studies, and mental illness."

In order to get Henry back to reality and stall the proceedings until Mitchell arrived, Gloria was prepared to spew bullshit all day long. And she was good at it. Professor Mitchell had been so grateful Gloria had found the missing Teasdale manuscript, was thankful for her hard work, and also wanted Gloria to trust her not only as an academic but as a friend. Gloria hoped she would be happy to help today. It was a big favor, but Gloria had been saving her chips for just such an emergency.

Gloria would do anything for Henry, just as he had done for her. To her great relief, her request had actually worked. A disheveled Margo Mitchell entered the examination room ten minutes later, uncharacteristically casual, dressed in jeans, a St. Cross sweatshirt, and a heavy wool coat. But at least she was there.

"Margo, please come sit with us," Professor Cook offered with familiarity.

Professor Mitchell approached the faculty side of the table, giving Gloria a kind but puzzled look as she sat down. She kept her coat on, noticeably uncomfortable next to colleagues more formally dressed and obviously prepared. But Professor Mitchell's stellar academic reputation at Oxford meant something, so it really didn't matter what she was wearing, even among distinguished colleagues. At this point in her career, she had nothing to prove. She was just a slightly gray middle-aged feminist scholar who was a bit embarrassed to be wearing her gym shoes at a formal academic hearing.

"So, Margo. Your research assistant was just explaining that you want our music doctoral candidate, Henry Young, to write a chapter in your forthcoming book about feminist poetry. Is this correct?" Professor Cook asked with incredulity, taking off his glasses.

Professor Mitchell looked at Gloria, who gave her a grateful smile as she subtly nodded her head.

"Absolutely, David. Mr. Young provides a very important multidisciplinary perspective," she said, seamlessly executing Gloria's *chutzpadik* impromptu plan. And then, looking directly at Henry, she added, "And I apologize for being late, Mr. Young. Emergency veterinary appointment for my dog, Fritz, who somehow swallowed a bottle of hand sanitizer."

Gloria and Henry shared a guilty smile at Fritz's suffering. Henry was back and ready to defend. He smiled appreciatively at Professor Mitchell and squeezed Gloria's leg under the table, even pulling at her skirt a bit. Gloria swallowed her own chuckle; with Henry, teasing and lewd behavior were always a good sign.

"Well, I am impressed, Mr. Young, but why didn't you tell me about this prestigious opportunity sooner? Being included in a Margo Mitchell anthology is quite an accolade," Professor Cook said.

"I should apologize, David. Henry has been talking to me about this, since I have done similar work on Stirling and the Victorian poets," Nicholas interjected in a quiet, deferential voice.

Henry gaped at his father.

Nicholas continued, "It was—is—an opportunity for us to reconnect as father and son, and I am sorry I did not insist he speak to you as chair first. You see, I was hoarding this special time with my son."

"Understandable, Nicholas. Shall we proceed? Are you ready for your opening remarks, Mr. Young?" Professor Cook asked politely with a new and noticeable respect for Henry's academic standing.

Henry smiled confidently. "Certainly, Professor Cook. In his work, *The Aural Poetry of Van Morrison*, published by Cambridge University Press, Peter Mills examines the unconscious poeticism of Van Morrison's lyrics in reference to Morrison's most powerful and acknowledged poetic influences—namely Joyce, Blake, and Yeats. Building on Mills, I argue that the connection between Morrison and poets like Blake, Joyce, and Yeats reflects what I call a fatalistic optimism, which is to say..."

As they had practiced, Henry impressed the committee, answering their rigorous questions with authority and challenging them with new questions. Nicholas and Claire appeared surprised, marveling at Henry's intellectual mastery of the material as well as his own innovative thinking.

But his *chutzpadik* loomate and dissertation tutor was not surprised at all. As soon as he started speaking, Gloria knew they had won—he had won. She put the annotated outline in her tote bag, relaxed as much as was possible in the uncomfortable high-back chair with its gaudy Jesus crest, and watched with quiet confidence as her very own British Maccabee handily defeated his enemies, both real and imagined.

7.

They were celebrating his triumph on the steps of the main entrance to Jesus College. Henry had passed the candidacy hearing with "high distinction," and Professor Margo Mitchell was so enthralled by his defense that she told Henry and Gloria she really wanted a chapter included in her forthcoming book that they would write together. Henry was flattered and asked if he could be the one to break the news to Liz and Sam that he was the latest feminist scholar to become their collaborator. They all laughed at the prospect, but he suspected Liz and Sam would not be laughing.

Before saying goodbye, Margo Mitchell had given them a strange look that Gloria could not quite decipher. It was obvious to Henry that Mitchell thought he and Gloria were romantically involved, but he kept this theory to himself. For many reasons, he could not talk to Gloria about that just yet. He was working up to it. He had a plan. And given the Hanukkah miracle that occurred at his hearing, it seemed quite possible. Anything seemed possible. *Tutto e possibile.*

It truly was a season for miracles. Henry's reputation at Jesus had been transformed. In one miraculous afternoon, he went from leper of the program to its greatest star. Various faculty and students leaving the hearing congratulated him on his forthcoming chapter and told him how interesting his work sounded. It also seemed like there were a lot of closet Van Morrison fans who now felt comfortable sharing a mutual obsession.

Henry was a bit overwhelmed by the accolades and felt like Gloria deserved most of the credit. He was about to ask her where they should spend the evening celebrating his candidacy paper as well as the first night of Hanukkah, when his father approached. Staring at Nicholas in warning, Gloria and Claire formed a protective circle around Henry. From outside the circle, Nicholas addressed him in an unusually quiet, nervous, and small voice.

"I just want to tell you, Henry. You did well in there," he said looking down as if noticing a scuff on his brown shoes.

"You did too, Dad," Henry answered softly.

His father was silent for an awkward several moments. Henry did not know what to say. Was it his responsibility to make his father feel comfortable? If so, how? Perhaps there had been too much intimacy for one day and they both felt a bit overwhelmed.

After another awkward stretch, Nicholas gave the group a weak apologetic smile as he walked away, most likely in search of a fortifying scotch. Henry wondered how long their bonhomie would last. He decided to give fatalistic optimism a chance. Things with his father would never be perfect, but they could be better. They both could try.

8.

Professor Mitchell had asked to see Gloria after the hearing. As Master of St. Cross, Professor Mitchell lived with her partner, Patricia Browne, in a well-appointed flat in a private area of St. Cross College beyond the central courtyard, well past the main common room and refectory. Because she was a senior research assistant and student at St. Cross, Gloria had been to the Master's residence on several occasions for various research meetings and social gatherings, but as she reached for the brass knocker on the oversized door, she was particularly nervous this time.

She was worried and confused. Professor Mitchell had told Gloria that she was delighted to have "helped out a bit" at a moment's notice with respect to Henry's candidacy hearing. And she even requested that Gloria and Henry coauthor a chapter for her forthcoming book based on Henry's "interesting multidisciplinary perspective on Van Morrison and the poetry of transcendence." But Gloria was nervous that Margo Mitchell was having second thoughts about the writing opportunity as well as the appropriateness of her impromptu participation in Henry's hearing. Had Gloria gone too far by calling the famous Margo Mitchell to the rescue?

Gloria was worried about the cryptic email she had received from Professor Mitchell that afternoon asking her to "stop by for an important chat before dinner time, if you please." *If you please. If you please.* The British were so polite, even when they were about to chop your bloody head off. *Place your head on the wooden block before the axe descends, if you please.* What was so important that required such urgency?

Gloria tried to block out Oliver's faint but relentless voice. Of course, in a small but grating way, Oliver was reminding her that she was an *incompetent, irreverent chutzpadik loser who would probably be kicked out of the program with all deliberate speed for impudently and arrogantly asking the distinguished Oxford professor of Poetry to assist dirty, messy Henry Young.*

And then the distinguished Oxford professor of Poetry herself opened the door barefoot, wearing a long red kimono with her hair piled high in a large white towel.

"Gloria, do come in," Professor Mitchell said with a wide smile.

"I'm sorry. I did not mean to disturb you. And thank you so much for helping today. You were amazing. But I can come back at a more convenient time," Gloria said, flustered, looking down in embarrassment.

She was taken aback by Mitchell's informal and uncharacteristically feminine appearance. Her perfectly pedicured red toes stood out on the black and white marble floor in the small entryway like little rose buds waiting to open. Gloria felt awkward being there and seeing her toes. The sense of intimacy put her off balance.

"No, please. I was just putting up some tea. Come join me," Mitchell said as she grabbed Gloria's hand, pulling her firmly into the flat with an undertow that was too strong and certain for any attempt at resistance.

Margo Mitchell brought a tray with tea and its accoutrements into the living room and set it on a large coffee table that was covered with a frenetic array of scholarly books and journals. Gloria immediately noticed the recently discovered Ted Hughes poem. Gloria knew that the BBC had asked Professor Mitchell to comment on its significance.

As if parting the Red Sea, she separated the books and journals into two sides to make room for the tray. The various scholarly works were adorned with dog-eared pages, Post-It notes, and bookmarks, giving Gloria the impression that Professor Mitchell was actively reading and digesting these twenty-plus books at once.

Knowing Margo Mitchell, Gloria thought it was entirely possible. Professor Mitchell was a voracious reader, an industrious scholar, and an extremely productive poet. Sipping tea, wiggling her red polished toes, and giving Gloria an eerie smile, Professor Margo Mitchell was as intimidating as hell.

Gloria took her cup of tea and looked at Professor Mitchell in earnest. She was sitting in a black leather chair by the fireplace, resting her feet on a matching black leather ottoman. Gloria wondered why she was not speaking. Why she was not telling her the important news that had to be delivered before dinner. Why there was no explanation about the urgent summons.

Margo Mitchell noticed Gloria staring at the portrait above the fireplace. It had been painted by Patricia, who was an adjunct lecturer in the Department of Fine Arts as well as a fairly accomplished artist in her own right. The portrait was painted shortly after Mitchell had undergone her double mastectomy. The look in her eyes was despondent and resigned. Her frail hands were resting on her diaphragm, underneath where her breasts used to be. In place of her breasts were two jarring, lonely scars, the only survivors of a brutal war.

The painting was disturbing but beautiful, difficult to look at but hard to look away from. It was one of those images that stayed with you for a long time. In the world of feminist poetry and feminist studies in general, the portrait was iconic. It was the cover of Mitchell's most famous book, *Love Letters to My Breasts*.

"Quite a painting."

"It is," Gloria said softly. "It's beautiful. I mean, I don't know if *beautiful* is the right word. It's just—"

"No. It is a beautiful painting. Disturbing and beautiful."

"Just like your poetry," Gloria offered in apology.

"Well, you should see Patricia's most recent work. Have I ever shown you her studio upstairs, Gloria?" Mitchell asked.

"No."

"Will you come with me?" Mitchell said in a tone that was more of a command than an invitation.

Mitchell once again grabbed Gloria's hand with that firm grip, pulling her up three flights of stairs with unexpectedly nimble bare feet. It seemed to Gloria that the second floor, which they hurried by, consisted of several bedrooms and bathrooms. Apparently, Patricia's studio was on the top floor.

The studio was almost all windows with a built-in skylight. Its architecture was different from the rest of the flat...the rest of the college, for that matter. The light was incredible, and the views of Oxford's dreaming spires were divine. There were paints and brushes and a large work sink. There was a shelf with a dozen or so canvases containing paintings in progress at various stages of completion.

And then Gloria saw what Margo Mitchell probably wanted her to see. There was a portrait in the corner of the room that was complete, quite literally. It was a naked Margo Mitchell, considerably aged since the *Love Letters to My Breasts* portrait from downstairs. It seemed contemporary to Margo Mitchell now, a little bit of gray by the temples and the same crow's feet by the eyes.

What was so remarkable was that where the scars were on her chest were now breasts. Full, supple, large breasts with light pink nipples. And Margo was cupping her breasts and smiling. Smiling at the artist. Smiling at her lover. Smiling as if they were exchanging a private joke.

In some ways this painting, which seemed more "normal" than the painting downstairs, was even more disturbing. Was this some sick joke? Was this a fantasy? Was it surreal? That was not Patricia's usual style; she was much more of a realist.

As if she read Gloria's mind, Margo Mitchell untied the belt of her kimono robe to show Gloria that the painting was quite real. Indeed, she had breasts, and she cupped them with the same proud smile that was in the new portrait. Gloria was shocked and didn't know what to say.

"You. Uh. Oh, God," she sputtered.

Margo Mitchell retied her robe quickly and said, "It's okay, Gloria. You can ask. I had reconstructive surgery two years ago. These are my breasts. Bought and paid for."

"But, how come?" Gloria did not know how or if she should be asking.

Mitchell spoke quickly, with an almost manic voice. "How come nobody knows? How come the painting downstairs has not been replaced with this one? How come I have a drawer of poetry about my new breasts, about feeling good about myself, about having a new lease on life, about making love to Patricia as a whole complete woman, about being happy? And how I cannot seem to publish these poems? My editor asks these same questions every week. She wants to publish my new work, but I'm afraid."

"What are you afraid of?" Gloria asked.

"I've made my success as someone who has been defined by illness, sadness, and hopelessness. Will they still like me if I'm doing all right? It's one of the reasons I was taken with Henry's paper today. I actually listened to some Van Morrison music this afternoon because it's exhilarating. Hopeful. Is there something about women that makes it so difficult for us to be defined by happiness? I mean, it's so easy and natural for us to be defined by sickness, by loss. Speaking of loss, did you hear about Ted Hughes' poem that was miraculously discovered two days ago at the British Library?"

Gloria had heard about the newly discovered poem by Hughes, titled "The Last Letter." Many scholars, feminist and otherwise, had scourged Ted Hughes for his behavior toward Sylvia Plath during their tortured marriage and for his apparent lack of remorse after her suicide. Hughes did not address Plath's suicide publicly until thirty-five years after her death, when he published his last poetry collection, *Birthday Letters*.

Many poetry scholars consider *Birthday Letters* one of the most important works of the twentieth century, especially when read in conjunction with Plath's own significant work and their sorrowful lives.

Hughes' poem "The Last Letter" had been found several days ago by Melvyn Bragg as directed by Hughes' second wife, Carol. The poem was found in an archive of papers in the British Library that had belonged to Hughes. The lost poem was in a notebook from the 1970s and recalls the moment when Ted Hughes first found out about Sylvia Plath's suicide, after she'd put her head in the oven with their children down the hall.

"Think about the last stanza, Gloria," Mitchell said in a trance as she started reciting the last lines of the newly discovered gem. The poem was powerful and haunting, and Gloria shivered as Mitchell spoke.

Mitchell said, "What about his use of the weapon imagery, Gloria? It's as if he's insinuating she chose sadness. She chose tragedy. Now, we can debate whether she chose or not. Whether she was mentally ill, he was mentally ill. We can look at how the bastard treated her. But irrespective of all those variables, I keep wondering whether we can actually choose happiness. And choose to embrace happiness. That is the message of Henry's hearing today. The message of Van Morrison's poetry and the poetry of transcendence. Are women writing about that? About choosing happiness? About choosing to be defined by happiness? Or, like me, are they writing about it but afraid to show it, keeping their happiness in the closet or attic studio."

They were silent for a long while.

Gloria finally spoke. "Why did you want me to come here? Is there something you wanted to tell me, Professor Mitchell?"

"I already told you, Gloria. I am telling you. Happiness. Grab on to it. Be defined by it. Choose it."

9.

They were climbing up their ladders with great success, so Henry suggested they go to Thirst to celebrate his candidacy hearing and the first night of Hanukkah. To his great delight, she agreed. It was Queen for the Queers night, and Thirst was crowded with a largely gay clientele, including Liz and Sam, who waved at Gloria but avoided Henry at all costs.

The dance floor was packed with what seemed like hundreds of patrons dancing boisterously to everyone's favorite guilty pleasure, Queen. "Bohemian Rhapsody," "Another One Bites the Dust," "Killer Queen," "Crazy Little Thing Called Love," "Somebody to Love," "We Will Rock You." Henry and Gloria were enjoying the outrageous dress and zealous dancing from the sidelines while eating deliciously unhealthy fried food that had not been prepackaged. Hanukkah miracle indeed! When "We Are the Champions" came on, Henry played the air organ and serenaded Gloria, who started to laugh.

"You really were a rock star today," Gloria said.

"Thanks to you, you clever thing. Calling in your favors with Mitchell. She must be very grateful you found that missing manuscript.

And turning my father into a human being for five minutes," he said, beaming at her.

Gloria responded, *"We are the champions of the world...*It was both of us, Henry. You presented your paper so well. You're an awesome scholar in addition to being a rock star."

When Henry went to get a second round of drinks, he noticed that Liz and Sam were conferring with Gloria.

As always, they ignored him when he returned to the table.

"So who is this superstar music student and feminist scholar who Mitchell wants to contribute to the book? She mentioned something about the poetry of transcendence? Van Morrison?" Liz asked.

"Henry," Gloria said with a sheepish grin.

"Who?" Sam asked.

"Henry," Gloria said loudly. "My Henry. This Henry."

Gloria pointed to Henry, who was doing his best to swallow his own grin.

"Hello, Elizabeth and Samantha. I am honored to be working with you on the book. It sounds like an interesting project," he said, taking care not to intrude on their personal identities.

Liz and Sam were more shocked than appalled. They smiled at Henry but did not utter a word. Completely speechless, they walked back to their own table in a daze, unable to shake their dumbfounded expressions.

Gloria was shaking her head. "I'm sorry, Henry. Liz is having some issues. She finally came out to her family last weekend."

Henry was curious. "How did it go? Happy ending?"

"Yes and no. Her father, who's this big lord or duke or sir something, was in shock at first, but when he recalled that the family estate was entailed strictly through the male line and that her *lifestyle* would not impact their *family heritage*, he calmed down a bit. Of course, Liz was insulted by his homophobic, misogynistic *expressions of understanding* and in retaliation asked whether she could inherit the estate if she had a transsexual gender-reassignment operation to become a man. Her Irish Catholic mother, who has no British sense of humor or sarcasm, proceeded to pass out. Liz said it was a long weekend, but by Sunday they were all drinking and laughing. She may even bring Sam to meet her parents on Easter."

Henry chuckled. "Too bad Jane Austen wasn't there to capture it in prose—British patriarchy at its finest. But I have always thought it extremely unfair and arbitrary that *Equanimity* passes to me and not to Claire simply because I have a *Y* chromosome."

"Still, in spite of your *Y* chromosome, you are being very polite and nice to Liz and Sam these days. Quite the recovering misogynist. There's no excuse for them still being so rude."

Henry smiled widely. "Please don't worry. The look on their faces when they discovered I was the feminist scholar Mitchell was raving about as well as their newest collaborator was well worth weathering their attitudes. And it was just about the best Hanukkah present I could receive. I do have eight days to get you a proper present, correct?"

"Not necessary. You already gave me a multitude of gifts," she replied, bashfully playing with her food.

"Such as?" he asked skeptically.

"Equanimity," she said, looking at him with a searching expression. "And I don't mean the kind that's entailed away."

Something had suddenly come over her. Gloria took off the formal navy blazer she had worn to the hearing. Henry hoped his tongue was not hanging out of his mouth like an idiot, but he could not stop staring at the tight camisole she was wearing without a bra. He watched as she loosened her ponytail and took off her shoes. He was even more amazed when she pointed her hard nipples in the direction of the crowded dance floor and dove in.

An uber-fast version of "We Will Rock You" started playing and she called back to him as she entered the fray, "You gave me this."

A bloody miracle indeed!

10.

Gloria was in Henry's room sifting through records, while he was running a bath, feeling sweaty from all their unanticipated dancing at Thirst.

When he turned off the water, he called out to her jubilantly as he slipped into the tub, "Amazing first night of Hanukkah, Gloria. I'm a real scholar and you're a dancing queen."

She selected *Moondance* and, as always, scratched the record when she placed the needle on the vinyl.

She knew Henry was grimacing in his bath. He pleaded, possibly for the tenth time that week, "Please, Gloria, do not scratch my records."

Gloria said her usual "sorry" but shrugged her shoulders, knowing very well it would happen again. It had become part of their routine and a metaphor for something. She just didn't know what.

Henry, soaking in the tub, started singing to the album with his throaty, soulful voice. Captivated by that voice, she followed it back into the bathroom. He did not realize she was standing behind the tub listening to him sing. As she listened, she quietly and methodically began stripping off and folding her clothes.

Unaware of her close proximity, he called over to the other room, "We've reached the tops of our ladders, Gloria. No challenges left. *We are the champions.*"

Gloria responded quietly, "There may be one more challenge, Henry."

Taken aback, Henry turned his head, utterly stunned by a very naked Gloria stepping into his warm bath.

Facing him, she straddled his long body, cupped his face with her soft hands, and pulled him toward her so she could give him the long-awaited kiss that had been building since they first met in this very bathroom months ago. Coming out of the kiss, Henry gently put his hands on Gloria's breasts. She closed her eyes at his touch, which caused her whole body to tremble. When she opened her eyes, he was looking at her as if she were the only woman in the world. A divine gift.

"I love you, Gloria," he said in a raspy voice she had never heard before.

"I love you too," she breathed, moving closer and feeling his erection under her thigh.

It was Henry's turn to pull Gloria close. He wrapped her legs around his body, pressed his chest against her breasts, and cupped her backside with his long fingers, as his soft lips and warm tongue eagerly initiated his own hungry, pent-up kisses.

Gloria and Henry were still in the bath hours later, having replenished the warm water and changed the Van Morrison albums several times over. She was sitting on his lap, legs extended over his, gazing at a sliver of the moon out the large window. She didn't care that her recently improved hands were getting pruny and wrinkled from staying in the water so long.

All she cared about was her Hanukkah gift. Her Henry. And the miraculous feeling of his lips on her bare shoulders.

11.

Henry woke up with Gloria on top of him. It had been hours, and they had fallen asleep in the bath. The wondrous, miraculous bath where they declared their mutual love. She was his great love, his loomate, his soul mate, his kindred spirit. And she felt the same. Bloody miracle indeed!

He kissed her shoulders and neck to wake her, but she did not stir. Her oddly heavy body gave off a strange blue cast in the now-lukewarm bath water, which was turning the lightest shade of red. That's when he saw the wound. He was panicked, but he couldn't run from the truth any longer.

Henry woke up alone in his bed amidst a mess of sheets, blankets, and circumstances. His nightmare terrified him, having seemed so real. Gloria's naked body, their admissions of love, the sweet kisses on her neck, and the pleasure of sleeping pressed against her luscious breasts—in so many ways, it had been an amazing night. A brilliant night. Quite possibly the best night of his life.

While most of him was delighted his chutzpadik loomate had initiated that first naked kiss in the bath and delighted by their declarations, he was also utterly terrified. He had developed a plan, which now made no sense. He had intended to talk with her about everything before attempting anything.

Full disclosure before Christmas had been his mantra, so that Gloria would be as comfortable as possible with his delicate circumstances. After all, they had to be careful. Very, very careful. Now, everything was messed up and topsy-turvy. He never thought she would be so bold as to make the first move. And what a first move. As amazing as it was, it was not part of his plan.

Looking around his room, he worried at her absence. His paranoia was on full alert. He hoped he had not made her feel uncomfortable in any way. His greatest fear was that she would flee. They had come so far together. He could not bear the thought of losing her now. He nervously checked for his pills, hidden in the red pouch under his bed.

"Good morning, Loomate," she said, startling him as she walked toward him.

He covertly hid the red pouch and went to kiss her pink lips, still cold from the frosty December air. She was wearing his oversized faded Oxford sweatshirt, and Henry immediately noticed she was not wearing a bra, still basking in the afterglow of their three-hour bath and half-naked sleep.

"Where did you run off to, sneaky girl? I missed you," Henry said, kissing her again as he slipped his hand under the sweatshirt.

"I decided to bring you breakfast in bed for a change. I've been combing the streets of Oxford for *sufganiyot*," she explained as she placed something sugary in his mouth with her velvet fingers.

Some red gooey liquid spurted out of his mouth, causing him nervously to pull away.

"Shit. Am I bleeding? Are you?" Henry asked, concerned.

"Henry, relax. It's just jelly from the donut. Sufganiyot are jelly donuts. A delicious Hanukkah delicacy." She moved closer to him, wiping the jelly from his mouth with her finger.

"Sorry. I must still be tired from..." he offered apologetically.

"It was awesome," she whispered and climbed on top of him. "I can think of another Hanukkah delicacy I want to try."

She made her way down his body, kissing his face, chest, and stomach. She lingered on his boxer shorts, kissing the elastic as she stroked the fabric above his responsive penis. When she started to pull the boxer shorts down, Henry gently stopped her, reluctantly pulling her back to the Northern Hemisphere.

"This Hanukkah delicacy is not exactly kosher, love. I don't know if now is the right time, Gloria," he said kindly, not wanting to hurt her feelings, and with great restraint because he wanted to feel her mouth more than anything.

"Maybe I should wait to go further, Henry. Sharing lovely germs like this is new for me. But I want to go further. With you. Birth control by New Year's?" she asked, shyly averting her gaze.

Henry wanted it all with Gloria—right now and every day. But he had to talk with her, and he was so scared. *Fuck, fuck, fuck,* he thought to himself as his erection and hopes were deflating. He needed Claire's help to devise a new plan. In the meantime, they could kiss, fondle, and do a hell of a lot of collective masturbating.

He gently cupped her face, pulling it toward him and, with the most loving voice he could muster, said, "No rush, Gloria. I am madly in love with you, and for a lot of reasons, both yours and mine, we need to climb this ladder slowly. One rung at a time. And let's fully enjoy each step. Shall we, love?"

"Yes," she said with a loving smile.

They spent the day enjoying ravenous kisses, luscious breasts, and sweet jelly donuts in the Northern Hemisphere. Henry would save the serious topics for another day. Today they were still celebrating Hanukkah.

12.

They had been cuddling and listening to Van Morrison music in his bed for most of the afternoon.

"If every day of Hanukkah is this enjoyable, I may convert," he said, playing with Gloria's long, wavy hair.

"I don't know if that's such a good idea," she laughed. "I think it requires ritual circumcision, and it would be a shame to take anything away from your adorable penis."

"Adorable?" he asked, feigning anger. "*Strong, virile, large*—a more manly adjective, please!"

"I thought you music students were the sensitive touchy-feely types and didn't care about macho labels."

"We are touchy-feely, whatever that means," he agreed as he touched and felt her all over, "but because we are music students, we need the macho labels even more."

"I assure you, Henry Young music student, you are all man," she said, stroking him as laughter was replaced by kissing.

Their passion was interrupted as Benjamin Britten's *War Requiem* bellowed from Gloria's iPhone, announcing a phone call or text message from her parents. She abruptly stopped kissing Henry to take a look at the ominous message. *Her worst fear.*

"Is everything okay?" Henry asked gently, tenderly kissing her forehead and nose as she pressed the keys of her iPhone to respond to their text.

"Hanukkah will not be so enjoyable tomorrow, I'm afraid," Gloria said in a serious voice, pulling away from him a bit as she put the sweatshirt back on and walked toward the window.

"What's tomorrow? What's wrong?" he asked with uncharacteristic paranoia.

She did not want to foist her parents on Henry. He was too good for them.

"My parents are coming to Oxford. Sounds like Mitchell had suggested they visit after my nervous breakdown. So, of course, they're coming months later now that everything with their Superstar is fine. They're hoping to meet you, which will probably be horrific," she apologized.

"Don't worry, love," he reassured, "I will be on my best behavior. I can be quite charming when I try, especially to strangers."

"You are extremely charming, but I'm not worried about them meeting you," she clarified. "Truth is, you are too good for them, and I just don't care what they think anyway."

After a long silence, she whispered, "It's just that I'm terrified they'll bring the OCD voice back. Oliver has been really quiet lately, even with the lovely germs we've been sharing."

"You've worked too hard and come too far," he insisted as he pulled on his trousers and walked over to the window.

"This happiness thing feels really good," she said, putting her hands together as if stifling a craving for hand sanitizer. He tenderly pulled her hands apart, placing both of her arms around his waist.

Holding her tight, he vowed, "If I can protect you from humorless militant lesbians, dead women poets, and Oliver, I can surely protect you from Frank and Gladys Zimmerman."

He had no idea how formidable the Zimmermans were, especially in combination with Oliver. Could Henry protect her from such a deadly partnership? Gloria gave him a weary smile and sighed as she allowed the full weight of her body to be supported by his strong, scarred arms.

13.

They were dining at Quod Brasserie, a trendy restaurant in a historic old bank building with haute cuisine, an extensive wine list, and beautiful views of the city. It was affiliated and shared its building with the Old Bank Hotel, where her parents were staying.

But the most significant criterion for Gloria selecting the restaurant was its rotten acoustics. The cavernous old space was an echo chamber, and with the jazz band in its bar next door, Quod was the loudest restaurant in Oxford apart from nightclubs like Thirst or the many loud and crowded pubs.

She hoped the jazz band at the bar, the boisterous talking of the patrons, the shuffling of the waitstaff, the clank of the Waterford glasses, and all the other sounds of the busy, trendy restaurant would drown out her parents as they droned on about the call from Professor Mitchell and their concerns about how she's doing.

But, like Itzhak Perlman performing with the Chicago Symphony last New Year's, Gladys and Frank Zimmerman could comfortably hold their own, no matter how thunderous the orchestra.

Gloria was sitting at a square table, flanked by her parents on each side. Her mother had bought her a red Burberry scarf for Hanukkah, and Gloria was wearing it tight on her neck like a noose. Feeling queasy, she could not eat or drink, but her parents were more than making up for it. The nervous energy was palpable as the dysfunctional trio waited for Henry, who would join them after his late seminar. Gladys consumed a half bottle of Bordeaux like grape juice, and Frank put so much bread in his mouth that his cheeks were bulging as if he had just had his wisdom teeth extracted.

Gladys and Frank took Henry's absence as an opportunity to interrogate. They took turns asking Gloria questions. She tried to answer, but she felt like she was playing tennis against a ball machine whose setting was too fast. Backhand. Forehand. Backhand. She could barely keep up.

"Doesn't Oxford have a decent place to get your hair blown? Your hair's so frizzy," Gladys commented, stroking the ends of Gloria's wavy hair.

"So is this...this guy..." Frank started.

"Henry," Gloria said for the hundredth time that day.

"Yep. Is he a Rhodes Scholar?" Frank asked as he stuffed more bread in his mouth.

"Rhodes is for international students, Dad. Henry is British. I already told you that," Gloria said, trying to contain her frustration.

"Did you gain weight, Gloria? Your face looks fuller," Gladys asked as she squeezed Gloria's cheek before eyeing the menu.

"Well, I am eating like a normal person, Mom, but most people would think that's a good thing," Gloria replied defensively.

"Is he...you know...into that feminine poetry bullshit?" Frank asked kindly, oblivious to his own impertinence.

"No, Dad. But thanks for speaking so highly of my field, which, for future reference, is *feminist* poetry," Gloria responded with more bitterness than sarcasm.

"You know what I mean. You should be with someone in law or medicine or business. Someone who can take care of you," he explained in earnest.

"You mean like you?" Gloria asked acidly. She softened, adding, "Henry takes amazing care of me. The best care."

"Did I tell you Suzanne Goldbaum's daughter is engaged? They both go to Penn Law School," Gladys said resentfully without looking up from her menu.

Gloria mumbled, "Mazel tov," with no emotion as she took a sip of her Diet Coke.

"Isn't there a place you can get facials?" Gladys asked, using her reading glasses to examine Gloria's nose closely. "Look at those pores. So many blackheads. I thought Oxford was supposed to be the *cradle of civilization.*"

"That's Mesopotamia, Mom" Gloria said, her hostility mounting.

"So is this Henry Jewish?" Frank laughed crassly, completely unaware of Gloria's anger. "Willing to convert?"

"Circumcised at least?" Gladys chimed, laughing with Frank. "We'll take what we can get."

Henry approached the table from behind, having caught the last several exchanges. When he confidently gave Gloria a kiss on the top of her head, she closed her eyes and sighed as if handing him a heavy bag she could no longer carry.

"I am sorry I'm late, love. My seminar ran until seven fifteen," he said warmly as he squeezed her shoulders.

And then offering his hand to Frank, he said, "You must be Mr. Zimmerman. It is so nice to meet you, sir." With his charming smile, he continued reaching to shake Gladys' hand with its spiky red nails. "Nice to meet you as well, Mrs. Zimmerman. I am Henry Young, the uncircumcised gentile recovering drug addict music student who is desperately and madly in love with your wonderful daughter. And how are you enjoying your visit to Oxford? First time here?"

The Zimmermans were quiet for once, a bit stunned. A relaxed and poised Henry sat down opposite Gloria and gave her a reassuring smile.

Henry pried the breadbasket from Frank's hands and offered it to Gloria. "Take one, love?"

Gloria took a roll, but her mother stopped the transaction midstream, grabbing Gloria's hand away and speaking in an eerily quiet voice. "Gloria?"

Gloria rolled her eyes at Henry and said, "What's wrong now, Mom?"

"Your hands. They look and feel so soft. What are you using, sweetheart?" Gladys asked with a strange expression, as if she might be happy for her daughter.

Gloria did not answer. How could she explain all that had happened with Henry? So many out-of-body experiences in such a short time. She took a bite of the warm, crusty bread and shrugged.

Gladys reached to touch Gloria's other hand. "Please tell me what you're using for your hands, sweetheart. Please."

This time it was Henry who answered. "I believe it is called Equanimity, Mrs. Zimmerman."

"Equanimity? Haven't heard of this miracle cream. Can you buy it in the States or online?" Gladys asked hopefully, desperately.

"No, Mom. Just here. Just in Oxford."

PART SIX:
CHRISTMAS
Gloria in Excelsis Deo

Jesus died for somebody's sins but not mine
Meltin' in a pot of thieves

Patti Smith, 1975
From "In Excelsis Deo"

1.

There were stark contrasts between this Christmas and last year's. Last Christmas, Henry had been a cynical, disillusioned, utterly apathetic fuckup who begrudgingly played organ at Jesus College Chapel. This Christmas, he was an optimistic, utterly smitten fuckup who was happy to play organ at Jesus College Chapel. The difference was clear—Gloria. How fitting that the finale of the Christmas concert would be "Gloria in Excelsis Deo." He had so much to be thankful for this Christmas— that Gloria was in his life and that, at this divine moment, his bare legs were straddling her beautiful backside while he rubbed her shoulders and kissed her neck.

"And you are sure you want to spend Christmas in dreary Oxford instead of the warm Caribbean?"

"With my parents, the warm Caribbean is Dante's *Inferno*," she replied, turning around to kiss him full on the mouth. "And anyway, I want my first Christmas to be with you. A traditional Oxford Christmas, if you please."

"I am hardly a traditional Oxford kind of guy, but I do play organ Christmas morning at Jesus College Chapel. Does that count?" he asked, pulling her close.

"Totally. And I want a Christmas tree. Outdoor ice skating. Gingerbread house. Christmas carols. Sitting on Santa's lap," she said with the excitement of a schoolgirl.

Inspired, Henry pulled Gloria onto his lap and asked in a deep, suggestive voice, "And what would you like for Christmas, little girl?"

Gloria pretended to think for a minute and then chuckled, "Hey, Santa, do you have a hard-on?" She moved her bum in his lap, only adding to Father Christmas' cheer. "You pervert."

"All your fault, you naughty, naughty girl," he said with a grin as he lay her back down on the soft, rumpled blanket.

2.

Claire was practically catatonic when Henry found her in an uncharacteristically untidy office. Something was dreadfully wrong. He had gone to her office wanting to talk with her about Gloria and his intention—or rather, his *need*—to be honest about everything. More than anything, he wanted to be honest, and he honestly wanted to make love with her. He could not wait much longer, but he needed advice about overcoming certain obstacles, and Claire was always an expert strategist.

But as soon as he saw Claire, he knew he would have to put off the important conversation yet another day. Claire was distracted and upset.

"Claire, what's wrong?"

"Nothing, Henry. This is a most inconvenient time. Can I ring you later?"

"What's the matter? Please let me help you for once."

"It's not your fault, Henry, but you can't help me with this. I need to handle this situation on my own."

"What situation? What do you mean, 'It's not my fault'? What are you bloody talking about?"

She looked distraught, but at the same time there was something settled and resigned in her eyes. And it looked like she'd been packing crates. Was she moving offices? Did Mars find out about Claire's involvement with Gloria? Had the Zimmermans contacted Mars? Was Claire being reprimanded?

"Tell me, Claire. Is this about Gloria and the Zimmermans? Did you get into some kind of trouble?"

She took a deep breath and said, "The Zimmermans contacted Mars, but they were complimentary. Very appreciative that I had— what did they say?—'solved their daughter's hand problems' or some rubbish like that."

"Then what happened? Why the moving crates? Was it taken the wrong way? Were there ethical questions raised?" Henry asked in earnest, determined to get to the bottom of this and find a way to help his sister. After all, this was his bloody fault.

"Yes, Henry, there were ethical questions raised. My distinguished chair, Dr. Alfred Mars, called me to his office, patted me on the head for receiving compliments, and then slapped me for not confirming that I was Gloria's doctor on record. I explained that she was your friend and we were informally helping her out and that the Zimmermans exaggerated and made assumptions about my involvement."

"So if Mars understood, why are you moving out of your office? Were you promoted again?" Henry asked optimistically.

Claire gave a steely laugh and responded, "Not exactly. The wise and upright Dr. Alfred Mars gave me a stern lecture about ethics and responsibility and said in a very self-righteous tone that 'he was willing to look the other way this time.'"

Henry lit up. "That's great! So everything is fine."

Claire continued, "And I said, 'Oh, that's odd; you're one to judge me on ethics, Alfred. You seem to have no problem with ethics when you're sticking your Viagra-inflated penis in my twat. Easy for you to look away then. Especially easy to look away from your Catholic wife and six children, you sanctimonious, self-righteous fucking arse. I'll talk to you about ethics.'"

They sat silently for a long while before Henry spoke. "Claire, you should not have to leave. Why are you leaving? He is the one in authority who took advantage of you. This is sexual harassment. There's a definite power discrepancy, and he crossed the line."

"Oh, Henry, we both crossed the line. Who am I fooling? You and I know I am still trying to get Daddy to love me. Whether it's Nicholas Young or Alfred Mars or some other old, uptight, cruel man who withholds the best part of himself. I should not be working here. I deserve better, so much better."

"You do, Claire."

"My baby does too," she whispered, rubbing her stomach.

"Baby?" he asked, astonished, although it made sense, since she wasn't smoking.

"I'm in the very early stages. And I'm not telling Alfred. He's not the kind of man I want in my child's life. I deserve what you and Gloria have," she said quietly as she started to cry.

"You do," Henry agreed as he reached out to console her with his strong, scarred arms.

He could not ask Claire about how to talk with Gloria. He had Gloria. That was way more than Claire had and way more than he deserved.

3.

As part of her traditional Christmas celebration, Gloria wanted Henry to take her to Winchester Cathedral's Christmas market. Winchester Cathedral was one of the largest and most beautiful Gothic cathedrals in all of Europe and the burial place of Jane Austen, Gloria's favorite novelist. It made a spectacular backdrop for her traditional Christmas celebration with its impressive limestone structures and bucolic woods. At Gloria's urging, they participated in as many of Winchester's traditional Christmas activities as possible, albeit in Henry's nontraditional, irreverent sort of way.

Both proficient skaters, they enjoyed the picturesque rink adjacent to the cathedral. Gloria focused on the trees surrounding the outdoor rink. With their erect trunks and symmetrical placement, they reminded her of the toy soldiers from the *Nutcracker*, diligently guarding Christmas. Henry enjoyed the skating as well but was inadvertently scaring children and adults alike, almost knocking them down, as he sped by, counting laps. Aware of the fuss he was causing, Gloria diplomatically asked Henry for a tour of the cathedral to get him off the ice.

Inside the majestic building, they listened to carolers sing in full Renaissance regalia, their voices echoing through the incredibly long nave of the cathedral. Gloria tried to enjoy their traditional hymns, but every time she looked at Henry, he was mocking them in one way or another. She hoped he would be more serious at Jesus College Chapel, where he was to play organ on Christmas. But she was happy they were having fun. She was not sure whether to sing along with the carolers or laugh with Henry, so she did both in a clumsy, cheerful mix of tradition and subversion.

At dusk, they watched the lantern parade, and even cynical Henry was taken in by the grandeur of the huge and colorful lanterns. Gloria thought Winchester Cathedral was the perfect traditional Christmas excursion. A winter wonderland, a scene from a snow globe, an advent calendar, and an English rendition of a Norman Rockwell or a Currier & Ives painting. Her perfect Christmas fantasy with her perfectly imperfect Henry Young.

While her family was not particularly observant, they were not among the reform and conservative Jews who celebrated Christmas. And even if they did, Oliver would have ruined it. Oliver had made it difficult for her to enjoy any day, let alone a holiday. For Oliver, holidays had been major germ events—too much unwrapped food and too many opportunities to exchange foreign germs through hugging, kissing, and other dangerous expressions of affection.

Oliver would be particularly worried about Gloria's intended expressions of affection this Christmas. If Oliver only knew about the germs she wanted to share with Henry before the New Year, he would destroy her. But it was Oliver who was extinct this Christmas, and happily, Gloria and Henry and their lovely germs were very much alive.

4.

enry wanted to contribute to Gloria's fantasy Christmas. He surprised her by decorating their flat. He had placed a medium-sized Christmas tree in her room by the bay window and covered it with handmade ornaments resembling mini album covers. The Van Morrison albums were near the top, but he also included their other favorite artists: Bob Dylan, Neil Young, the Doors, Tom Petty, the Who, and many others. For sentimental reasons only, he even included Queen, toward the bottom. Of course, the tree was adorned with a Van Morrison figurine as its angel, the one true god they worshiped every day.

Henry had hung mistletoe all over the ceiling of both bedrooms and the loo. He wanted an excuse to ask for as many Christmas kisses as possible while he figured out a strategy for taking their relationship further. On the mantle of her bedroom, he had placed an ornate gingerbread house that he had purchased from the food halls in Harrods. And on the green door of the gingerbread house, he wrote with red frosting, *202 A&B*, the numbers of the flat they shared at St. Cross—his true equanimity.

He was delighted at Gloria's face when she first saw his Christmas decorations. She said, "Oh my God" over and over again, exclaiming that she was "totally blown away" by the "fucking unbelievably awesome" Christmas decorations from her "totally incredible, amazing loomate and soul mate." Her Jewish-American-Princess-Surfer-Girl accent always pleased him and made him chuckle, as it belied her extraordinary intelligence, academic accomplishments, and bluesy Chicago roots.

They squabbled over album placement for practically each and every ornament. And Gloria made sure they kissed under all sections of the mistletoe so that "no leaf or vine would be left behind." Her excitement at this, her first Oxford Christmas—her first Christmas of any kind, for that matter—was infectious. Along with Gloria, Henry also felt innocent and new, in spite of his scars.

They were standing by the mantle, examining the ornate gingerbread house.

"Can we have a bite?" she asked, always the schoolgirl impatient to open presents.

"Claire and I have a tradition," he offered. "The person with the worst Christmas memory gets to break off and eat the door. It is a big honor. I should warn you, I always win," he explained, adjusting the purple-frosted chimney.

"Don't be so sure," she said with a confident grin. "Christmas break in the ninth grade. I was on the forensic squad, a public-speaking team, and I'd made it to Nationals, a big speech competition that took place the first weekend in January. I was so nervous, being the youngest person to qualify from my state. I'd get sick, vomiting and convulsing at least three or four times a day, worrying about the competition, having the most awful anxiety attacks. The forensic coach and assistant principal urged me to withdraw, saying the pressure to win coupled with my OCD was detrimental to my health and against the mission of my wonderfully progressive Francis W. Parker School. But my wonderfully *unprogressive* parents would positively not allow it. It was Christmas Eve, and I so clearly remember my father yelling at the assistant principal on the phone, 'The Zimmermans are not quitters! Gloria's my Superstar. I won't give your school one more dime if you pull her from the competition.'"

When Gloria went to break off the door, Henry stopped her.

"Pretty good, Loomate, but now it's my turn," he said with his own confident smile. "On Christmas when I was seventeen, I overdosed badly. I was robbed and left beaten in a bad part of London. Police found me and discovered that I had been involved, myself, in dealing drugs. They took me to a special hospital for juvenile offenders from privileged backgrounds. My father didn't visit me until the third day after my arrest and even then only because Claire made him. First words out of his drunken mouth when he saw me were, 'It's a good thing your mother's already dead from cancer; otherwise you would have killed her, and on Christmas.'"

Henry thought he had won, although he had to admit, they both had made it through dreadful Christmases. Gloria didn't say anything, but he saw her tear up. She closed her eyes and inhaled a deep breath for what seemed like ages. She emptied her lungs as if blowing out past demons.

Holding herself a bit lighter, she offered a compromise. "Okay, you get the door. But I deserve the chimney, at least."

Henry nodded and said, "Deal," as he offered his hand so they could shake.

Still holding her much-improved soft hand, he kissed it gently. He was surprised when she in turn rolled up the sleeve of his shirt and kissed up his arm, making sure to touch each and every track mark.

Henry was not one to cry. Even when his mother died and his father abandoned him, he did not cry. Even when they gave him his diagnosis, he did not cry. He just couldn't cry. But Gloria kissing his arm almost made him feel like crying.

The mood turned light again as Gloria broke off the door and laughed as she fed it to Henry, sloppily getting frosting all over her hands and his mouth. As he licked the frosting off her hands, sucking her soft fingers, they momentarily forgot their ghosts of Christmas past.

5.

Gloria thought it had been a perfect Christmas Eve as she was lying in bed with a sleeping Henry and carefully examining the wonderful Christmas tree he had decorated just for her. She did not want to appear ungrateful, but upon closer examination, she did have some issues with the patriarchal placement of some of the mini-album ornaments. Since Henry was sleeping, she decided to rearrange them a bit, hoping he would not notice.

But being the music fanatic he was, he noticed her unauthorized interventions as soon as he awoke, turning from Santa to Grinch in two seconds flat.

"What happened to the Clash's *London Calling*? Only one of the greatest albums of all time. What's wrong with you?" he asked in a groggy voice but awake enough to notice it in the garbage.

"Okay, fine," Gloria responded, taking the ornament out of the garbage can and placing it back on the tree.

She didn't want to talk about Oliver's infatuation with the Clash. She didn't want to talk about Oliver this Christmas or ever. But she didn't want Henry to think she was ungrateful. He had worked so hard on the tree.

"And why is Joni Mitchell's *Blue* so close to the top? Did you move it without consulting me?" he asked as he shook himself awake.

"Henry, I'm a feminist poetry scholar, for Christ's sake. *Blue* and Carole King's *Tapestry* and *Janis Joplin's Greatest Hits* are the only female ornaments on the upper half of the tree. You need to allow some more women near the top. And there should be more female artists on the tree in general," she said with a bit more self-righteous indignation than she had intended.

"What about Patti Smith? She's a girl...woman. She's near the top. And she covered Van Morrison's 'Gloria,'" he said in defense of his tree.

She gave him an irritated look. He softened her with a kiss, which led to more of the same. She was trying to hold on to her argument, but it was impossible with dangerous-dimpled Henry kissing her. She found herself on top of him as he lifted her tank top and cupped her breasts.

For a brief moment, he broke away from the kissing and looked up at her with an evil grin. "See, I do like it when women are on top."

He was incorrigible and irresistible, and he knew it. She laughed at him and purposefully taunted him with her breasts, brushing his face and pulling away. She knew it was driving him crazy and thought her feminist colleagues would be appalled that she was using her sexuality to put a man in his place, beneath her body and on the bottom of her Christmas tree.

Before she gave in to his and her desires, she said, "I do love spending Christmas Eve with you, Henry Young, even if you are a misogynistic *ANTI*feminist."

When she started kissing him again, she was surprised when he moved slightly away and pulled down her shirt. He hesitated for a long while, staring at her with an unexpected somberness as if he just remembered he had something important to say and was struggling to find the words or nerve.

She stroked his furrowed brow to reassure him and reclaim their former Christmas cheer. But there was a melancholy and worry in his face she had not seen in a while.

"An antifeminist who loves you very, very much," he said in a serious voice that did nothing to assuage her concerns. Something was wrong.

6.

The weather on Christmas morning was cold but bright. Henry awoke early to find the most divine Christmas present lying next to him naked and sleeping under his blanket. Today was a day to put all fear and anxiety about talking with her aside and to celebrate his two favorite Jews: Jesus Christ and Gloria Zimmerman. Taking in her naked silhouette, he had to admit she had a slight edge over Jesus. Saint Thomas Aquinas and his mind-body split be damned.

He kissed the nape of her exposed neck and whispered in her ear, "Happy Christmas, Loomate. I love you."

Gloria stirred and moaned and turned over. Her beautiful eyes still closed, she was dreaming of Christmas, no doubt, as Henry quietly slipped out of bed to get ready for the Christmas concert.

He arrived early to Jesus College Chapel so that he could rehearse with the choir. When they rehearsed their finale, "Gloria in Excelsis Deo," he could not help but sing along. The music was joyful.

Gloria in excelsis deo
Et in terra pax hominibus bonae voluntatis
Laudamus te
Benedicimus te
Adoramus te
Glorificamus te

It was a song about his girl. All he could think about was how much he praised, blessed, and adored Gloria and whatever god had brought her to him.

She would be walking through the doors of Jesus College Chapel in less than three hours, and he couldn't wait. If she was the impatient schoolgirl, he was her impatient schoolboy. This was the first Christmas in a long while that really felt like Christmas.

In awe of the bright sunlight illuminating the stained glass, Henry knew he was a blessed man. Whether it was called Jesus or Hashem or Van Morrison or some dead woman poet he hadn't heard of, there was a god, and that god loved Henry in spite of how messed up he was. He realized that Van Morrison's fatalistic optimism was no different from Christian redemption or Jewish *tikkun olam* or Buddhist enlightenment. In epiphany, Henry knew that Van Morrison's sacred song "Beside You" was ultimately about the power of healing—healing oneself, healing each other, and healing the world. Gloria in Excelsis Deo.

7.

She woke up Christmas morning to the sound of "Gloria in Excelsis Deo" playing below. As she listened to its triumphant melody, she heard excited feet pattering on the stairs, running as fast as they could to greet her and the expectant Christmas Day.

"Mummy, Mummy...it's time! It's time!" a boy and girl shouted as they jumped onto the king-sized bed, tackling her with hugs, kisses, and tickles, the best Christmas presents. They brought over her favorite camel cashmere robe, coaxing her to come downstairs so they could see what Father Christmas had left under the tree.

Once in the living room, the children ran to the tree, but she looked toward the piano. She was looking for the man who was playing "Gloria in Excelsis Deo," her song. She was looking for her inspiring poet, father of her children, her husband, Henry.

"Gloria in Excelsis Deo" was blasting from the alarm on her iPhone. Henry had obviously changed the song and increased its volume so she wouldn't sleep through his concert. Whether it was Oliver's dormancy, sleeping in the same bed with Henry, or eating unwrapped carbs, Gloria was sleeping more soundly these days than she ever had. It was difficult to wake up, especially when Henry was not there to pull off the blanket and prod her to find clothes for warmth in the chilly room.

It was especially challenging when she was having such a lovely dream about having a family with Henry. A normal family. She wondered if she should even call it a dream. Weren't dreams supposed to be out of reach? Maybe *goal* and *plan* were better words. Rubbing her soft hands on her cheeks, she knew the best present was having Henry in her life.

But she was an impatient schoolgirl celebrating her first Christmas, so she was also excited about exchanging tangible presents with him after the concert. She made sure her present for him was under the tree, but she had not seen his present for her. She wondered where he was hiding it.

She had two hours to get dressed and have a quick breakfast before heading to Jesus. She was naked and wrapped in Henry's duvet as she rummaged through a pile of clothes on the floor, looking for Henry's old Oxford sweatshirt, a favorite piece of lounge clothing that she'd recently absconded.

She liked wearing it as she tidied up and got ready, as it was fairly cold in their flat this time of year. Since most of the students were on holiday and most of the colleges were closed, Henry thought those Oxford cheapskates had turned the heat way down everywhere, including St. Cross, even though its many international students were still in residence and it was open all year.

As always, his room was a mess, and it seemed like the sweatshirt was nowhere to be found. She checked under his bed, where there was another huge pile of dirty clothes he had hidden from view. After the New Year, she was going to have a talk with him about letting her do his laundry and organize his room a bit. He had told her his mess helped him feel creative, but this was ridiculous. She finally found the sweatshirt with its sleeves tied around a mysterious red-zippered pouch. She wondered if Henry had hidden her Christmas present inside.

A small black box, perhaps? Was her dream of starting a family with Henry coming true already? The impatient schoolgirl waiting for Santa, she just couldn't resist. She opened the zippered pouch enclosing her present, only to find a bottle of prescription medication. But as Gloria read from the label of Henry's pills, her wonderful dream became her worst nightmare. She grabbed the laptop from his desk and started mercilessly pounding the keys. It just couldn't be true.

8.

As he listened to the sermon, Henry scanned the gallery of seats in frantic search of Gloria, but he couldn't find her anywhere. She was the most punctual person he knew. So he couldn't help but worry and feel paranoid. Had this all been a cruel joke? Was he being punished for past crimes and misdemeanors? Was he being punished for the way he had bastardized "Gloria in Excelsis Deo" in past years?

> *Glory to God in the lowest*
> *And to people of bad will for fucking teasing me*
> *We praise you for taking my mother*
> *We bless you for denying me a real father*
> *We adore you for getting me high*
> *We glorify you for making me sick*
> *We give thanks to you for fucking nothing*

Henry was desperate to tell whatever god would listen that he was sorry. He didn't mean it. Please excuse everything. He was so grateful for Gloria. Please let her show up.

9.

Her hands were shaking as she read and reread the label of the bottle, desperately hoping she was missing something. She tried to be an objective researcher. She was not going to panic until she had all the facts. The only fact she knew for certain was that the label read, HENRY YOUNG, ATRIPLA, TWO TABLETS DAILY.

She had to remind herself that these were six meaningless words. They were just words. Dumb, stupid, idiotic words. They could not steal her dreams and bring Oliver back. They had no power until she gave them meaning and accepted that meaning. They were just six words.

She was a Rhodes Scholar doctoral student. She was a researcher, for Christ's sake. She had to do research to find out what they really meant. Moreover, she was a nuanced and thorough researcher who always read primary sources. Surely, there was more to this than those six meaningless words.

Accessing Oxford's online medical database, Gloria quickly found over seventy-five studies about the efficacy and uses of Atripla. Gloria's hands were shaking as she scrolled down the list, frantically reading each abstract summary, looking for something that might indicate this nightmare was not what it seemed. Three studies were particularly compelling.

A trial performed in Nigeria involved prostitutes taking Atripla proactively to prevent sexually transmitted diseases. Gloria could work with this. Maybe because Henry had been an intravenous drug user, he took Atripla as a precaution in case he might ever use or share needles again and end up on the street. After all, he had overdosed and was found on the street when he was seventeen. That was reasonable.

A trial in South America tested Atripla as a treatment for an advanced form of herpes. Gloria nervously wiped her sweaty forehead with the sleeve of Henry's sweatshirt, contemplating whether he might have herpes. She thought herpes might make sense, given his hesitation toward fellatio and his reticence about having intercourse in general. She could work with herpes; it was treatable, especially in Western industrialized nations. They could live with herpes.

The third study concerned children in India born to HIV-positive mothers, who received Atripla as a prophylactic to prevent them from being infected as well. Again, this was more proof that Atripla was used for prevention of HIV and not just treatment. Perhaps he was taking it as a precaution. Always better to be safe than sorry.

An adept researcher, Gloria could not deny the fact that most of the studies concerned Atripla's use as a combination retroviral drug for the treatment of individuals infected with HIV. These studies were quite promising; Atripla increased life expectancy by as much as thirty or forty years, giving most HIV patients a normal life span by significantly delaying the onset of AIDS.

While this was positive news, Gloria could not accept that Henry was infected with HIV. No matter how unlikely, she needed to know firsthand if there was a possibility that he was taking Atripla for herpes or prevention or for any other fucking reason.

He was not infected with HIV! He could not be infected with HIV! HIV was not a lovely germ at all. It was the worst germ possible. He must be taking Atripla for something else. She needed to talk to a real live person with knowledge about medication. A real live person who would tell her there was a possibility that Henry was taking it for some other reason, that he was okay, that he did not have the worst germ possible, that Christmas was real, and that life wasn't over. My God; hers had only just begun.

10.

loria was in a desperate search for a pharmacist, or as the British would say, a "chemist," who could give her a professional opinion about Henry's pills and whether she had the right to believe in Henry's famous fatalistic optimism.

As she stood on the empty cobblestone street, in front of Rowland's Chemist Shop, the sign on the door discouraged her, as it read, CLOSED THROUGH THE NEW YEAR. HAPPY HOLIDAYS! All of the charming Tudor buildings that lined the street were decorated for Christmas but closed Christmas Day. For blocks around, everything was closed; in so many ways, Oxford had become a ghost town. The many church bells made her feel that much lonelier.

The security guard at St. Cross had suggested she try the John G. Clifford Chemist Shop on George Street. The shop was dark, and a sign on the door read, CLOSED FOR CHRISTMAS. Gloria took Henry's bottle of pills from her pocket, shaking them in frustration as she headed to the next chemist shop on her list. It was also dim inside Buckden Pharmacy, but Gloria was hopeful since there was no sign on the door. She anxiously rang the doorbell, hoping that the chemist lived above the shop and might hear her. She was getting desperate, and the tears were starting to well up.

Gloria's eyes were red from crying by the time she found Kaplan Pharmacy miraculously open on Christmas. Jerry Kaplan, an Orthodox Hasidic Jew in his late sixties, wore a long white beard, yarmulke skullcap, and tzitzit religious strings from his vest. He looked like a Jewish Santa Claus with his round reading glasses low on his nose, protruding belly with black vest, and jolly smile.

There were quite a few customers in his shop because he seemed to have a monopoly on Oxford's Christmas drug business. And like Santa, he was in good cheer but a bit overwhelmed by all the customers, as well as his five young grandchildren, who ran around the store in Hasidic garb like boisterous elves pulling on each other's strings.

"Sorry for the delay, Miss. My wife and daughter are visiting her sick sister in Chicago," he said, smiling as he took out a handkerchief to wipe the sweat collecting on his shiny forehead.

Gloria handed him her prescription. "I'm from Chicago."

"Long way from home," he said as he read from her prescription. "I will have this Luvox filled in ten minutes, Miss Zimmerman. Is there anything else I can help you with this Christmas?"

Gloria handed him Henry's bottle of pills and asked quietly, "Can you please tell me what these are for?"

Jerry adjusted his round reading glasses and examined the label closely. He looked up at Gloria with recognition but shook his head. "I am sorry. I absolutely cannot comment on someone else's medication, Miss Zimmerman. Can you talk to this young man yourself?"

A completely dejected Gloria looked like she was about to burst into tears again. Jerry, moved by her despondent eyes and noticing her Oxford sweatshirt, motioned for her to step behind the counter.

He gave her Henry's pills back as he spoke in a hushed voice, out of earshot of other customers. "While I cannot comment on any specific case, I can comment generally. Let's say you as an Oxford student were doing a research project and asked me about certain medication in the abstract, without regard to anyone in particular, I might be able to answer a few questions. Hypothetically, of course, because you are a student."

Jerry winked at Gloria, who gave him a grateful but worried smile in return. Gloria put Henry's pills in her coat pocket as she started formulating life-and-death questions for her Jewish Santa Claus.

11.

Gloria staggered through the Gothic limestone campus to a cacophony of bells from all the various chapels and churches celebrating the birth of Jesus Christ. But as she made her way through the stone gates to Jesus, the bells rang in elegy, waking Oliver.

He spared no mercy.

I knew he was dangerous. But you wouldn't listen. He could kill you. His germs could kill you. His dangerous, deadly germs could kill you. HIV is the worst germ possible. And Henry has the worst germ possible. Don't go to him. Run. As fast as you can. Run. Run. Run. While you're still alive, run.

Gloria relinquished her Christmas dream to Oliver. All she could see as she walked through the Jesus quad was Henry and their fantasy children, all practically dead from advanced AIDS, their bodies infested with horrific purple welts, branding them with the worst germ possible. The most dangerous and deadly germ possible. But where was she? Was she dying too?

Lifeless, Gloria opened the door to Jesus College Chapel in the middle of "Gloria in Excelsis Deo." But she could not hear the joyful Christmas music. She could not hear the chorus. She could not hear the organ. She could not hear Henry playing and calling her name. As she entered the chapel, the only voice she heard was Oliver's. Henry's organ and the choir were drowned out by Oliver's rendition of Patti Smith's version of "In Excelsis Deo." It was the only song she heard. *Jesus died for somebody's sins, but not mine.*

12.

Henry finally saw Gloria as he accompanied the very last chorus of "Gloria in Excelsis Deo." She was so late, and he had been so worried. As the concert ended, an uncharacteristically disheveled Gloria was slowly snaking her way through the rows and pews to where he sat at the organ. Her unhinged appearance utterly terrified him.

She took a bottle of pills from her coat pocket and slammed it on the organ bench. His hand was shaking as he picked up the bottle and read the label as if he had never seen it before. But he had. She knew everything.

"Did you forget your pills, Henry?" she asked with acid in her voice.

Members of the choir peered at them, and Henry spoke quietly as he went to put an arm on her shoulder. "Can we talk about this in private, love?"

"Don't touch me. Keep your hands off me," she barked, swatting his arms away.

"I didn't know how to tell you. I was going to tell you. I was just waiting for the right moment." He wanted to pull her close.

"When? After unprotected sex? Or right after I swallowed your semen? After I got pregnant and passed HIV to our child?" she asked bitterly.

More people were looking at them now.

"We did not do anything risky. I made sure. I would never," he said in a quiet, intense voice.

"You lied," she said, avoiding his eyes, more subdued now.

"I didn't want to scare you."

"Because I'm a germophobe and would be completely freaked out, knowing I've spent hours with you in bed, sharing saliva and touching the soft skin of someone with HIV, the worst germ possible for a freak who has spent her life avoiding germs? Too bad I didn't swallow your semen; it would have been a poetic way for me to die. Much more flourish than my dead women poets. The head in the oven is so cliché, and the fur coat with carbon monoxide poisoning is not at all politically correct these days."

"I...didn't want to ruin...us, scare you away," he offered, trying to get her to see the truth in his eyes.

She laughed, but her laughter was bitter and manic as she finally turned to look at him. "Well, congratulations, Henry. Like everything else in your life, you fucked up. You messed up. You ruined it—ruined us."

Henry got as close to her as he could without touching her.

He reached out with his voice, desperate to reassure. "We could have a happy life, Gloria. My condition is stable. The medication works well. These days people live long and happy lives with HIV. I can live another twenty, thirty, forty years or more. Have a future. A happy ending. Something I never thought about or wanted—until I met you."

Gloria looked searchingly in his eyes for a long while before falling into a front pew. She covered her face and began to cry, as if she had come to the chapel to pray for the health of a loved one with a terminal disease. But this wasn't a simile; it was true. He had a fatal condition, and he had kept it from her. Was she praying for him? Was she praying for them? Did they have a chance?

When the tears were finally gone, all Gloria could muster was a hoarse whisper. "Oliver is telling me to run."

13.

Gloria ran out of the chapel, eager to be far away from Henry and his terrible germs. As if Oliver had arranged it, there was a bus outside the gates of Jesus marked CHRISTMAS SUFFOLK RAF. She had no idea where her getaway bus was going, but she didn't really care. She needed to get away. Oliver had told her to escape Henry and his deadly germs as quickly as possible. She had no choice.

She boarded the crowded bus, which was filled with people of all ages, their clothing and moods in keeping with Christmas cheer. Gloria staggered to the back of the bus, pausing by a twenty-year-old shopgirl, the only passenger with an empty seat.

"Happy Christmas. Wanna sit down? I'm Millicent," the girl said in a voice entirely too happy for Gloria's current state.

Gloria ignored Millicent, visibly repulsed by her jolly manner, unkempt appearance, and disorganized stuff—a large purse, satchel of gifts, bulky coat, and disgusting food on her filthy table tray.

Oliver was now wide awake and very distressed. Of course he was sending her mixed signals, wanting her to run away from Henry but disgusted by the germ-infested bus. He was impossible to please. But he was all she had.

Too many germs. Too many germs here, and too many germs with HIV-infested Henry. Too many germs and you'll die. HIV and you'll die.

14.

They were on the grounds of *Equanimity* sitting in the small family cemetery on their estate. The marble headstone at their feet read, *Sally Young, beloved wife and mother, who brought music to so many and lived fully although precious time was slipping away.*

Henry read the headstone over again as Claire placed a potted poinsettia at its crown.

"She'll come back, Henry," Claire said softly, adjusting the Christmas plant.

"You don't know that," Henry said in frustration, wondering where Gloria was and whether she was safe.

He had looked everywhere, but she was nowhere to be found. Where was she? Was she safe? He worried that she was suffering alone and without her medication.

"I know she'll come back. She's in love with you," Claire said.

"She looked at me like I was tainted with germs, Claire," Henry spat. "Like I was the most disgusting, deadly, vile creature she'd ever seen. She was crazed. Out of her mind. And so hurt. Devastated."

"She's just in shock. Scared of you getting sick. Dying young," Claire explained more like a psychologist than a sister.

Henry backed off. It wasn't Claire's fault he was in this mess. And Claire had her own burdens.

He felt the cool marble with his mother's name. "Good thing Mum isn't here to see what a messup I am."

"Mum would be very proud of you, Henry. The way you helped Gloria fight her OCD. How impressive you were at your hearing for your candidacy paper. Opening yourself up to love. That's what she wanted for both of us. I hope someday I'll be open to real love. And I'm so glad you'll be the most important man in my baby's life," Claire said, putting her hand on his shoulder and speaking more like a sister than a psychologist.

15.

Gloria struggled to pass Millicent to get into the window seat. When she was finally settled, she squirmed around, trying to get comfortable. Adding to her discomfort, Millicent was humming Christmas carols in a loud, crass voice as she tapped along with red fake nails on a matching red Coke can. Gloria closed her eyes and covered her ears, trying to tune out the aluminum clamor, especially when Millicent started singing "Gloria in Excelsis Deo."

Oliver had come back with a vengeance. Oliver's alarm bells competed with Millicent's cackling.

Annoying, loud, vile, fetid, heinous, germ-infested prostitute. Stop. Stop. Stop. Can't take it. Can't take it. Too loud and disgusting.

An unsuspecting, cheery Millicent unwrapped what looked like a chicken sandwich. The look and smell of the vile food as she stuffed her face, getting mayonnaise all over her lips and cheeks, sickened Gloria. She frantically searched her coat pockets for remnants of her safety pouch to help her calm down. But she had nothing left. No hand sanitizer. No Van Morrison. No gloves. No Sylvia Plath. No pills. She was completely trapped with no way out. Oliver was her only security, but he was losing it.

Need to get out. Need to get out. Need to get out of this vile, fetid, heinous, germ-infested bus. These dirty people. Dirty chicken sandwich. Vile, fetid, heinous, germ-infested chicken sandwich.

Desperately, she turned toward the window so that her back was facing Millicent. But facing the window had its own problems. Gloria could not help but notice how dirty the window was. *Vile, fetid, heinous, germ-infested, dirty window.* She just could not get away from the dirt and germs. On the window. On Millicent. On the chicken sandwich. In her mind.

Vile, fetid, heinous, germ-infested window. Vile, fetid, heinous, germ-infested bus. Vile, fetid, heinous, germ-infested chicken sandwich. Vile, fetid, heinous, germ-infested prostitute. Stop. Stop. Stop.

At the height of her anxiety, when Gloria thought it could not get any worse, Millicent's phone rang. Her cell was hiding somewhere in her globs and globs of vile, fetid, heinous, germ-infested stuff, but she did not know where. Trying to answer her phone before losing the call, Millicent knocked over her Coke can, spilling the cold brown liquid everywhere, including in Gloria's lap.

If Gloria had been pulled tight like a rubber band, this was the moment when the band broke. She snapped.

Gloria lost control and started shrieking, "Look at me! I'm a fucking mess, you fat bitch! I'm a fucking mess!"

Millicent and other nearby passengers quieted down in shock to stare at an absolutely mortified Gloria, who sat impotent and guilty. Once again, Oliver had messed up everything.

16.

If St. Cross seemed empty, their flat was desolate. Henry walked into the sparkling clean loo, tossing his bottle of pills from one hand to the other. He looked at himself in the mirror and read Gloria's notes: *Henry Young's an awesome scholar and totally worth staying up late for!* In the wake of their recent intimacy, she had since added, *who is very sexy!!*

In a decisive instant, he opened the bottle of pills and poured them in the toilet. He flushed and watched as they spun through the water in search of a more worthy home. He retrieved glass cleaner and a paper towel from a cabinet and removed Gloria's messages. When the mirror was wiped clean, he grabbed the red marker and instead scrawled *HIV* on the clean glass. Because of the symmetry of the letters, he was happy they were legible in reflection. No mistaking the fact he had HIV, even if the letters appeared *VIH*— Very Idiotic Henry.

Finally, he stepped into the empty bathtub fully dressed, sitting with his legs extended in utter silence and looking out at the abandoned quad. He had no idea what to do or think. He knew he had HIV, but he did not know much else. He knew he was not a scholar. He knew he was not awesome. He knew he was not worthy of staying up late for. He was especially not worthy of his medication.

And he knew this bathtub, where he had peed and cleaned and made the deal with her and kissed her and dreamed of killing her was the only place on earth he felt safe, a tiny lifeboat in a very stormy sea. But the tub wasn't really a lifeboat without Gloria. No life without Gloria. He played with the faucet most of the afternoon, ruminating about stormy seas and that depressed Japanese student who drowned.

17.

Another flood, Coke spilled everywhere, and everything was soaking wet. Gloria was mortified and contrite as she helped wipe Millicent's tray table and dry the items Millicent was removing from her flooded purse.

"I am sorry. I am so, so sorry. Please let me help," Gloria pleaded.

"Bollocks! Everything's ruined. And that was my good Lancôme blusher," Millicent said in frustration.

"I am so sorry I yelled. I was totally out of line. It's been a really hard day, and I lost it," Gloria apologized, shaking her head in mortification.

"We've all been there. And I spilled the bloody Coke. Are you okay? You seem very sad," Millicent said with concern, lifting Gloria's chin with her sharp nails.

"I'm fine. I'm fine," Gloria insisted, trying to dry Millicent's wet and filthy hairbrush with the bottom of her sweatshirt.

Millicent noticed Gloria's sweatshirt and asked, "Go to university?" Gloria nodded, and Millicent continued. "What do you study?"

"Postgraduate studies in poetry," Gloria said meekly, as if agreeing with her father, that her field was meaninglessness and utterly self-indulgent.

"I like to rhyme all the bloody time," Millicent said with a smile, in a feeble attempt to validate Gloria's professional identity. "I'm a shopgirl, not a poet. In case you didn't know it."

Millicent continued to survey the contents of her purse, wiping off various items damaged in the spill. Millicent found a soaking-wet picture of a young man in a military uniform and placed it on her chest, unsuccessfully trying to wipe it dry with her Christmas sweater.

"Bollocks!" she uttered in disgust.

"Here, let me try," Gloria offered as she gently took the picture from Millicent's chubby fingers.

Gloria carefully used her absorbent sweatshirt to wipe it off. It was almost dry when she handed it back to Millicent, who carefully received her treasure.

Lost in the picture, Millicent said, "I'm visiting him for Christmas. Most of us are visiting loved ones on the base. Home temporarily for Christmas. That's my boyfriend. Actually, my fiancé, Andrew. I like saying *fiancé*. We're getting married New Year's Eve. Mum wants me to wait for his time in Afghanistan to be over."

"What do you want?" Gloria asked, unexpectedly engrossed.

"As many happy days married to Andrew as can be. In a bloody wheelchair. Or in a pine box. Doesn't matter. Love is love. Rises above anything, everything. Time and space are powerless. Kneel down to love. Know what I mean?" Millicent asked as she kissed Andrew's picture.

Gloria smiled at Millicent in perfect epiphany, knowing exactly what she meant. Millicent was wrong. Millicent was a poet.

And then Gloria recited,

> *Let me not to the marriage of true minds*
> *Admit impediments. Love is not love*
> *Which alters when it alteration finds,*
> *Or bends with the remover to remove:*
> *O no! It is an ever-fixed mark*
> *That looks on tempests and is never shaken;*
> *It is the star to every wandering bark,*
> *Whose worth's unknown, although his height be taken.*

Love's not Time's fool, though rosy lips and cheeks
Within his bending sickle's compass come:
Love alters not with his brief hours and weeks,
But bears it out even to the edge of doom.
If this be error and upon me proved,
I never writ, nor no man ever loved.

"You *are* good. Real Oxford material," Millicent remarked with a wide grin. "You should have that poem published—at least online. The Internet is filled with sites that will put up new work."

"My friend William wrote it," Gloria clarified.

"Tell him he's good," Millicent winked, as if assuming he was Gloria's boyfriend and had written it for her.

Millicent dried off her makeup bag and opened it to assess the damage. She found red, sticky lip gloss and applied it on her lips, kissing the air a few times to blend it in. Finally, Millicent found a bottle of hand sanitizer. She used it to clean her hands and then offered it to Gloria.

"Your hands must feel sticky from the mess. Here—" she said.

Gloria was frozen, staring at the hand sanitizer with wide eyes like a former junkie. But Oliver was smaller and quieter than before.

Please clean your dirty, germ-infested hands. Please. Please. Please. For me? I just want you to be clean. Safe. Protected. No germs. Please clean your hands, Gloria. I just want you to be okay.

It was the first time in all the years since she was diagnosed that Oliver addressed her by name. He was separate, truly and finally externalized. Gloria took a good look at her hands. She inspected them on both sides, finger by finger. She marveled at their beauty. She closed her eyes and rubbed them on her cheeks. Her face registered their softness and serenity in spite of, or maybe because of, their stickiness.

Gloria knew she had reached the top of her ladder and could finally use her much-improved hands to wave goodbye to Oliver, her beloved and dreaded OCD voice—her protector, her surrogate parent, her bodyguard, her jailer, her jealous lover, her crutch, her overbearing friend who tried to take care of her for so long. She did not need him anymore. It was time to let go, to break up for good.

Oliver's voice turned uncharacteristically soft like Henry's as he spoke with quiet desperation. *But you need me. You're not okay, Gloria. We've been through so much together. I'm here to take care of you. I just want you to be okay. Free of germs. No germs. You won't be okay with germs.*

"I'm okay. I'm fine."

But the germs. You're not okay.

"I'm okay. Really, I'm okay. Thank you for everything. But I am okay now. My hands feel good. I feel good."

"Okay. Just offering, you know. Stay calm," Millicent replied, wary of another eruption. "Not a big deal, just offering hand sanitizer. I'll put it away."

"Thank you, Millicent. And I think I forgot to wish you a Merry Christmas when I first sat down."

"Over here we mostly say 'Happy Christmas,'" Millicent corrected gently as if pleased to be educating someone from Oxford.

Gloria was holding back tears now; Millicent had educated her in so many ways.

"Of course, Millicent. *Happy* Christmas. *Happy. Happy. Happy.*"

18.

Henry was ashen in the empty tub as he stared out the window at the dark Christmas night, feeling nothing, feeling numb. But then he thought he was going mad when he saw an apparition by the sundial that looked like Gloria. This would have been the perfect moment for drugs, especially Valium. He hated going mad sober; awareness was both a blessing and curse. Was that Deuteronomy?

He closed and opened his eyes, but the hallucinatory Gloria was still there. He got out of the tub to take a closer look. Pressing his face to the window, he saw that indeed it was the real Gloria. She had come back.

He quickly splashed water on his face, trying to bring himself back to consciousness when the loo door opened. She was out of breath from running up the stairs. In spite of the stained Oxford sweatshirt she was still wearing, her face was soft and glowing, *a Christmas angel in the first degree.* Was that Van Morrison? "Tupelo Honey"? Was she here to stay? Did he have a chance?

Nervous and desperate, Henry started talking with the urgency of someone making a last appeal on death row. He was talking to save his life, as if this were his only chance. Babbling. Explaining. Pleading. Begging. Incoherent free-association. He was making no sense whatsoever.

"Gloria, I was scared. I am so sorry I did not tell you. I wanted to tell you. I was planning on telling you before anything happened. All things considered, my condition is under control and I'm healthy. I take my medication. I love you so much, and I just couldn't bear the thought of losing you. Were you okay today? I was so worried. Looked everywhere. I didn't know how to tell you. You hate germs, and my germs are particularly egregious. But I never did anything that risked your health—I would never."

She was quiet, listening to him go on. And then they were both quiet for a long while.

"I'm still scared," he finally said in a small voice.

"I'm scared too," she said in a neutral tone he could not quite decipher.

Was she coming back? Was she coming back to him? Was she coming to retrieve her belongings? He felt the desperation bubble up and pour out of him all over the bloody loo floor. The messiest floor in all of Oxford.

"Gloria, I don't know what to say, what to do. I want to touch you, but I understand if I've lost that right. If my germs make you uncomfortable. If I'm too tainted."

"Shh, Henry. Shh," she soothingly reached out with her soft hands.

Treading lightly, he placed his hands in hers. He was skating slowly and carefully now. She pulled him close with a firm grip, guiding him into an embrace.

He wanted to say so much more. He tried pulling away for a brief moment to look into her eyes and explain how he felt. "Gloria..."

She stopped him, forcing him back into the hug. She leaned her head against his chest, listening to his frantic breathing, his frantic heart. When he started to speak again, she placed a soft hand over his mouth.

"No voices, Henry. Let's just listen to the quiet. It's still Christmas."

19.

Christmas was almost over, and once again Gloria was standing by her Christmas tree, inspecting the ornaments. She smiled, noticing that during her transformative bus ride to nowhere, Henry had moved all the women musicians near the top just underneath the ring of Van Morrison albums. She picked up a wrapped present from the bottom of the tree and gave it to him.

Handing him the small rectangular box, she said, "Only a few minutes left of Christmas, and we forgot to exchange presents."

Henry opened the box to find the two tickets to the Van Morrison concert.

Overwhelmed, he said, "So you're..."

She finished his sentence, "The crazy, obsessed fan with Obsessive-Compulsive Disorder who overpaid. Guilty as charged."

"Did you buy these out of guilt?" he asked, delicately stroking the tickets as if he had retrieved them from the rare-book archive.

"Not really. More like hope," she said softly. "Van Morrison's fatalistic optimism."

Henry put the tickets on the mantle and reached for another present under the tree.

He handed it to Gloria, "For you, my crazy, obsessed Van Morrison fan."

Gloria carefully removed the wrapping paper to find Sally and N.'s *Moondance* album.

It was her turn to feel overwhelmed. "Sally and N.'s *Moondance*. Messed-up cover. Scratches. Romantic inscription." She looked up at Henry. "It's perfect."

"I added my own inscription as well. Underneath," he said, and then, chuckling, added, "And I know you'll add more scratches."

Gloria smiled and started reading from the back of the album.

25 December 2010

Dear G,
Please give our Crazy Love a chance.
I may be messed up, but I will love you
my whole life (however long). No one could
ever love you more.
H.

He carefully studied her face. He looked confused, probably not knowing what to make of her reaction. She did not say a word; not because she did not know how she felt, but because a Christmas dream was coming true. Maybe not her original Christmas dream, but a different one, equally compelling and the same in its essentials. Poor, insecure Henry thought her silence was a bad sign. How could she explain? Where to start?

With desperation again, he asked, "Do G. and H. have a happy ending, Gloria? I need to hear it from you. Please tell me how it ends for G. and H. What happens to them?"

"I can tell you they're going to see an awesome Van Morrison concert in a few weeks, Henry. But beyond that, I don't know *exactly* how it ends," she said, trying to be encouraging but honest.

He still looked dejected. He didn't get it. And fatalistic optimism was his bloody concept.

Gloria moved closer. "I do know their ending is happy because they are together. Because they will love each other, in spite of and because of their scratches, their whole lives, no matter what happens." She laughed quietly before adding, "And you know that between the two of us, there will definitely be more scratches."

Gloria put her soft hands on Henry's cheeks as the tears welled up in his eyes. "Oh, Henry. Don't you know? All Christmas stories have happy endings. Even messed-up ones like ours."

Silent tears finally poured down Henry Young's face as Gloria placed gentle kisses all over his scratchy, dimpled cheeks, trying to catch every last tear.

PART SEVEN

NEW YEAR'S EVE

Lovely Germs

i like my body when it is with your
body. It is so quite a new thing.
Muscles better and nerves more.
i like your body. i like what it does,

ee cummings, 1925
From "i like my body when it is with your"

Oh child to never wonder why
To never, never, never, never wonder why at all
Never never never never wonder why at all.

Van Morrison, 1968
From "Beside You"

1.

Henry was waiting impatiently in his room with his ear at the loo door. Gloria had planned a surprise New Year's Eve celebration and would not let him see any of her efforts until everything was just right. Bloody perfectionist! He contemplated using his screwdriver to pick the lock, but his head knew he would get into trouble, and his body would not allow him to undermine the romantic plans he had in store for the evening.

His knocking and voice were getting louder as his impatience grew. "I thought we weren't supposed to lock doors. I'm going to huff and puff and break this door down. This is taking way too long, Gloria."

"Patience is a virtue," she called cheerfully through the door.

"Fallacious assumption that I care about being virtuous," Henry retorted with a mischievous smile as he retrieved the screwdriver from his desk.

He heard her laugh as she said, "Did I hear *fellatio*? I love it when you talk dirty, Henry Young."

"Now you're really driving me crazy," he responded, fondling his screwdriver a bit before putting it back in the drawer.

"Speaking of *crazy*—," she said, and he heard her put Van Morrison's "Crazy Love" on the turntable, indelicately scratching the record when she placed the needle.

His angry voice was tinged with affection. "God help me—you're going to damage every record I own. It's a good thing I love you so much and you have such luscious breasts. Otherwise, I would be very angry indeed."

She responded indignantly, "What is this *I own* crap? You told me we were sharing everything, including all records. Are you a man of your word, Henry Young?"

"Always," he muttered, hoping there was not even one ounce of truth in her joking.

Adorned with a *Happy New Year* tiara, a giddy Gloria peeked her head out of the loo door and jubilantly announced, "Well, in that case, I can let you in. Ready? Close your eyes."

Covering his eyes, she guided him to sit opposite her on a thick carpet that must have been in the open space between the bathtub and sink. When she let go of his eyes, he looked around in amazement at the utterly transformed and outrageous loo.

The blazing fire in the fireplace surprised him because she had always been reticent about the mess it would make. White helium balloons covered the ceiling. The claw-foot bathtub was downright dirty, as in filled with dirt; Gloria having planted it with three fragrant red rose bushes. Where did she find rose bushes this time of year? Impossible!

His—actually *their*—record player was resting on the covered toilet seat with their favorite Van Morrison albums leaning against the mirror, which once again read, *Henry Young is an awesome scholar*, although Gloria had added the appendage, *and also a sex god*. The shelves held about ten votive candles, illuminating the delight in her eyes as she watched him take it all in, overwhelmed, enchanted, confused, and for once, speechless.

"You've never been so quiet, especially in the bathroom. Do you like it?" she asked, making a grand gesture with her arms like the ringmaster of a circus.

"Totally fucking awesome, like you," he said still overwhelmed by the décor, as well as the tight silk blouse she was wearing.

He leaned over to kiss her. She complied but pulled away when he tried to expand upon the kissing.

"As always, I love your enthusiasm, but tonight there is an order to things," she explained as she placed three covered silver trays between them.

"Isn't that a little OCD?" he asked gently.

"Not at all," she replied, "it's about a deal we made."

"Another deal?" he laughed. "I really should write these things down."

Her wide smile undermined the entitlement in her voice. "Several months ago, in this very bathroom, you told me that if I ate dinner on this messy bathroom floor I could have, and I quote, "any big heaping reward I wanted." Tonight, I intend to fulfill my end of the bargain, and I hope you'll fulfill your end. Are you up for it?"

The dangerous creature had no idea just how *up for it* he was.

He tried to contain his romantic cravings as he took a deep breath and asked, "So this carpet is for a New Year's picnic?"

"Exactly," Gloria answered as she lifted the cover of the first tray, revealing two small bowls with brightly colored pills and a bottle of spring water.

"Voila! First course is our appetizer," she announced, kissing her fingers like a master chef. "Lovely Luvox for me, so that I can keep sitting here next to a big pile of dirt as I dine with my man. And appetizing Atripla for you, so that you can be sitting here—well, sitting here at all."

Henry bowed his head, taking Gloria's soft hands in his, as they prayed with mock solemnity, "Thank you, pharmaceutical gods and overpaid CEOs, for enabling us to reach this wonderful day and for many more days to come and for incredible returns on Frank Zimmerman's biotechnology portfolio."

"Amen," Gloria agreed as she placed Henry's pill on his tongue and handed him the bottle of water.

He did the same for her. After they swallowed their pills, he tried to kiss her but again was gently rebuffed. Gloria had an agenda and appeared unconcerned about the torture her tight blouse and pink tongue were inflicting. The dangerous creature was driving him mad.

But she didn't care. There was, after all, an order to things. She lifted the lid on the second silver tray to reveal two McDonald's burgers.

Laughing, she said, "Your favorite US import."

He leaned over the tray to kiss her, muttering, "Second-favorite."

Gloria started pulling apart one of the Big Macs with her fingers, and the gooey mess got all over her soft hands. She fed him a bite, allowing him to lick the residue from her fingers one by one, which only fueled the sexual tension and his ravenous desire. He was aching as he went to kiss her again, but as before, she gently pushed him away.

The next activity on her agenda involved a bottle of sparkling apple cider she retrieved from the sink, where it had been chilling on ice.

"Virgin champagne to wash it down?" she offered, opening the bottle.

Looking around, Henry asked, "No glasses for a New Year's toast?"

Gloria laughed. "That's so passé, Henry. So OCD of you. So last year." She raised the bottle and said, "Here's to sharing lovely germs in this New Year: scratched records, toilet paper, a bottle of apple cider, and lots of love."

She took a swig straight from the bottle, without even cleaning it with an antibacterial wipe. He was impressed.

She handed the bottle to Henry, who raised it in his own toast, "Here's to the unlocked bathroom door that brought me you, saved my life, and is beckoning for me to show you how much I love you in the next room."

He took a swig from the bottle and started to stand up. Couldn't she see how excited he was? He could hardly contain himself; he needed to be lying with her in his messy bed with her hands all over his body making more of a mess. But she was insistent on torturing him as she pulled at his leg for him to stay seated on the bloody carpet.

"Not before dessert," she said firmly. "Ready?"

He nodded reluctantly. She lifted the lid of the final tray to reveal five boxes of latex Durex condoms stacked on top of one another as if she were building a little house with blocks.

Henry laughed in delightful surprise. "Fifty condoms. Ambitious, aren't we?"

She smiled with confidence. "Oxford overachievers."

He was serious now and spoke quietly. "Are you sure, Gloria? Not too risky with my HIV?"

She was getting exasperated. "I read like a hundred studies about this, Henry. Using latex significantly reduces any risk of passing HIV. It's fine. It's better than fine. It's great."

He needed to make sure she felt comfortable as he tried to hide the desperation in his voice. "But why, Gloria? Any risk of infecting you, however slight, is too much. Aren't you scared of dying?"

"I'm more scared of not living," she answered confidently. "I've spent twenty-two years completely miserable in a hermetically sealed rare-book library. I love you—everything about you, including your risky germs, scratches, and filthy rock T-shirts," she explained with mild frustration at having to answer the same question over again.

He continued to sit motionless while Gloria carefully moved the dinner trays off the carpet. Even though technically she was the virgin and he was the one with "experience," it was she who moved with self-assurance and certainty, while he sat there like an idiot not knowing how to respond or what to say. She moved closer so that their knees were touching. His whole body shuddered, and he almost came in his pants at the touch of her noticeably improved soft hands on his cheeks.

With a penetrating gaze, she said, "*Never, never, never, wonder why. It's gotta be. It has to be.* Van Morrison, 'Beside You,' 1967."

"Your hands feel so soft. Henry Young, almost 2011," he whispered as he gently moved her shoulders back so that she was sitting opposite him again, their eyes locked.

Gloria moved in again and started kissing various parts of his face while uttering intermittently, "My hands are soft thanks to you. Now, you told me you were a man of your word. I want my reward, goddamn it. This carpet is very comfortable. I tested like twenty carpets before I found the right one, the softest one."

Henry chuckled, enjoying her kisses. "Always the researcher. So prepared."

He finally felt the confidence to act. He slowly and methodically unbuttoned and removed her clothes, as if she were a rare porcelain doll he did not want to break. He then removed his own and held her close, their naked bodies entwined on the soft carpet.

"I love you, Henry Young," she said, a little breathless.

"I love you more, Gloria Zimmerman," he responded with more conviction and honesty than anything he had ever said in his entire life.

"Always so competitive," she laughed.

But she was serious again, handing him a box of condoms and speaking with urgency. "Prove it, Henry. Show me, Loomate. Right now. Right here. On this carpet. In our dirty, messy, germ-infested bathroom."

Henry guided Gloria until they were lying tangled and naked. Their words were quiet murmurs between eager, hungry tongues and urgent, exploring hands.

"Soft carpet. Clever girl," he said, nuzzling his face in her breasts.

"Happy girl," she moaned.

"Happy New Year," he whispered in her ear, stopping for the briefest moment to take in her face.

He was relieved that she did not seem to notice his trembling hands as he feebly attempted to release one of the condoms from its packaging. After several tries, with protection in place, he carefully positioned his long, lean body on top of her delicate frame.

She ran her fingers through his hair as her hands moved down the side of his neck and over his shoulders. Clutching his back, her hands, now soft and white, pulled him into her to the deliberate and uneven and ascending rhythms of Van Morrison's "Beside You." At long last, Gloria and Henry made love.

They devoured each other all night long and into the next year, a first meal for two people who had been starving most of their lives. At some point between an orgasm and sleep, as Henry was tracing the contours of Gloria's breasts with his long, gentle fingers, she gave him the most magnificent smile. He was particularly moved by her eyes. For once, they were completely happy—not a shred of concern. They reminded him of Van Morrison's final chorus in "Beside You." *To never, never, never, never, wonder why at all. It's gotta be, it has to be.*

Before drifting into peaceful sleep, Gloria realized she was no longer a dweller on the threshold. She had crossed. Gazing at the waning fire, she recalled it was an imperfect metaphor for love. As Van Morrison sang, *the fire's still in me and the passion burns.* So the real fire would never fade, always aglow in the memory of Henry's bright eyes and Van Morrison's expectant music. Staring at Henry, Gloria silently gave thanks to him and their god, Van Morrison, for *Astral Weeks* and all the out-of-body experiences they shared these past five months and would undoubtedly share for the rest of their lives, however long.

She also paid homage to Oliver and her dead women poets for delivering her to this glorious place, having seen her through many lonely—or rather, *empty*—years.

As she finally drifted into unconsciousness, Gloria knew that this new year was and would continue to be decidedly different. Her exhausted rapture was mirrored in Henry's blissful face. It was long past midnight when Gloria and Henry were sleeping in quiet and total embrace, ringing in the new year and their new life together in the messy bathroom where they first met, breathing in and out.

> *Open and just hold the lantern in the doorway,*
> *For the freedom of it*
> *And you take the night air through your nostrils*
> *And you breathe in out, in out*
> *And you breathe just like that, just like that*
> *You may not know it's got you until you turn around*
> *And I'll point a finger at you, point a finger at you*
> *You say which way, which way*
> *Beside you, beside you*
> *Oh child to never wonder why*
> *To never, never, never, never wonder why at all*

Van Morrison, 1968
From "Beside You"

EPILOGUE: ANOTHER AUGUST

Brand New Day

Emma used her chewed-off fingernails with the remnants of black nail polish to take off large sunglasses, revealing sad, despondent blue-gray eyes. Emma, dressed in an eclectic combination of Goth and preppy, put her sunglasses atop her wavy red head of hair and adjusted her large black tote bag, which was filled with the evidence of her anguished existence at Oxford—a heavily annotated Sylvia Plath book, Dante's *Inferno* in Italian with choice relatives penciled into various circles of Hell, daily two-pack quota of cigarettes, headphones, angry leather journal, and her aunt's "emergency" Valium, which she had stolen the night before she traveled to Oxford. Damn, only four pills left.

What was she doing running away again? Nothing really helped except maybe the Valium and Van Morrison, preferably in combination. Perhaps that's why she escaped to the Van Morrison section of this dusty old record shop, which very fittingly was called Dusty Vinyl Record Shop or something similarly quaint.

Emma was mindlessly rummaging through a stack of Van Morrison records when one caught her eye. She carefully handled the torn, messed-up cover. She was about to put it back when she noticed some stray marks on the other side of the record jacket. It was covered. Like a tattoo artist displaying her wares, there was ink splattered everywhere. It was covered. Curious, Emma started reading.

To Sally,
Please believe in our Crazy Love.
n.

25 December 2010

Dear G,
Please give our Crazy Love a chance.
I may be messed up, but I will love you
my whole life (however long). No one could
ever love you more.
H.

Emma was a bit stunned. Her automatic defensive reaction was to scoff at the ridiculous inscriptions. She didn't care about Sally, N., G., or H.—or X, Y, Z, for that matter. This alphabet soup of lovesick bullshit had no bearing on her pathetic life. She put the album back; she wanted no part. Her story was not a love story. She could hardly stand herself, let alone anyone else.

But she hesitated for a long while, staring at a photograph of a young and hopeful Van Morrison on the scarred old wall with its peeling yellow paint. She remembered reading somewhere that being a Van Morrison enthusiast requires a certain degree of—shit, what did the author call it? Fatalistic optimism or some other god-awful cliché?

Emma always supposed she was the atypical Van Morrison fan who could not be happy even when listening to "Bright Side of the Road" or "Days Like This" or even the lively "Wild Night." There was just too much black in her life, she thought, as she examined her chipped nails. But a strange feeling came over her and caused her to pick up the worn *Moondance* album. Why not buy the damn thing? It was only three pounds, for Christ's sake.

The cashier, an Oxford student she thought she recognized, reached for the album with a grin. She could hardly read the faded writing on his vintage rock shirt. Led Zeppelin? The Doors? Tom Petty? Working in this shop, he probably knew a lot about music. Did he like Van Morrison? Was that why he was smiling?

Hesitantly, Emma placed the album on the counter. When she put her three pounds down, he pushed the money back and brushed her fingers. Oh fuck, she thought, he must have read the back of the album with its love confessions. Did he think she was a hopeless romantic or just a hopeless loser? She pulled her hand away and started chewing the remaining black polish off her thumb.

He watched her walk toward the door. She was about to open it when she hesitated, feeling his steady gaze. She thought she might have seen him at the Bodleian Library, or maybe in her large Italian Literature class. Perhaps she'd come back and talk to him about music. To her surprise, that actually seemed possible. As she thought about the cashier, the *Moondance* album, and this dusty old shop, anything seemed possible. Tutto e possible.

And then as she placed the album in her large black tote bag, she realized she never checked the bloody record. She took the record out of its inner sleeve and examined the vinyl closely. Jesus, so many scratches; like her, it had been through hell. Was it even worth three pounds? But then, placing it back, she noticed writing on the other side of the inner sleeve. Apparently, mysterious H. had added a postscript. She handled it delicately. The paper sleeve was old and thin, like parchment. So much writing—it was a fucking novel. A fucking novel addressed to her?

P.S.
1 July 2070

To whomever owns this record after me,

Please know this scratched-up Moondance brought my wife G. and me together. Truth be told, G. is responsible for most of the scratches, and I apologise on her behalf. In spite of the scratches, we made love to this album for many years. We even made a couple of books about Van Morrison's music, or "poetry" as she would say. I still cannot believe some considered me a scholar as well; she was the academic superstar, and I was merely the arse who carried her books and loved her dearly.

Unfortunately, we never made any children. Our nieces and nephew, two German shepherds, and her adoring students were our affectionate surrogates. That is why I know she would want me to leave this album back where we found it. From Dusty Vinyl to Dusty Vinyl and all that. Is that Genesis? I digress. Forgive the ramblings of a crazy old man. My wife was always the better writer and the more ruthless editor.

She has been gone several months now, and my writing and life are not quite the same. But who am I to complain? We had over sixty glorious years, sixty Aprils with sixty anniversaries. We celebrated every last one in a hot-air balloon, of all things! This past April was no exception. She insisted on the bloody balloon ride over our favourite Oxford landmarks, even though the weather was brisk and her doctor required we bring an oxygen tank and nurse. She always said precious time is slipping away so we should live until we die. And so she did.

But to me, she will never be gone. Every day, I listen to Van Morrison's music and think of our precious time and how she gave my messed-up life hope, purpose, and love. You deserve the same happy ending we had. Indeed, it is a brand new day. Your brand new day. Don't lock the loo door.

Your balloon is waiting.

H.

Emma did not know who H. was—she didn't know his name or where he lived or to whom he had been married or how his wife died or why they never had any children.

The only thing she knew was that he was some messed-up soul who, inspired by this messed-up Van Morrison album, found love and a happy ending. Emma didn't know if she could ever have or was even worthy of this album or its promised happy ending. She didn't know if she even believed in happy endings. But she could be open to the possibility. She could try.

Before losing her resolve and following H.'s directive, she quickly put on her sunglasses and lifeline headphones. And then blaring Van Morrison's "Brand New Day," Emma opened the unlocked glass doors of Oxford Dusty Vinyl and headed into a sun-drenched August afternoon, open and ready for a brand new life.

It was time to try.

When all the dark clouds roll away
And the sun begins to shine
I see my freedom from across the way
And it comes right in on time
Well it shines so bright and it gives so much light
And it comes from the sky above
Makes me feel so free makes me feel like me
And it seems like yes it feels like
A brand new day

Van Morrison, 1970
From "Brand New Day"

ACKNOWLEDGMENTS

I could not have written or brought this book into the world without the expertise, care, and belief of some amazing people who include (in alphabetical order): Allison Adler, Jeannie Aschkenasy, Elli Cohn, Margaret Cohn, Ruth Efrati Epstein, Ellen Fiedelholtz, Patricia Frey, Ilyce Glink, Michael Gregory, Amanda Holly, Lenore Kayne, Saree Kayne, Gina Mondragon, Laine Morreau, Lynda Prior, Eliza Rose, Sr. Frances Ryan, Becky Sarwate, Catharine Sprinkel, Rachel Wizner, and Claire Young. Thank you for believing in Gloria, Henry, and me.

FOR DISCUSSION

1. Why do you think the author titled the book *Oxford Messed Up*? What are the different ways the phrase "messed up" is used in the book? What are the implications of its various uses? Can being "messed up" be a good thing?

2. Do you see this as a traditional love story? How is the book similar to and different from other novels with romantic plotlines you have read in the past, and how do these differences or similarities affect the general themes of romantic love in this work?

3. How do Van Morrison and his music affect and inform Gloria and Henry and the other characters in the novel? Why does the author use Van Morrison music as the link between these two isolated souls?

4. How do Gloria's dead women poets and the other poets referenced affect and inform the characters in the novel? How is poetry a language for both isolation and connection?

5. Why does the author set so many of the novel's high and low points in the claw-foot tub? What is its symbolism for Gloria, Henry, and their relationship?

6. OCD's internal struggle is not usually portrayed in mainstream media. How did this book inform your knowledge of OCD? Did you have any misconceptions about OCD before reading it? How do you feel now? What has changed and why?

7. Gloria describes Oliver as both a protector and jailer. What did you think of him? Did your feelings for him evolve as you read? Has there been something in your life that gave you security but was not good for you? Were you able to let it go?

8. Would this story have been different if told in the first person? How would it change if told from Gloria's point of view or Henry's? As it exists now, what devices does the author implement to place the reader inside the minds of Gloria and Henry?

9. When Gloria asks Henry whether he believes in happy endings, he replies, "In theory." But by the end of the novel, he seems to be converted. When does this transformation occur? Does Gloria undergo a similar metamorphosis? Do you think *Oxford Messed Up* has a happy ending? Do you believe in happy endings?

ABOUT THE AUTHOR

Andrea Kayne Kaufman is chair of the Department of Leadership, Language and Curriculum at the DePaul University College of Education in Chicago. She is an educator and attorney who earned a bachelor's degree from Vassar College, a master's degree in Education from Harvard University, and her Juris Doctor from the University of Pennsylvania Law School.

Kaufman's unique shared focus on education and law has made her an award-winning expert in the area of school law, and she has published and spoken widely about special education law, education civil rights, the No Child Left Behind Act, cyberbullying, and other legal and political issues impacting students and schools.

Kaufman draws inspiration for her writing and life from poetry, Van Morrison's music and other classic vinyl, her daily walks along Lake Michigan, and her time spent with her husband and two children in their equanimity-filled Chicago home.

Andrea is currently working on her next novel, *Parent Over Shoulder*.